JOHN ELLSWORTH

LA JOLLA LAW

BOOKS

Vinci Books

vinci-books.com

Published by Vinci Books Ltd in 2024

1

Copyright © John Ellsworth 2019

The author has asserted their moral right to be identified as the author of this work in accordance with the Copyright, Designs and Patents Act 1988

This work is a work of fiction. Names, characters, places and incidents are the product of the author's imagination or are used fictitiously. Any resemblance to actual persons, living or dead, places and incidents is entirely coincidental.

All rights reserved. No part of this publication may be copied, reproduced, distributed, stored in any retrieval system, or transmitted in any form or by any means, including photocopying, recording, or other electronic or mechanical methods, nor used as a source for any form of machine learning including AI datasets, without the prior written permission of the publisher.

The publisher and the author have made every effort to obtain permissions for any third party material used in this book and to comply with copyright law. Any queries in this respect should be brought to the attention of the publisher and any omissions will be corrected in future editions.

A CIP catalogue record for this book is available from the British Library.
Paperback ISBN: 9781036700263

Printed and bound in Great Britain by Clays Ltd, Elcograf S.p.A.

By John Ellsworth

THE THADDEUS MURFEE LEGAL THRILLERS

The Defendants

Beyond a Reasonable Death

Attorney at Large

Chase, the Bad Baby

Defending Turquoise

The Mental Case

The Girl Who Wrote The New York Times Bestseller

The Trial Lawyer

The Near Death Experience

Flagstaff Station

The Crime

La Jolla Law

The Post Office

The Contract Lawyer

THE MICHAEL GRESHAM THRILLERS

The Lawyer

The Defendant's Father

The Law Partners

Carlos the Ant

Sakharov the Bear

Annie's Verdict

Dead Lawyer on Aisle 11

30 Days of Justis

The Fifth Justice

Lies She Never Told Me

Girl, Under Oath

Lawyers in Gray

SISTERS IN LAW

Court Order

Hellfire

The District Attorney

Justice in Time

Chapter 1

La Jolla California was a hilly seaside community within the city of San Diego. It occupied seven miles of curving coastline along the Pacific Ocean within the northern city limits. The population last night was reported at 46,781. Today the number was one less.

The La Jolla climate was mild, with an average daily temperature of 70.5°F, which perhaps explained why Reginald—Reggie—Pelham was wearing a Speedo. He had just climbed out of his backyard lap pool when Jonesy, his manservant, delivered his cell phone to him at poolside. "Call from the missus," whispered Jonesy.

With one hand holding his towel, Pelham grabbed the phone from Jonesy and shouted, "What? It's three o'clock here. It must be midnight in Paris! Why are you up so late?"

"You'll never believe what just happened," trilled Victoria Pelham.

"What?" Reggie said sardonically, "You've got another five followers on your Instagram account? Or maybe another ten on your fashion YouTube channel? Whoop-de-doo."

"Now, Reggie, no reason to be bitter about my success."

"I'm not bitter. I just don't get it. Why would people want to look at what you wear?"

"Darling, I'm a fashion icon! That's why!"

Reggie let out a long sigh. "Victoria, why did you call me in the middle of your night?"

She let out a loud laugh. "I just sued you!"

"Jesus help me," said Pelham. "This doesn't even approach funny, Vicki. I've got enough on my plate right now to keep ten of me busy." Pelham felt his bowels loosen way down low. He knew what fear felt like. But he was determined not to give it away. "You sued me for what, dare I ask?"

Victoria didn't respond. She was taking her time, drawing out his pain. Pelham thought he heard her yawn before she finally said, "I filed a shareholders' suit against you. I'm going to have you removed as CEO. Ta-da, darling, sleep tight."

In less than five minutes, Pelham was on a call with corporate counsel. "Jesse," he cried, "Vicki just called. She's filed a shareholder suit against me. She's seeking to have me removed as CEO. Can she pull it off?"

Jesse Matina, corporate counsel for Reggie's brainchild, SkoolDaze, was quick on the draw. "Her counsel just dumped the lawsuit papers on me, Reggie. What say you go inside, take a long, hot shower, and let me call you back. The lawsuit is close to a hundred pages long, so it's going to take me the rest of the afternoon to scan it and run it by some of my guys. Then I'll get right back to you."

The phone line went dead. Pelham sat there, poolside, a

sweaty shaker of martinis on the table next to him with a tiny mound of cocaine on a mirror with a single-edged razor beside it. He leaned back and pressed an index finger across his lips, the perfect posture when he contemplated. So many things were going wrong, mostly what Victoria had learned about him before she left for Paris, that he felt himself quaking inside at the thought of losing SkoolDaze to her. SkoolDaze was his precious app, the precocious child he'd never had, his heaven-sent baby. It was an app that he, a pure tech genius, had developed when inspiration struck one night while he was doing a line of coke in the men's room of Gillies in Texas.

The inspiration was this: an app that placed a CCTV camera inside your kid's schoolroom and let you monitor the kid's school day whenever you wished to virtually drop in. Each camera was directed at the teacher at the front of the classroom but none of the children. The child's smartphone would then broadcast the child's remarks to the teacher. It was based on voice-recognition technology that Reggie had taken a step further.

The app also allowed parents to communicate with one another, with the teacher, and to hold classroom meetings. The icing on the cake? The app allowed parents to collaborate and hire subject matter monitors for any class to ensure the children were receiving the right curriculum.

The app had been venture capitalized out of Silicon Valley 24 months earlier and was now up to 500,000 users plus installations, yielding a market cap of $150 million. If Reginald Pelham lost his CEO-ship to Vicki, it would be the end of the world for him. More than anything, Pelham needed SkoolDaze, and SkoolDaze needed him.

He tended the small mound of cocaine, sculpting it with

the razor blade into a short ridge of zoom. Holding the mirror to his nose, he sniffed, tossed his head back, and tried to imagine Victoria returning home to him. But as the drug coursed through his veins and his heart pounded, he knew she never would. She was in love with Francis Vichy, her French lover, who did hair for *Vogue* in Paris. Francis was 20 years younger than Pelham, 40 pounds lighter, and had a full head of hair. But there was more, and Pelham knew it. Francis Vichy was a poet, a man of the people, and a listener. He was all those things Victoria needed in her life, all those things that Pelham had never been and would never be.

Divorce had always been imminent, had always ridden on the tip of their tongues, always shaded their discussions. The only remaining question, the only *serious* remaining question, was…what would become of SkoolDaze and the couple's other assets? There was the home in La Jolla, the condo in New York City, and the apartment in Paris. Add to that a few miscellaneous games and toys including the Gulfstream jet, the Cirrus jet, the 60-foot yacht moored at the La Jolla Yacht Club, a money market fund of no less than $45 million, and various IRAs plus other retirement vehicles.

And speaking of vehicles, there was a Rolls-Royce used by Pelham when he needed to travel north the 45 miles to Los Angeles on business and pleasure, plus the usual Porsches and vintage machines. The largest holding was their real estate in La Jolla and its environs. The Pelhams owned two restaurants, three high-rises, and six houses along the beach. They also had a house in San Francisco and a horse farm outside Nashville. There was a ski lodge in Telluride, and the dive boat was tied up in Greece.

Pelham aligned another snort and was just getting ready to take it onboard when his nephew, Butchy, and his entourage stepped out of the patio doors.

"Hey, Unc, we are off to the studio. So we'll see you later, yeah?" Butchy was the lead singer of a boy band called Boyz 'N Luv, a foursome churning out number one singles, one after another. The other three young men hung back behind Butchy, fiddling on their phones. While they were recording, Reggie let them stay at the mansion. There was plenty of room, and for the most part, he enjoyed the energy they brought to the house.

"Yep, we'll see you later."

Butchy turned to leave with the others, but Reggie reminded him, "Remember the party this weekend. You have the photoshoot here with the president."

Butchy snorted. "That old dude? Yeah, Dad told me." Butchy's dad was also his manager and Reggie's brother-in-law.

This generation had no respect, even for the President of the United States. "I heard he's paying you guys well and you don't even have to perform. Just take a few pictures and then you can party. No big deal."

Just then, Reggie's cell phone chimed. Jesse was getting back. He waved Butchy and his band members away. "I've got to take this."

Once the boys were out of earshot, he waded right in. "Don't worry about my feelings, Jesse," he said steadily. "Give it to me like it is."

"It's not pretty, Reggie, and I'm not going to blow smoke. She's brought up the whole Hawaii fiasco. She also brought up the off-the-book's transactions and the Thai women."

"The invisible deals... Where in the hell did she get that info?" Pelham drummed his fingers on the arm of the chair. Vicki...she was a sly bitch.

"You never seem to remember, Reggie, that Vicki has friends inside SkoolDaze, too. You can just assume, henceforth, that anything you do inside the four corners of your company is going to get back to Vicki and her lawyers. The good old days of cowboying every sweet young thing that catches your eye out on the sand and selling off pieces of technology under the table are over. You have a new full partner now, even though she owns only ten percent of the stock. Repeat this to yourself every night at bedtime. 'Vicki is now an equal or greater partner whether I fucking like it or not.'"

"So are you going to defend me or what, Jesse?" asked Pelham.

"Are you out of your tree? I still have to make a living here in the Valley. Never forget it was Vicki's dad who believed in you enough to put up fifteen million when your banknote had been called. If I defend you here in Silicon Valley, her father will have my head on a platter, and I'll never do deals again. You won't find a lawyer in all of California who'll take this case."

"So, what, you're just dropping me here to fend for myself?" Pelham hoisted himself from his chair and started pacing the length of the pool.

"Nope, I have an old law school friend I'm going to call."

Pelham stopped across from the diving board. "Name of?"

"His name is Thaddeus Murfee. He's practicing in Colorado, last I heard, but we were close enough I think I can talk him into at least coming to La Jolla and meeting with you."

Pelham squeezed a fist and released it with a slow breath. "I'm hosed without you, Jesse. I'll leave your replacement up to you."

"He is one of the smartest lawyers I've ever known. If you can score his services, he'll save your company for you. If you don't, I hate to think what might happen to you, to Vicki, and to SkoolDaze when the litigators are done with the three of you."

"Please tell him up front how much I appreciate any help he can give me and how price is not an issue."

"That reminds me…price *isn't* an issue. This lawyer has made enough money in the practice to buy and sell both of us *and* your father-in-law. It isn't money that's going to persuade him to come to your rescue."

"So what will?"

"Down on your knees, praying like the son of a bitch you are. Have a good evening, Reggie. I'll put in my call to Thaddeus right now."

After Pelham hung up, Reggie stepped up onto the diving board. It was time to row some money out in the boat, his doubletalk to his banker to transfer funds offshore to the Caymans where Vicki might miss it when she came snooping around, looking for hidden assets. The people Reggie dealt with were too smart for any lawyers she'd come up with. Numbered accounts never lied, as long as they weren't in Zurich where nobody with any brains hid their Fuck You money anymore.

"Cayman Islands, here we come!" cried Pelham as he topped out on his purposeful belly flop off the three meter board and prepared to crash down into the perfect blue water below. He knew there would be rougher landings than this one. The thought flashed through his mind as he belly-planted in the water.

When he resurfaced from the flop, Reggie drew a deep breath with his face out of the water then exhaled mightily, sinking to the bottom of the pool. He sat there, arms crossed, refusing to give an inch.

Chapter 2

"Dickless wonder!" Safari Frye mumbled to herself. "You actually called a junior officer a 'dickless wonder.'" She felt like she had been set adrift in a mindless sea of fresh vegetables at the Safeway store. When did she first start thinking she could call junior detectives 'dickless wonders'? She knew there would be hell to pay with the chief. Just as soon as she located a pre-made salad for lunch.

She was avoiding all organic produce. She loved the stuff, but it cost nearly twice as much as the regular. The young woman with the purple-tinged hair just ahead of her steered her cart to a freshly sprayed plot of organic Romaine. "Is it really that much better than nonorganic?" Purple said aloud to no one in particular.

"I can't tell the difference," said Safari from behind. "Besides, how are we supposed to know it's really organic when it's just more lettuce?"

"What, you don't trust Safeway?" Purple said with a note of feigned incredulity.

"Let's just say I'm a little jaded."

"Me, too," she said as she selected a head of lettuce that looked like all the others.

Safari needed to head back to the police department. If she dashed through the self-serve checkout, then there would be just enough time to stop at the Starbucks up by the entrance. Cops lived on coffee; Safari was no different.

As Safari browsed the pre-made romaine lettuce salads, some with croutons, some with egg, two teenage girls came up behind Purple and jostled against her as they were playing "grab ass." Purple was thrown sharply against the display case.

"Watch it, Tootsie Roll," said the teenager with the tattoo sleeve on her arm. "Your cart jumped right in front of us."

Purple turned around, her eyes flashing. "What in the hell are you talking about? You just crashed into me."

"Hey, watch your mouth, Tootsie Roll. I might have to wash it out with some of that Tide in aisle fifteen."

Safari watched as Purple's hackles went up. She stepped out from behind her grocery cart and bellied up to tattoo girl. "That, I'd like to see," she said in a caustic tone. "Run, get your Tide box. I'll wait here."

Tattoo girl waited a beat too long. She took one step back, and the spell was broken. There would be no Tide box after all. Purple turned her grocery cart as if to return to her shopping, but as she took a step, tattoo girl snaked a leg out and tripped her. Then, in a blink, the two girls were running full tilt to the other end of the store and were gone.

Safari, witness to the incident, came around and bent down to help the young woman to her feet.

"Ouch!" she cried, "I think it's twisted." Safari took a step back. Purple struggled, trying to turn onto her knees and then stand, but one knee refused to take the weight. "If you could get behind me and lift, I think I can make it."

Safari went behind, grasped her elbows, and lifted. Purple was very light, and all but floated up onto her feet. "Thanks, I can handle it now."

"No problem, but they're lucky they ran."

"Oh, yes, I see the gun on your belt. And the badge. You're a police officer?"

"Detective. In fact, I detected a crime just now."

Purple laughed. She had shoulder-length dark hair in an expensive cut and the kind of pert nose plastic surgeons aim for. Safari herself had a similar nose, and though she had always liked it, she thought her eyes too widely spaced. The young woman's eyes were almost a deep violet color, and her face was in perfect symmetry. Safari wouldn't mind looking as put-together as Purple, but Safari would lose the tiny nose ring that Purple boasted and could only be discerned up close. Safari wasn't much for over decorating.

The young woman's knee suddenly buckled, and she grimaced.

Safari said, "Hang on, and I'll grab the produce manager. We'll get some ice for that knee."

The produce manager was quick to help and returned with a bag of ice and an offer to get a wheelchair. Purple declined the wheelchair. She said she would find a place to sit down and ice up for a few minutes. She leaned on Safari who steered her to the front of the store where she took a seat in Starbucks. Safari helped her lift her leg onto the chair across from her and placed the ice on her knee.

"Thank you," said Purple. "Hey, I don't even know your name."

"Safari. My dad was a jungle enthusiast who actually never went on one. A safari, I mean. What's yours?"

Purple adjusted the ice on her knee. "Janet. Janet Ringley. How does someone young as you get to be a detective?"

"By calling other detectives terrible names like dickless wonder."

Janet was fighting a full-fledged smile from erupting. "You called another detective a dickless wonder?"

"I did, and now my boss is waiting to see me. It ain't gonna be pretty."

Janet laughed. "I can't imagine why. I called my ex a fuckhead, and he hit me. Now we're separated. Some people just have no sense of humor. So, did your detective turn you in?"

Safari took a seat adjacent to Janet. "He filed a sexual harassment charge, of all things. It sounds kind of funny, at first, but it's actually as serious as a heart attack. I should've known better. I have a feeling I'm going to have to apologize to the dickless wonder I called a dickless wonder." When Safari laughed, her shoulders shook.

Janet could see she was going to like her new friend. Wait, did she just call Safari a new friend? It had been so hard in La Jolla meeting anyone since her arrival over a month ago. She had moved here with Jamison, her six-year-old, looking to make a new start away from LA where the fuckhead lived. La Jolla was beautiful, and traffic was nonexistent, but the differences in net worth were staggering. She had found La Jolla and its people much wealthier than in LA, where many were barely scraping by.

"So when's the hearing on the sexual harassment charge?"

"Friday morning. I can hardly wait," Safari deadpanned.

"Then we should meet up for a drink Friday night and celebrate your win. Are you married?"

"I'm in love with a guy but we aren't together any longer. It's complicated. What about you, you said there was an ex?"

"It's not complicated. He's a fuckhead, and I'm a pretty nice person. We got married when I was way too young and didn't know any better. But he looked better than my situation at home, so we ran off and tied the knot."

"Got it."

Janet tried flexing her knee. "Ouch! *Fuck*, that hurts! Pardon my French."

"No need, cops talk worse than sailors. I'm going to get us some coffee. Name your poison."

"Just a dark roast with extra cream. Nothing fancy. I'm a real plain Jane at heart."

Safari went over and ordered then turned and stood with her back against the counter, waiting on their coffees. From the side, she studied her new friend. Safari had a habit of memorizing facial features. She supposed it came with the territory of being a detective. She never forgot faces though she did forget names and often referred to them in her head by a nickname, known only to her. Like the way she'd called Janet "Purple." The coffee came, and she went back to the table.

Janet said, "Thanks so much. What about Friday night? Can I buy you a drink to repay?" She wasn't desperate, but she was so close in actually making friends with a real, living person who didn't drive a Maserati, she didn't want the opportunity to stray.

"I don't see why not," Safari said with a smile. "I've got a feeling I'm going to need more than one drink after they get done with me Friday."

Just then, a young police officer in uniform came through the front doors and sized up the two women. His face lit up, and he approached them. "Hey, there. It's me, Roddy Smith, your next-door neighbor."

Janet smiled and gave him a sheepish look. "I didn't recognize you. I'm sorry. So...you're a cop?"

Without being asked, the uniformed officer sat down with the two women. "I am. I've been on the force eighteen months now. I'm looking to make detective in the next year," he said with a certain sense of self-satisfaction. Janet shot a look at Safari, who almost imperceptibly shook her head. She meant to let it play out and see how far Officer Roddy Smith would run with it.

"I hear detectives make a lot of money," said Janet. "Maybe you can afford to buy a house and get out of apartment hell when you make it."

"Well, maybe..." He looked down at the table. She must have said something wrong.

"Hey, listen," she said to him with a big smile, "It's just my dream, so I assume everyone has the same."

That seemed to do the trick, and he smiled back at her. "So," said the young officer, all but ignoring Safari, "what do you do for jollies in this town? I know you're new."

"We were just talking. We're going out for drinks Friday night. Care to tag along?"

"That sounds cool, but I don't know if I can make it. I think they're going to have me working with the detectives on a stakeout Friday night. But if they don't, I can meet up and hang."

"What case will you be working Friday night?" asked Safari. When she sat back, her sport coat opened, clearly displaying her gun and badge. The young officer, upon seeing the hardware, suddenly went from mahogany to cocoa skin color.

"Oh—oh—you're a detective?"

"I'm a supervisor. I would be supervising your stakeout Friday night. Except, guess what? We don't have any stakeouts on Friday night. This wouldn't be something you're cooking up on your own, would it?"

The young officer checked his watch. "Oh, my god, I just ran in for coffee. My partner is waiting outside. Gotta run."

When he was gone, the women laughed with their heads thrown back. "That was pretty cool," Janet said.

"You mean pretty cruel," said Safari. "But he had it coming."

Janet again flexed her knee and winced. "I wonder if I could lean on you to get back out to my car. I think I'll be okay after that."

They made their way out to Janet's VW convertible. "I'll just call and have groceries delivered."

"How will you get from your car to your apartment on that knee?" asked Safari.

"The security guy in the parking lot will help me. He's always on duty."

"If you're sure. Otherwise, I can follow you home and loan you my shoulder to lean on."

With a shake of her head, Janet fired up the VW and smiled. "You have a card? I'll call about Friday night."

Safari gave the girl one of her business cards and returned to the store. She had just enough time to grab a salad and head for the office.

Friday night and a new friend. She wondered if the cop would show up. It might be fun to go just to find out. She had them put her prepared salad inside a bag with ice. Lunch was only a couple of hours away so it would keep.

Then she jumped into her Ford Interceptor and tromped it.

Time to face the chief and the harassment charge. It wouldn't be pretty. Why in the hell had she ever said such a thing?

She chided herself, *You said it because you have a habit of talking before you think sometimes.*

Yes, she thought, it was grow-up time.

Chapter 3

Safari Frye knew that the reprimand was justified. After all, she had referred to a junior grade detective as a dickless wonder, and he had gone running to the Chief of Detectives and immediately made his complaint against her. His name was Eugene Michaels, and he was all of 28 years, a graduate of SDSU in police science, with five years patrol under his belt. He had been an outstanding patrol officer, but as the chief knew, getting high marks as a patrol officer and making the grade as a detective were like night and day. Chief of Detectives, Aaron Adamson, had filled out the proper forms, put the complaint in line for hearing, and was prepared to interview Safari late that afternoon when she returned from the field.

The Chief's beat, Northern Division, served a population of 250,000 people and covered 41 square miles of San Diego County, including La Jolla. The Northern Division office was located at Eastgate Mall, which was where Safari was headed. She called dispatch, had Adamson tipped off she was running late, and spent the rest of the ride waiting for his angry call which, fortunately, never came.

At the Eastgate Mall parking slots marked POLICE ONLY, Safari nosed her vehicle in, got out, popped the trunk, and unloaded her 12-gauge shotgun and her M-16, slipping the magazine and shells into her valise. After slamming the trunk shut, she two-fingered a cigarette out of her side pocket and applied the Bic flame. She inhaled as many puffs as possible walking from the car to the police department, then smushed the ciggie out in the smoking receptacle before she jerked open the door. Right at the hallway, straight ahead thirty steps, second door on the right, Safari stuck her head inside the chief's office, brightly announcing she had arrived. Chief Adamson scowled and waved her inside.

She stepped inside without speaking and fixed the chief with her piercing gaze. He returned her look, slowly shaking his head.

Safari Frye was a shorter woman with the build of a gymnast and plenty of muscle. She was pretty enough with long blond hair that she normally wore in a tight ponytail. Something that looked professional enough with her blazer and jeans or khakis yet didn't get in the way when she was in a bit of action.

Other cops felt comfortable having her cover their backs since she'd proven herself twice under fire. She'd won the admiration of the entire detective squad when she engaged in a firefight down at the beach, taking out a vested shooter who was armed with an automatic rifle with only the help of her Glock 17. She pinned the man down, aggressively moved toward him, and had shot him in that three inches of flesh between his vest and helmet where the only fatal target could be found.

Chief Adamson knew her value, and as she waited, the look on his face clearly told her that he considered the sexual harassment complaint a joke. Nevertheless, his bearing said his duty lay before him, and he would do everything he could to discharge that duty. That would include gathering all evidence in the case and letting the chips fall where they may, even though Safari might be found guilty of the charge and her job put in jeopardy.

He stood and pointed across his desk at the visitor chair on his left. She sat down, unbuttoned her blazer, and brushed a hank of strong-willed hair that had escaped her hairband from her forehead. She said, "And the winner is?"

"Back off, Frye. When there's a winner, you'll be the first to know, but it ain't yet. I'm going to hand you a copy of the complaint filed against you by Eugene Michaels, and you're going to take it home and study it overnight. In the morning, you're going to present me with your remarks and response in writing."

He passed the complaint to her. She weighed the documents in her hands. "What are we looking at here chief? Am I going away for a month without pay?"

He shook his head. "I'd be happy with that result right now. In fact, I'd sign off on that result right now, if that's as bad as it got. However, Downtown takes sexual harassment claims very seriously, so seriously that you might even be out of a job if this stands."

Despite her cool exterior, Safari shuddered where she sat. "You have got to be kidding! I could lose my job over calling the dickless wonder a dickless wonder?"

The chief dropped his hands on his desk. His scowl deepened. "Get up and shut the damn door! We're going to have this out right now."

Safari did as ordered. She then sat back down, but

without crossing her legs this time, maintaining a more erect posture. "All right, I'm all strapped in, why don't you give it to me straight?"

Chief Adamson peeled his readers from his eyes and rubbed his hands up and down on his face. "You are a very difficult woman." He slowly shook his head side to side, displaying his disbelief. "You know, Safari, you're the one dick I know I can put on any case in the office and get the result that case and that victim deserves. You know that. But your attitude sucks and has ever since you moved from junior grade to senior level detective. I frankly don't know why. Are those bad boys making it that hard on you that you have to overpower them with words? I know it's not that you're afraid of the street, and I know it's not you're afraid of any man in uniform or out of uniform under this roof. So why don't you explain to me just why you're so fucking hard for me to work with?"

Safari nodded, at the same time counting to five before she replied. Then, "Let's just put it this way. Outside the walls, every day, people are counting on me and the men I supervise to keep them and their families, not only safe, but alive. They're counting on me to hunt down the man who raped their twelve-year-old daughter, the gang bangers who knocked out grandpa at the mall, and the armed robber who took down North Bay United Bank and shot a teller just for the hell of it on his way out the door. You know what that makes me, Chief? It makes me very short-tempered with the men I supervise to help me take care of those people. And when one of my men tells me he has to be home by six o'clock because his wife needs him to help set up for her bridge party, yes, I get very pissed, and I'm very likely to call that same man a dickless wonder. Do you really want me to put all this in writing and drop it on your desk in the morning?"

"Believe me, Detective Frye, I dream those same nightmares you're dreaming. But I've learned never to call a dickless wonder a dickless wonder to his face. Or even to her face. That's the difference between me and you. And that's the thing I hope you're going to get the opportunity to learn out of this. And I say 'I hope' because there's a chance you might not be working here once this chicken comes home to roost."

Safari felt her face burning. She was suddenly very thirsty, her mouth as dry as tissue paper, and she was seeing red. It wasn't fair. Male police officers called each other the same name and worse, much worse, every hour of the day, and nobody ever filed a grievance over any of that. But when it came to her, a female in a position of authority, suddenly the brakes were slammed on and it was a whole new ballgame when she resorted to the same terminology about one of them. It was a double standard; she knew it and chief Adamson knew it. She smelled the stink of retribution all over the grievance because, if any male detective called Detective Michaels the same thing, there might have been shouting, there might even have been curse words, but there wouldn't have been a formal grievance. But she was a woman, and women who had fought so hard for so long for equal treatment at work were now receiving that equal treatment, and much worse, in the form of very petty grievances being escalated into very major grievances like the one just now on the Chief's desk.

She should've known better—she did know better—and she should've kept her mouth shut instead of lashing out at Michaels. The paperwork was a useless exercise; she had already learned the lesson. It wouldn't happen again, no matter how much of a dickless wonder another detective—even a female detective—acted like.

"Just drop it on my desk in the morning, Detective Frye, and we'll go from there." He glanced at the door and leaned forward confidentially. "Off the record, I'll do everything in my power to protect you because the whole thing is bullshit and everyone knows it, including Detective Michaels."

Detective Frye sadly shook her head and shrugged. The reality of what she'd done was sinking in. She had been wrong and, yet, she had been right, too. But just now, the wrong was on the front burner. "Thank you for that. Honestly, I don't deserve it. I dropped the ball and shot off my mouth, and I should've known better, but a bridge party? Seriously?"

"We're done here, Frye. Don't you have some place to be?"

"In fact, I'm headed home to take a shower, change into my skimpies, and drop in on some friends down at the beach where I just might trade a drug beef for some names."

"All right, then, in the morning."

"In the morning."

Chapter 4

Safari hurried home and parked her car in the carport. She went inside, removed her gun and badge, and changed clothes. The khaki slacks, white shirt, and tan blazer went back into the closet. Standing there with her arms crossed, she selected a pair of Levi's, a navy blue T-shirt that read *Chargers*, and hiking boots. It was January, cool outside, and would be quite cold down along the beach. She took a quick shower, dried and did her hair, and then dressed.

At the rear of the carport was a small locked storage closet where she kept her Harley. At one time, she had worked as a motor cop and had never gotten over her love of motorcycles. She donned her leather jacket, gloves, and white helmet, then wheeled her Harley into the driveway. She took a seat on the bike and settled in before she kicked at the stand. The bike was heavy, but she liked that. It was solid and safe. She twisted the throttle once, then hit the electric start button. She downshifted into low and eased out on the clutch. Adding throttle, she rolled out of her drive.

Back uptown she went and turned left for the beach on Avenida de la Playa. Traffic was light, and she arrived at Shores five minutes later. Shores was a restaurant and hotel sitting directly on the beach at La Jolla. It featured great lounge acts, three dollar whiskey, and all the networking one could stand in a night. Safari spun her motorcycle around, then backed it into a space just outside the front doors as it was still early enough the professional crowd hadn't hit yet. She stowed the helmet in the top box and locked it. Then she was inside, keeping an eye out for her mark.

He hadn't arrived yet, as near she could tell, so she sidled up to the bar and ordered a beer on draft. She dropped a five, tasted the beer, and turned her back to the bar.

Halfway through her beer, she spied Randy Combs coming through the front door, dragging his bad foot behind, the sure sign of a less than competent motorcycle driver. He saw her and approached the bar.

"Guess what I've got?" he said around tobacco-stained teeth. "I've got a name for you."

"Sure you do, but the question is always the same with you, Randy. Is the name any good, or is this just another ruse by you to beat a drug rap? Now, you'll get yourself knocked off if anyone who's anyone sees you talking to me. I strongly advise you to go back to the men's room and wait for me there. Give me five minutes."

Combs did as instructed. Safari dawdled. She nursed her beer, carefully draining it over the next five minutes to allow any curious eyes to wander elsewhere. Then she replaced her glass on the bar and slipped around to the hallway and down to the men's room. Without announcing, she strode inside and found Combs running water in the far sink and poking at his hair with a black comb. He had been at it a good five minutes and yet it still looked far from perfect. He needed a haircut bad.

Safari approached. "All right, who are we talking about, Combs?"

"Guy's name is Kenneth Chesley. He's a rider out of Oakland and wears all the wrong colors. Chesley is a guy you don't want to just walk up to and strike up a conversation with. He would just as soon crack your head open as look at you. Of course, a pretty thing like you, it might be a totally different story. So who knows?"

"Let's be sure we're on the same page. I'm looking for the guy who sells the smack to the guy who sells the smack to the guy who sells the smack. That Kenneth Chesley?"

"The same. Put this in your affidavit—your CI has been to Chesley's hotel room and seen the scale, the kilo of heroin, and enough cash to fill a bedroom. He's room 11 at the La Jolla Biltmore Hotel. That should get you your search warrant and should get me off the hook on my beef."

Combs was talking about the affidavit the district attorney would supply for Safari to sign, convincing the judge she had a confidential informant who had supplied the evidence that the warrant for the hotel room was legal and justified. Once the warrant was issued and in hand, Safari would set up a raid on Chesley's room and see what the sweep turned up.

The Biltmore Hotel was a hole in the wall. Two levels of rooms with a rickety wooden external staircase. The police had been there many times for multiple infractions, but always found the same ratty people in rooms with old heavy drapes and bedspreads from the seventies. Some had small kitchenettes with stained stove burners where the inhabitants used to cook their heroin or meth.

"You get a pass if the bust proves useful. Not until, Randy. You know the drill."

A man wearing a blue serge suit entered the bathroom. He spotted Safari and froze in his tracks. "Oh, am I interrupting?"

She smiled. "I was just leaving. Have a great evening."

Safari surfaced in the bar minutes later and almost ran head-on into her sister, Elaine Frye. They said hello and hugged. Then Elaine grabbed Safari by the hand and insisted she join her crowd at a booth near the windows. Safari didn't resist, even though she was hungry and wanted to hit a drive-thru on her way back home to type up her affidavit for the search of Kenneth Chesley's hotel room. But she thought one more beer wouldn't hurt anything, and she did want to catch up with Elaine.

But her heart fell as she approached the table. Sitting on the right, closest to her, was Max Schnell. Max was the last person she wished to see, but it was too late to just veer away and leave her sister standing. Elaine slid into the booth on the left-hand side, leaving the only remaining seat the one next to Max.

Safari closed her eyes, shook her head, and edged in beside him, taking care that their legs and hips did not touch. He sensed her there and turned to look. "Hey, Safari. Long time."

She didn't turn to look, but only stared daggers at her sister. She had purposely steered Safari to her table where she knew Max was having a drink before he went on the bandstand and played. Elaine remained engaged in conversation with the girl to her left, refusing to meet her sister's angry eyes.

He asked gently, "How you been, okay?"

"Yes," she said, avoiding eye contact. "I'm surviving." She made a point at not asking how he'd been. She didn't want to know if he'd moved on, found someone else.

"Hey, if you don't have anything going on Friday night, the band is playing at Reggie Pelham's mansion for his party for the president. I could put you on the guest list."

She fiddled with the label on her beer, peeling the paper off in strips. "I heard about that. We've got extra blues on security when his motorcade comes in from the San Diego airport."

He nudged her with his shoulder. "So, do you think you'd like to go? Not every day you get to rub elbows with the President of the United States."

She chanced a quick look at him, and his smile practically made her melt. She remembered that smile; it was one of the best things about him. She didn't give a rat's ass to see the president, but Max? Well, he was more than special.

"I dunno…"

"Well, how about this. There's no one else I'd rather ask so I'll put your name on the guest list. You can come or not. Up to you."

If she could face down a gunman with an automatic rifle, she should have enough bravery to look the man she loved in the eye. So she did, even though it hurt more than anything. "I'll think about it."

"Good."

He stared at Safari for a moment, and she knew—*she knew*—he still loved her. His brown eyes framed with long lashes, the spider webs at the corners of his eyes, his shoulder-length hair mussed but perfect nonetheless.

If she stayed here a minute more, she'd drag him out to her bike and ride him home to her place. So she cleared her throat and rose. "I have to leave." She eyed her sister and playfully made she was shooting a gun at her.

Max said with a chuckle, "It's really great to see you anyway."

She was close to tears. Max had been an important man in her life. It had ended badly, and she still was carrying a torch. She loved the guy, but she'd ended the relationship. She couldn't be with a man who didn't understand her job, how much of herself went into every day as a detective. He'd complained that her job had always come first. Then her fosters and Little Sisters. Everything before him. She'd argued his music and band was the same, but they'd never been able to come to an accommodation. Her job and love for children always would come first. Didn't mean she'd loved him any less. But that's how it was.

That concluded their conversation since Safari chugged down her beer, grabbed her bag from the table, stared a final dagger at her sister, and fled the place. The Harley jumped to life, and she was gone. Back up the canyon she drove, leaning into the curves, ignoring the tears that threatened to blur her vision. It was time to prepare the affidavit for the raid, grab some dinner, and watch the LA Chargers on *Monday Night Football*.

Then, with a sigh, she remembered the response for Chief Adamson. He would be waiting for it tomorrow morning. She swerved into the parking lot of the package store she frequented, went to the drive-thru, picked up a bottle of Stoli, and went on home. It was going to be a long night, and she didn't want to spend it alone, yet she didn't want human company either. The vodka would just have to suffice.

Just inside her front door, her cell phone chimed. It was

her Little Sister, the girl she mentored as a Big Sister. She answered the call. "Carrie, is everything all right?"

"No." The voice was tentative, and Safari could tell the twelve year old had been crying. "Safari, can I spend the night at your house?"

"Why, honey, what's wrong?"

"She's drunk, and her boyfriend's hitting me again. My jaw hurts like crazy. And he chipped my front tooth with his hairbrush."

She felt like she'd been shot. She carried the girl very close to her heart. For years, Safari had been fostering young girls. If not fostering, then she was their Big Sister. Not only did she want to give them a good life, but she wanted to show them that a woman could do anything, be anything. She understood their circumstances often didn't lean toward this possibility, but Safari tried her best to boost their confidence, and she loved them with her whole heart.

And here and now, what hurt Carrie equally hurt Safari. "Okay, where are you? I'm on my way."

"I'll be waiting at the 7-Eleven. Can you get me there?"

"Sure, I can. Have you called your caseworker?"

"I got her recording so I called you. I'm glad I did."

"Give me thirty minutes. I'm going to drop in on your mom first."

"Oh, God, Safari, don't make me go back there tonight."

"Don't worry, honey, I wouldn't do that to you."

"Okay, bye."

Without stopping to change her clothes, Safari headed back out the front door and settled into the driver's seat of her SDPD Ford interceptor in midnight blue. She backed out of the driveway and left with a squeal of her tires. Carrie lived less than a mile away.

She slid to a stop in front of the familiar block house and rushed up to the front door. She rapped her knuckles hard on the aluminum frame and rang the doorbell at the same time.

Carrie's mother, Maryjane Dillon, cracked the door and peered out. "Oh, Jesus, not you again."

Safari glared at the woman. "I warned you if he touched that child again, I'd be back in person and I'd run your ass in. I made a call, uniforms are on the way, and I swear to God you're not getting out of jail for at least a year. But this is my special warning to you, delivered in person. If either of you ever touch Carrie again, I'm going to make you disappear."

Safari waited for a response, but when there was none, she said, "You have any doubt in your mind what I'm saying is true? Because if there's any doubt, you'd be smart to let go of it right now. Now…you enjoy the next twelve months in jail, and when you get out, you don't come looking for Carrie. In fact, you don't even say her name. Now where's the asshole you're shacked up with? He's going in on a felony assault charge."

The woman swayed away from the door and made a smacking sound with her mouth meant to indicate she was taking none of what Safari said seriously. At that moment, Safari pushed her way inside and swung at the woman with a hard right hand. Her fist connected with Maryjane's nose, and blood flew everywhere. The woman sagged down to the floor and sat there stunned, her legs splayed in front of her. She began vomiting down her chest.

"Oh, hell," muttered Safari as she made her way beyond the woman into the bathroom. She unrolled a swirl of toilet paper, dampened it under the spigot, and returned to the mother. She forced the ball of wet tissue into the mother's hand and told her to wipe her face.

At that moment, she heard a voice from behind, outside on the porch, the voice of a young police officer wanting to know what was going on. She told him to come inside. She had arrived to protect the child, and the woman had tried to assault her. It was a small lie, but she was more than done with Carrie's abuse. How anyone could hurt a child, put them in a situation where they were afraid, often scared to death of what might happen to them, was beyond understanding for Safari. She'd had a decent upbringing, a solid, supportive family so it was something unfathomable to her but happened all the time.

She then turned the scene over to the two officers and made her way back outside. At her car, she stopped and looked back at the house. "You were warned, bitch," she said.

She then jumped in her car and left for the 7-Eleven where Carrie waited. Chief Adamson's report would have to wait and the affidavit for a search warrant might not happen until tomorrow. Safari pounded the steering wheel and cursed.

It would've been a long night at law enforcement chores, but now she had her Little Sister instead.

The rest of the world could just wait.

Chapter 5

Carrie was munching a Dolly Madison cupcake and washing it down with a purple Slurpee when Safari arrived. When she walked up to the girl, she immediately saw the paper napkin wrapped around her upper forearm and held in place with a wrap of silver tape. "All right," said Safari, "what is it?" She pointed at the makeshift bandage.

"Nothing. I got hurt."

"Hurt? How?"

"The asshole hurt me."

"Your mom's boyfriend, Kenneth Chesley, hurt your arm?"

"Yeah. He was mad at me. I mean, like really mad."

"What did he do, hit you?"

"He burned me with a cigarette."

"Oh, Jesus, take that off and let me see, please."

When the girl unwrapped the silver tape, the napkin fell to the floor. There, in a perfect half-inch diameter, was the concave burn, the blackened flesh agape.

"Oh, Jesus. We've got to get that looked at. Come on and let's climb in my car."

"Where're we going?"

"Where? To the hospital. You've got to have a doctor take care of that."

"It does hurt. It's throbbing, actually."

"I can tell you've been crying." Safari could see that Carrie's eyes were all puffy and red. A person would have to be blind not to notice, but Carrie was holding it together now. Barely. "Why aren't you crying now?"

"I don't want anyone to see me. It embarrasses me to cry in public."

Safari gave Carrie a big hug. "I know I talk about how strong a woman can be, but it's okay to cry, to show emotion. That's different."

And as soon as Safari had her arms around Carrie, she'd sniffled, letting out the emotion she had so painfully held in for the last twenty minutes.

They climbed inside the car and buckled up. "What else did he do to you?" Safari said, the height of suspicion in her voice.

"He hit me. But he hits me all the time, anyway."

"Then why did he burn you?"

"Because I wanted money for my flow."

"Your flow? Do you have your period?"

"I just got it. I didn't know what to do. I asked my mom to take me to the store for pads or something, but she was drunk and waved me off. Then Ken said he'd take me if I showed him what I was talking about."

Son of a bitch. I'm gonna kill that bastard. But to Carrie, she said, "What exactly did he ask for?"

"He wanted me to show him my underpants or something, I don't know. I just wanted something for the blood, but now I wish I had stolen the money out of my mom's purse and shut up."

"You're not going back there, Carrie. Do you hear me?"

Carrie started crying. "No! I love my mom. I don't want to lose her."

"Honey, your mom is drunk every day. She brings these assholes home constantly, and we have to come get you. It's not normal. You can't keep on living like that. You're going to stay with me for a while."

"I'd like that. Just please don't put me into foster care. I'll get raped in foster care, and I don't wanna be raped and have someone's baby. I'm never having kids."

Safari wasn't sure where Carrie had heard that stuff about foster care, but her fears seemed real so she didn't say anything. All types signed up to be foster carers for the money only, the monthly stipend they received from the government for every child. There were some good families though.

"If the case worker allows it, you're welcome to come live with me." Safari left the 7-Eleven parking lot and pulled into traffic. "My precious girl, I'm so sorry this happened to you. Do you still need something for your period?"

"I stole some napkins at 7-Eleven and stuffed them in there. Maybe we can get something at the hospital?"

"Don't give it another thought. We'll get you all fixed up, and we'll talk a little about it."

"Really, we don't have to. I had health class. This is old stuff."

"We'll talk anyway. It'll make me feel better. As your Big Sister."

Carrie looked out the window as if resigned. "Okay."

Safari continued driving toward Scripps Memorial Hospital on Genesee Avenue. It was after seven o'clock, and traffic was thinning. As they drove, she studied Carrie out of the corner of her eye. She'd known kids with terribly difficult starts in life but never as difficult as this girl's. She had worked with Carrie as her Big Sister for just about six months, and the entire time the child's living conditions at home had continued to slide downhill. Just in the short time she had known Carrie, her mother had gone through a succession of five boyfriends, all of whom were live-ins for anywhere from twenty-four hours to three weeks. It was a pattern: get drunk, bring a man home, support him. Carrie's mom made good money as a software tester in Carlsbad, so Safari never understood why Maryjane didn't go for a nice working man. But for some reason, she didn't. She'd always end up falling out with the scum boyfriend, he would leave, and her mom would break down in tears and go on a bender. That left Carrie to do her own self-care while mom was checked out in that exosphere she created around herself, that place where she went to get over the life she created and created again.

Safari pulled in under the emergency room sign and put the SUV in park. Anyone who bothered to look would see it was a police vehicle and leave it alone, which was fair enough. She actually was there on police business, bringing a crime victim to the hospital for treatment.

Inside, Safari waited while Admissions went through its protocol and even found a previous record for Carrie, a fractured arm, and gathered her insurance information and personal data. She was then taken to a curtained examination table without the usual interminable wait like in most ER situations. Since there was severe pain, Carrie was moved ahead in line of the headaches, belly aches, and other common complaints in hospitals serving a wealthy population.

Safari stood next to Carrie's bed and held her hand. A female doctor, Dr. Elizabeth Murray—thank God for that—appeared through the curtains, accompanied by a female nurse. When they began with questions, Safari badged them and said she would remain while they treated the girl's arm and discussed her flow. She wasn't about to leave her charge with anybody.

After numbing the site, they cleaned the burn and went to work on the wound, applying an antibiotic cream. Then they dressed it carefully with dry gauze. When the doctor asked Carrie about a tetanus shot, she appeared scared, shrinking back under the sheets. Dr. Murray looked to Safari, who shook her head slightly. "We'll get it done later."

Dr. Murray acquiesced and, finally, they heard Carrie's whispered questions and commentary on her flow—whispered because another patient now occupied the adjacent curtained examination area. The nurse went to retrieve a supply of feminine products while Carrie and Safari waited. Upon her return, she demonstrated how the products should be used.

Following the child's discharge, along with a short supply of pain pills, Safari drove them to her apartment, and they went inside. Safari hung her motorcycle jacket on the hooks by the door while Carrie slumped down in the couch.

"I have a guest room," Safari said, taking a seat beside Carrie on the couch. "It's your room now, at least until the judge says you have to go somewhere else, if that time ever comes. I will fight that ever happening. I want you here. I want you living with me now. Your other situation has failed you miserably."

Carrie began crying. "I miss my mom. I hope she's okay."

Safari slid over and rubbed Carrie's back. "Honey, your mom brought home an animal who burned you with a cigarette. She doesn't deserve your tears right now. I understand, though, if you need to cry and let out some of your grief. But let's keep mom in perspective. I know you love her and worry about her, but just for tonight, let's let mom look out for herself, okay?"

"O-okay," Carrie huffed between sobs. "Do you think Ken is still there with her? I'm scared for her."

"Did you hear that call I made on my radio while we were driving home? I requested police officers go to your mom's apartment and arrest him. He needs to be taken into custody ASAP before he hurts another little girl or another mom. I expect the police have him by now."

"I hope they put him in jail forever."

"I do, too. For what he did to you, I expect him to go away to prison for a long time. Many years."

Just then, Safari received a call from dispatch. She went into the kitchen, away from Carrie, where she could speak freely. "Go on, dispatch. Detective Frye here."

"Officers responded to the apartment complex on Faraday Road. There was no answer, so they went through the door with their battering ram. The place was a mess. A woman's body was found in the main bedroom. She was wearing jeans and a white peasant blouse that had been pushed up around her neck. On the side of her neck was a peacock tattoo in green and blue. Sounds like your minor's mother?"

"I think so. I'll check it out with my visitor and get back. Cause of death?"

"Initial investigation of strangulation with the window shade cord. She was garroted."

"Roger that, dispatch. Assign a detective outside my team, please, if you haven't already."

"One step ahead of you, Detective Frye. The captain didn't want to create a conflict by assigning you or a team member to the case since you have the minor daughter of the victim."

"Leads?"

"Boyfriend. Neighbors say he was there and left. We've got a description and an all-points bulletin."

"Notify me when you have him in custody. I'd like to sit in on the interview."

"Roger that, Detective Frye."

"Roger that. Frye, out."

"Good night, Detective. Out."

Safari jammed the phone back inside her jean's pocket and made coffee. She poured a glass of OJ and took it to Carrie, who had left the couch and living room and was now familiarizing herself with her new bedroom. She was walking around the room, touching items briefly before moving on.

"Have you read all these?" asked the girl, pointing to the waist-high bookcase filled to overflowing with police science and crime scene books and manuals.

"Every one. It was part of my college courses."

"You went to college?"

"I did. I even have a master's degree in justice studies. Big stuff, huh?"

The girl smiled. "I might like to do that someday."

"You definitely can. We can start working toward that now."

"I think it's a good fit. I hate criminals."

"Definitely a start." Safari didn't know how to approach the tattoo any other way than directly. For what reason would she have to ask about Carrie's mother that way? So she just laid it on the line. "Tell me about your mother's tattoo."

"She loves peacocks. She has it on her neck."

Safari sighed. Telling Carrie about her mom was probably one of the worst things Safari had to go through. Right along with the pain of breaking up with Max. But in many ways, this was worse. With children, their pain, and therefore your pain, was the most intense emotion in the world. "We need to talk about your mom. There's been a bad thing happen."

Carried turned on her bed toward Safari who had taken a seat next to her. "What happened? She got arrested?"

"Worse."

"Somebody hurt her?"

"Somebody killed your mom, Carrie." Safari grabbed the young girl's hand. "I'm so sorry."

The girl erupted in paroxysms of tears and wails. Safari folded her arms around, rhythmically rocking back and forth with the girl's sobs. For several minutes, she was inconsolable, but then it slowed, as grief will, and Safari was able to say a few small, simple things about her love for the child and the safety Carrie would find in her home. But it helped very little, as Carrie was stuck in the house with her mother, still trapped in that old reality. It was going to take more than loving words and a few days. It was going to take a long time. But Safari was untroubled. She had all the time in the world.

Carrie wasn't going anywhere.

Not over Safari's dead body.

Chapter 6

The call came an hour later from dispatch: Kenneth Chesley had been taken into custody while at the Shores Hotel where he'd started a fight with the house band's guitarist and got eighty-sixed. The uniforms on the call had recognized him and notified the detectives they had their man in custody. It was all downhill from there. Dispatch had asked if Safari wanted to be there during the interview of Chesley. Safari told them yes, but she was going to have to pass as she had the decedent's child with her. She had notified Department of Children and Family Services that she had the child and was waiting on the caseworker.

The caseworker came out after nine o'clock when Carrie was already in bed, asleep. She re-opened Carrie's case and advised Safari they had made house calls before to Maryjane Dillon's house. It had been only a matter of time before the line was crossed when they could remove the little girl from her mother's house.

Wasn't that typical? Safari thought. It was only after it

was too late that things got done in the current system. Now Maryjane was dead and Carrie was without her mom.

Temporary placement was granted to Safari, who told the caseworker she would like it to be made permanent if possible. That would take time and court participation, of course, so everything was wrapped up that could be wrapped up by ten o'clock when the caseworker left Safari's home.

Safari called her captain's voicemail to advise she'd be taking a personal leave day tomorrow while she got Carrie situated and spent some time with the child. She also said she intended to take Carrie to Chesley's initial appearance before the judge the next day and let the child see that her mother's killer was being prosecuted and held in jail and was no longer a physical threat. She figured that was as good a therapy as any.

Chapter 7

Sunset North Sound was a state-of-the-art recording studio set back 150 yards from the white sands of La Jolla. It was owned and operated by a consortium out of Los Angeles that was always actively looking for the next big act for next year's Grammy Awards. The studio was built around a Neve console. Its outboard racks were full of the latest gear from Germany and Japan, each rack unit crackling and sparkling with LED lights, begging to be put in line on the next track.

A La Jolla producer by the name of Rita Reynolds was in the chair Wednesday afternoon, mastering the CD of a chart-topping boy band called Boys 'N Luv. Seated next to her was her best friend and sound engineer Joan McIntyre, a comely 22-year-old just out of the Musicians Institute in LA, who looked up in awe at the producer, Rita, who already had two Grammy nominations to her name. Rita triggered the talkback mic and said soothingly to the four boys gathered around the Neumann mic in the talent room, "That was incredible, guys, but give me one more take just for the hell of it." Joan created a new track and hit record. The countdown click kicked in, and the boys began singing in four-part harmony.

Rita turned to Joan and said, "These guys are really dragging today. Too many late nights."

Joan shook her head and stubbed out her cigarette on the console ashtray. "I was out with them last night. My head is still pounding. Butchy talked about you."

"What did he say?"

"He said he thought you were the best producer on the West Coast."

Rita felt her heart jump. "That's all he said?"

"He also said he was madly in love with you. *Not*."

"Ha ha, funny lady. Just look at him out there singing lead. I love how that blond hair sweeps across his forehead in that sexy way. He makes me tingle in all the right places."

Joan scowled. "Get over it, girl. He's nine years younger than you. His mother would have your scalp. Not to mention his agent. Not to mention LA. That's all you need right now."

Rita moved two sliders on the console and sat back. "Hey, will you be going to Reggie Pelham's bash Friday night?"

Joan twisted the skin on her elbow and examined a small black mole. She considered the wisdom of her friend Rita attending a party where Butchy would be in attendance, too. He was but sixteen while Rita was twenty-five. It was an accident waiting to happen. She had tried to warn her best friend that having sex with a juvenile was not only declasse *and* illegal but could actually ruin her career as a top West Coast music producer if it got around that she was fucking the talent.

"I know what you're thinking," Rita said. She smiled her

most malevolent smile. "What if I told you I've already tapped that? What would you think of that?"

"I think you're insane. I think you're laying everything on the line for a piece of boy tail. It's nuts."

"Butchy Penrose is much older than his years," Rita said. "I peg him at about twenty-one in the way he handles himself and the way he views the world. He's a very precocious boy—man. Oh, my God, what am I saying? I need to have my head examined."

The boys finished the take and pulled off their headphones. Butchy shook a cigarette out of pack from his front pocket and lit it with a big inhale. He stepped up to the microphone and leaned into it. "Hey, Rita, I think we nailed it that time. I feel a big party coming on. Is the control room ready to hit the streets with us?"

Rita hit the talkback button. "Negative on that, Butchy. You guys are on your own tonight. The big kids are going to do their own thing."

"Come on, it's not the same without our big sisters," Butchy whined. He was baiting her, and Rita knew it, but for once her sense of self-preservation prevailed, and she stood her ground.

"You had your chance with us, kiddo, and you blew it," Rita teased. "There are no second chances with us." She laughed over the talkback mic so that Butchy knew it was all in fun. When they were young, a lady couldn't be too careful. Butchy was the youngest, then Jonny and Sammy were nineteen, and the oldest was Dusty at twenty. They'd all changed their names so they ended with *y*. It was all part of the big marketing wheel they rode. It was supposed to be cute, memorable, easy for the girls to name.

But Butchy wasn't going to go away that easily. He

pressed the button on the talkback mic again. "Hey, are you guys going to my Uncle Reggie's party on Friday?"

Rita spoke, "Joan and I will definitely be there, but we'll be playing like we don't know you guys, so find someone else to talk to. Someone your own age." Rita wondered whether Butchy could hear the tone of regret in her voice when she'd said *someone your own age*.

If he heard the regret, he wasn't letting on. "Hey, if you are too goody goody for us, maybe we need a new production team. What you say guys, do we need a new team?"

All four members of Boys 'N Luv jumped up and down, hooting and whistling. "New producer! New engineer!"

One of the boys, Dusty Zamboa, walked to the bench along the wall where the main doors stood. The boys had dropped jackets and serapes and bags along there when arriving hours earlier. Dusty pulled his vest from under the pile and dug out a cigarette, a Mexican brand. As he did, a small handgun slipped halfway out of the vest's waistband pocket. Dusty shot a look around. Had anyone seen? The other boys in the band knew he carried heat; he was from Rosarito, for fuck's sake. That's where he'd learned to drum on the sidewalks with plastic buckets and homemade drumsticks.

He shrugged into the vest, making sure the gun was snugged deep inside the pocket and there was no outline printed through the cotton material. Then he turned back to the others. He saw Rita, the producer, frozen on Butchy, where she had been since the album sessions began. It was disgusting; the bitch was in heat.

Rita's breath caught in her throat. She shivered underneath her oversize T-shirt and her latex tights. How on earth could she ever tell anyone that she was totally in love with Butchy Penrose? Twenty-five-year-old women didn't get a free pass when it came to seducing sixteen-year-old boys. She was already frightened of what she had done. But it had felt like cocaine had felt before she got clean and sober: one kiss or one touch was too much, while a million touches or kisses were not enough. She had to admit she was head over heels. Even now, sitting beside her, Joan must have sensed there was something going on. She'd even given her the side-eye followed by an eye-roll.

She was acting like an oversexed sixteen-year-old girl in heat for the first time. Her thoughts dashed ahead to Friday night and the party at Reginald Pelham's house on the beach. Everyone was going to be there, which left her no choice—she would have to be there or be talked about behind her back. Naturally, she would be there. She decided to ask Joan to accompany her and to stick with her at all times Friday night so that she didn't do something crazy like try to get Butchy alone in a dark corner. Speaking in the privacy of the soundproof booth, Rita said to Joan, "Any chance you could accompany me to Pelham's Friday night? I feel like I'm going to need a friend to lean on, a friend who won't let me out of her sight if I try to run off and be crazy."

"Just how crazy are we talking about running off and being?" replied Joan.

Rita shut her eyes and grimaced, fighting it back. But then it came out anyway, "I shouldn't tell you this, but I bedded that boy already. Oh, my God, what in God's name possessed me?"

"TMI! TMI! Don't say another word. I don't want to be a witness when the cops come around asking questions. I know you think I'm kidding, but I'm not. Underage sex never works. Someone always gets caught and has to pay the price. My God, girl, what were you thinking?"

"That's just it, I wasn't thinking. I was touching myself and getting off, which made me wind up in bed with Butchy. I have to go Friday night, but I'm really begging you to come with me," said Rita.

Joan didn't immediately answer. She was a sound engineer and right above her was Rita, a full-fledged producer. But Joan knew Rita was really nothing without Joan's technical genius. So, she had to admit—for Joan was good at self-examination—she was jealous of Rita. Were something to happen Friday night and Rita got canned, that would leave Joan to finish the album. There was no one else the studio had to turn to who knew the songs and the engineering and upcoming production like Joan. She had her finger on the pulse of the album. Even now, with Rita still at the controls, she was there mainly because of Joan, who'd engineered Rita's last four outings. It was Joan who gave her just about everything good she had. Still, a little recognition—a Grammy, maybe?—would be wonderful. Then she answered Rita's question: Would Joan watch over her Friday night?

"Don't worry, honey, I'll be right there with you. And I promise I won't let you get alone with Butchy. Still friends?"

Rita clapped her hands together. "Still friends. Thank you, thank you, thank you."

Joan couldn't stop feeling deprived the more she thought about it. Rita was even getting the choice of all the men that came along, a seat that Joan might like to occupy every once in a while, thank you very much. She'd stewed about it in the past, but the more she thought about it now, the more her jealousy moved her from resentment to hatred of Rita.

Thirty minutes later, as everyone was heading off to lunch and Joan was, again, heading out alone, Joan wondered what bad thing might happen to Rita Friday night that would get her booted off the album. She caught a glimpse of herself in the reflection of the studio glass and tugged at the long red bangs that swept across her forehead and obscured one of her eyes.

She didn't know, exactly, what that bad thing might look like, but she knew this—there would be a gun involved. A gun not unlike the gun her father kept at home in the drawer of his nightstand. It had pearl handles and a snub barrel. It was the type of gun that would fit easily inside Joan's jacket pocket. The type of gun that would nicely fit in the palm of Rita's hand.

It was done. The decision was made. There would be a gun.

Chapter 8

Safari, with Carrie in tow, arrived at half-past nine for Kenneth Chesley's ten a.m. initial appearance. They found a seat in the back of the courtroom, as far away as possible from where Chesley would stand before the judge. While Safari wanted the girl to see and hear what happened with her mother's killer, she didn't want the child close enough she might be traumatized by the experience. She was there to learn, not made to suffer.

The courtroom filled slowly with family and friends of those with an initial appearance today, court personnel, and the usual rubbernecks. Just before ten o'clock, a long chain line of prisoners was brought over from the jail. In their highway orange jumpsuits and the long chain, Safari was reminded of the hot peppers on the vine growing beneath her kitchen window.

Judge Weinaur appeared at ten sharp, and court was called to order. The clerk began reading case names, starting with the oldest first. An hour later, after a bathroom break for Safari and Carrie, the name of Kenneth Chesley was called.

Outwardly, the man didn't look like much. His dark hair was thinning, but he still pulled it back in a ponytail. His face was nondescript, dark eyes, low brows, a biggish nose and a cleft in his chin. He was just under six feet with sloping shoulders, and if he had a belly paunch, Safari couldn't tell under the orange jumpsuit.

He was un-manacled from the chain and came forward, hands cuffed behind his back. Two deputies, one on each side, had him pinned between. His court-appointed attorney stood off to the side.

Said Judge Weinaur, "Your name for the record?"

The defendant said, "Kenneth J. Chesley."

"Mr. Chesley, what is your usual occupation?"

"Road manager for touring bands."

"And your address?"

"Currently at the Biltmore Hotel."

"Permanent address?"

"Haven't had a permanent address for years. Like I said, I tour with different bands. We're never home."

"How long have you been in La Jolla?"

"Couple of weeks. We're parked here while our touring schedule gets some dates dropped and added. We're small potatoes, and we'll move on without warning."

"Well, sir, that confirms some of the court's concern. You stand accused of murdering Maryjane Dillon. Counsel, have you seen the charging document?"

At the mention of her mother's name, Maryjane Dillon, young Carrie jerked in her seat. Safari felt this and draped a protective arm over the child's shoulders.

The public defender, a willowy woman with a wave of short blond hair, longish on one side and quite short on the other, answered, "We have, Your Honor. Defendant waives reading in court."

"Mr. Chesley, you have the right to have an attorney present and representing you at all stages of these proceedings. The court notes that the public defender has been appointed and is appearing with you just now. Do you understand this right?"

"I do."

The judge then ran through a litany of rights and explanations applicable to the case. He then took up the question of bail. "Does the defendant have a motion?"

"I do," said his lawyer. "The defendant requests that bail be set in this matter. While the defendant doesn't have a large number of contacts with the community, he also has no record of failing to appear in any court anyplace in America. He is gainfully employed and would like to return to the work of managing the band's tour. Respectfully suggest bail in the amount of fifty-thousand dollars."

"Counsel?" asked the judge of the district attorney.

"That must be intended as a joke, Judge," said the district attorney, a young black man with beautiful teeth and a quick smile. "Fifty-thousand dollars bail on a first-degree murder case would make the national news it's so preposterous. I can see the headlines now. 'Come to California and murder your enemy. Go free with only five-thousand dollars down.' The state has read over the defendant's financial forms, and while it looks like the defendant has only minimal assets, bail no less than one-million dollars is the standard in these cases and should be ordered in this case. But let's even take another step back. Should there even be any bail allowed? That's the real question. Here, the presumption is great, and the proof is strong of first-degree murder. The defendant was stopped by police only three miles from the victim's house in his Toyota Corolla. Fibers found in the Corolla's carpet match the fibers used on the Venetian blind cords in the victim's bedroom window. So the presumption he did commit the crime is far beyond a reasonable doubt. The proof is not only strong, it's overwhelming given the match between the defendant's knife blade and the cords used to strangle Ms. Dillon. This defendant is a threat to the entire community, and to turn him loose on the people of California would be to betray the court's duty."

Judge Weinaur nodded as the DA sat down. "Mr. District Attorney, the court is well-aware of its duty to the community and the state, but it is likewise aware of its duty to set bail. The court is of the belief that the defendant won't be able to make bail, no matter how much it is, based on the defendant's financial statement submitted to the court. That being the case, bail is set at one-million dollars. Usual conditions of bail will apply. Lady and gentleman, is there anything further?"

"No, Your Honor," said the defense attorney. "Thank you, Judge," she added, and meant it for she had done her job.

"Setting bail in this case is astonishing," Safari said to Carrie when they were safely outside in the hallway, out of earshot of the courtroom's occupants. "I've never heard of bail in a first-degree murder case with this kind of proof."

"What did the man mean about the Venetian blind?" Carrie wanted to know.

Safari realized the little girl hadn't been told of the manner of her mother's death. Great, now she got to tell her the sickening story of how her mother died. She knew it would be terribly upsetting, so she decided to avoid answering just yet.

"I didn't quite follow all that," Safari said. "I'll need to talk to the arresting officers before I can tell you."

"Please talk to them. I want to know what they meant. I'm thinking if there are cords from the Venetian blinds, it must mean the asshole used the cord to choke my mom."

When Carrie started cursing under her breath, Safari took the child's hand and began moving them toward the elevators. The cursing continued all the way down the hall, mostly directed at Chesley, but she also included all the other assholes that had come before him.

They rode downstairs and then walked out through the police exit to Safari's waiting police vehicle. They piled inside and buckled up.

"Did you understand most of it?" Safari asked before she started the sedan.

"I got it, I think, except the cord thing. Chesley's charged with first-degree murder. He could go to prison for life."

"Yes, he could."

"Well, he should. Mom was a lot of things, but she didn't deserve to die. First, he burns my arm and then he kills my mom. Welcome to La Jolla, asshole, where you can do whatever you want to people and get out on bail."

"I don't think he can come up with the money," Safari told the child. "I looked at his financial information online. He's got jack shit to post bail."

"He is jack shit."

"Jack shit it is, then," Safari said, and they high-fived as Safari fired up the Ford Interceptor.

"Hey, if he gets the money and gets out, will you save me from him?"

"Oh, honey, he won't hurt you again. He's got bigger problems than you."

"Says you. I know he'll want to come after me. I just know it."

"Why's that? Why do you think he would be after his victim's daughter?"

"Because I saw him cut the window blinds. He was mad 'cause my mom kept opening them up at noon to get him out of bed. I saw him take his knife and cut them so she couldn't do it again."

"Good grief. You're a witness. I'll have to tell the detectives."

"Do you have to? Can't they find him guilty without me?"

"Maybe yes. But if the case fell apart, and you didn't testify, you'd grow up hating yourself. We need to tell the dicks what you saw."

She squirmed in her seat and looked down at her hands. "I don't want to, but okay. Just tell them not to use me unless they have to, okay?"

"That I can do."

"Okay, then."

"Okay," Safari said, grabbing and squeezing Carrie's hands still knotted on her lap.

Chapter 9

While everybody who was anybody at Pelham's party was engaged in deep conversations or deep joke-telling or deep making out, a stranger arrived in town Friday, checking into his room just two miles from Reginald Pelham's house on the beach. The stranger was from Durango, Colorado where he was a lawyer. His name was Thaddeus Murfee. Thaddeus was married, early forties, and the father of many children. He was six-one, 195 pounds on the scale at the 24-Hour Fitness, his hair was brown-blond, and he wore single-vision eyeglasses that turned dark in the sun. He had been around the block with the mob in a case fought fiercely with them and had come away owning a Las Vegas casino which, along with other earnings, when sold brought in $400 million.

Last night he'd been in Las Vegas because a law school roommate—Jesse Matina, corporate counsel of SkoolDaze—had called about Reginald Pelham. Jesse had asked nicely. Thaddeus had resisted at first, but then Jesse promised

Thaddeus several youth programs would be able to continue operation in Las Vegas if Thaddeus prevailed in La Jolla, so Thaddeus had agreed to come to La Jolla and have a look. That was all, just have a look.

Thaddeus parked his rental at La Valencia Hotel and went inside to register. He had reserved the Villa King Ocean suite for its king-size bed and ocean view. While in his room, he changed into coral-colored slacks and a white cotton shirt with a coral collar and left for Reginald's party. He was to meet with his prospective client that night at the gathering. Reginald had invited Thaddeus there to talk and had promised complete privacy away from the crowd.

When Thaddeus arrived at six p.m., he was shown into a library stuffed with mysteries and thrillers. He took to looking over the volumes while waiting. Just then, the door opened at his back, the light switched off, and he heard a giggling couple make their way across the floor to an overstuffed couch. Then, before he could even speak, he heard clothes being whipped off and the sound of two lovers moaning. "Hey," he said as soon as it started, "did anyone see me back here?"

"Christ!" cried a female voice.

"No cameras!" cried a youthful male voice.

"Whoa, whoa," said Thaddeus. "I'm a lawyer. I keep all secrets entrusted to me." With his words, he couldn't help but laugh. In a way, what he'd just heard and observed was a secret and, on the other hand, he'd never reveal any of it.

The young woman, tucking in her shirt, stood from the couch and approached him. "I'm Rita. Who're you?"

"Thaddeus Murfee. I really am a lawyer"—he handed her his business card—"and I really will keep my mouth shut. What I heard here, what I saw here, it shall stay here." He made the sign of someone zipping his mouth shut. Then he smiled, and Rita was dazzled. The guy was adorable and older than her, just her type. She was quickly forgetting about Butchy, the young man peering over the top of the couch.

"You're new in town," she said with a wide smile.

"Just got in. I'm supposed to meet Mr. Pelham in here any moment."

"Have a drink with me after?"

"Why not?" he said, again with a laugh. "My wife won't mind, and I don't drink. It ought to be a barrel of monkeys."

"Hey!" the young man said. "I'm right here, Rita. What the hell?"

She laughed, blatantly ignoring the kid on the couch. "Can't blame a girl for trying, especially with a guy who looks like you."

Thaddeus nodded, turning away suddenly as the door opened. Reginald Pelham came strutting grandly into his library, hand-extended.

"Hey, I'm Reggie. You're Thaddeus?"

He was ignoring Rita and his nephew, the boy toy.

"I'm Thaddeus. I think these two desperadoes were just leaving."

Rita and the young man sailed right past them, right out the door.

"So," Thaddeus began, "troubles with the business? Jesse mentioned something like that."

"Please sit." Reggie motioned to the couch that Rita and lover had just vacated and took a seat himself at the chair adjacent. "Wife trouble, and now she's filed a shareholder's suit against me."

Thaddeus sat and crossed his legs, hooking his hands

around his knee. "She's trying to knock you out of the CEO position?"

"Exactly. She's claiming I'm double-dealing my company, selling assets it owns under the table, and wasting corporate assets in pursuit of young women."

"Are you doing those things?"

"Yes and no," Pelham said without hesitation. "You know how it is."

"Actually, no, I don't know how it is, Mr. Pelham. But if you are doing those things, or have done them in the past, are you ready to stop doing them if I defend you and help you with a second chance?"

"Whew, brother, yes! I can't lose my company, Thaddeus. It would be the end of me."

"Good, then there are some things we can talk about."

Chapter 10

Air Force One touched down at Marine Corps Air Station in San Diego. The presidential motorcade was formed and moved out for La Jolla and the home of IT billionaire Reginald Pelham.

The president, a slender, ex-mayor of a large Midwestern city, sat sandwiched between a Secret Service agent and the First Lady. He was an older man and up for reelection next month. In fact, the purpose of the La Jolla visit was to get a photoshoot with the young and upcoming boy band, Boyz 'N Luv, a strategic play to try to reel in the millennials, where his ratings sucked. He needed the younger votes if he wanted to spend a second term in the White House.

As the President's advance Secret Service contingent entered the grounds of Pelham's estate, Joan McIntyre, recording engineer and best friend of Rita Reynolds, realized she needed some place to hide her father's pearl-handled revolver. What had she been thinking to bring a gun when she'd known the president would be at the party for his photo op?

Joan hadn't been thinking. That was the problem. She'd only seen red and felt her rage directed at her friend and co-worker, Rita.

She dashed through the house as the Secret Service was entering and setting up its electronic gates, then charged upstairs, where she settled on a bathroom where a loose ceiling tile could be bent down and the gun inserted just above. It was loaded and ready for action.

While she was there, Joan pulled out her flute and smoked the last of her crystal meth. She needed to calm the fuck down, stay steady until she could set it up so Rita went down for murder.

Ace Moynahan, lead agent of the presidential Secret Service detail, set up a security checkpoint at the entrance to Pelham's home. His agents then shepherded all the guests and employees to the front of the home and began searching them and scanning them before they returned inside. Joan, Rita, and the boys, even though they lived there, had to go through the gates.

While this process was ongoing, Secret Service agents skilled in technology went meticulously through the house with their electronic devices, searching for explosives and weapons. Bomb sniffing dogs helped in this endeavor, and the necessary wiring schematics were traced as well. An hour later, all the employees and two thirds of the guests had been readmitted to the house, and the party was back in full swing.

The presidential motorcade came up the circular driveway and diverted to the back entrance of the home. Doors opened, and the President and First Lady were ushered inside by armed agents. They were taken down along a hallway that interconnected with the guest house, itself a small mansion, fully staffed with its own cook, servants and, now, Secret Service agents. The President and First Lady took the opportunity to change clothes and freshen up before going out poolside and joining the party there. Reginald Pelham was beside himself with glee, for he had scored major marks in the game of wealth by hosting the President and First Lady in his home.

Delbert Hicks of the *Denver Post* managed to get the first picture of the President, First Lady, their host, Reggie Pelham, and the boy band Boyz 'N Luv. The President and First Lady held hands with Reggie on their left and then his nephew, Butchy. On their right were Jonny and Sammy, with Dusty on the far end. Butchy had wrapped his arm over his uncle's shoulder in a casual stance, as did Jonny and Sammy; they playfully locked in a scuffle when the photo was snapped. Only did Dusty take on a tough hip-hop type stance, standing a bit separate from the rest. The photograph was broadcast around the world, and immediately petty jealousies arose among other members of the press in attendance.

As the alcohol flowed and lowered inhibitions, the mood of the party became more and more excited and then even exhilarated. Cloistered poolside were partygoers who had taken to cabanas, breaking off into small knots of their own choosing and species. Inside one such cabana, the one closest to the high dive, there was a frolic underway involving Rita, Butchy, Joan, Dusty Zamboa, the two other band members, Jonny and Sammy, and a dozen others.

At some point in the evening, Joan began speaking with Addison Bayer, an eighteen-year-old freshman at UCSD in premed. Addison was head over heels in love with Butchy, but no one there knew it, and she was reserved enough that no one would ever know it. As Joan spoke with Addison and they traded stories, an idea formed in Joan's head. "Just for laughs and giggles," Joan at one point said to Addison, "how would you like to play a trick on Butchy?"

"I don't think so," said Addison. "Tell the truth, I'm quite fond of him and don't want to tease him."

Joan brushed her off. "Trust me, I know Butchy from the studio, and he loves nothing more than a great practical joke. If you really wanted his attention, this is the way to do it. In fact, I'm so ready to have a few laughs tonight that I would gladly pay you a hundred bucks just to make a pass at him."

"I don't think so. I don't do stuff like that."

"Believe me, he would absolutely love it if he found out later you had been paid off to do it for me. Like I said, Butchy is a great practical joker."

"Hundred bucks? Just for making a pass at a guy I kinda like? You're making this very hard to resist. Show me the money."

Joan dug down into her pocket. It was the time of high rollers and big spenders. A hundred bucks was nothing. She pulled out a Benjamin, concealing it in her hand, and passed it to Addison. Addison opened her hand for a brief second, checked out the denomination, and tucked the bill inside her short's pocket. She then nodded and shrugged. "Oh, well," she said. "I want to check my makeup. Be right back."

Addison headed for the house, found an open bathroom, and did a quick touchup. She then returned to the cabana with a fresh gin and tonic in hand, downed half the drink, and came up behind Butchy.

Butchy had been stalked all evening by Rita, who just wasn't able to leave him alone, despite knowing better. As

Joan had followed Rita during the earlier hours, it was clear Rita's bad angels were running her show, and she wasn't going to back down. Rita intended to go home with Butchy that night, and Joan couldn't have that.

Addison had touched a fragrance called *Oh Man!* behind each ear. It was one she had picked up at Ordly's on Rodeo Drive in Hollywood. Leaning in from behind, her fragrance got his attention, and he felt warm breath against his ear. His head snapped around, staring at Addison head-on. "Whoa, who's this?" said Butchy, obviously surprised and happy.

"I'm Addison." With those words, the young woman leaned even nearer and placed her lips against Butchy's. She pushed, opening her mouth for his tongue to play across her teeth.

Rita missed none of it.

Chapter 11

Pelham returned to the home library where he'd left Thaddeus while he posed for pictures with the President. He found his maybe-lawyer waiting for him there, seated in an overstuffed chair and reading from a textbook on key advances in computer science since 2015. "Hey," said Pelham. "Thanks for waiting."

Thaddeus shut the book. "Not a problem. You've got the President here, and I'm going to guess that takes precedence." He smiled. "At least for members of the President's party. But let's not get into that. Let's get back to some of those things your wife wants you done in for. I take it your R-and-D people have developed technology that isn't applicable to your current IT architecture and you've parlayed some of those developments into cash payments. Maybe offshore cash payments?"

Sweat broke out across Pelham's forehead and he leaned his weight against the back of the leather couch. "Guilty. You know me too well, Thaddeus. Yes, I've done some of the things you mention. All told, between fifty and sixty million in undisclosed earnings."

"Undisclosed to SkoolDaze, I get it. But undisclosed to the IRS, too?"

"That's right. Unreported income from the sale of company assets."

"So we're defending not only your wife's case but there's also the possibility we'll be defending some form of IRS claims. Maybe revenue only, maybe criminal. We'll hold the latter for discussion on down the road. But for now, if I get involved, we're going to need to go back and assign a capital basis to those assets you sold off and report the net gain on amended IRS filings. Are we together so far?"

"Yes, we are," said Pelham meekly. "Reveal the sales to the IRS. Check."

"And we're going to need to enter the transactions on the company books in the form of adjusted entries. This should be done without delay."

"But doesn't that just prove my wife's case against me? We're giving her the ammunition she needs to nail my ass to the wall."

"We are and we aren't. Chances are, she's going to find out about these things anyway during discovery of the underlying case. We beat her to the punch by adjusting the books and take some of the wind out of her sails. We'll come up with a compelling rationale why those entries have been delayed. That much I can help you do. Then we'll justify the delay, and that will blow up a good portion of her case."

Thaddeus set the book he'd been reading onto the end table. "The chasing after young women part—that's personal stuff, and I think that goes nowhere in the context of a shareholders' suit. Sure, there's some commingling of personal and corporate funds, but it's a closely-held corporation, a family corporation, and that kind of stuff is inevitable. People see their businesses as their own ATMs. It gets fuzzy. Like I said, this kind of stuff I'm not so worried about. Your big worry is the sale of company assets without reporting to the IRS. Let me handle that, and I think we can make that go away."

Pelham finally took a seat on the couch. "Jeez, man, I'm loving what you're saying. When can we get started?"

"In the morning. I plan on being in La Jolla for the next few days. Maybe you can have your CFO get some records together for me?"

"Whatever you need. Just ask."

"And I'm going to need a couple of hours of your time to help me track down and isolate the unreported sales. That stuff worries me. That's up first."

"Can do. Just tell me where and when."

"How about tomorrow, my hotel, La Valencia, at ten a.m.?"

Pelham clapped his hands together. "Done. I'll be there."

AS THADDEUS WAS MEETING with Pelham, Safari Frye was pulling her undercover vehicle under Pelham's portico where all vehicles were being searched by the Secret Service before being allowed to proceed onto the grounds. She badged the agents, but that had no effect—they searched her vehicle anyway, running a mirror beneath her car and shining lights into the interior. A contraband-sniffing dog finished the search, and Safari was finally waved on through.

As much as she didn't think it was a good idea to come here as Max's guest, she couldn't help being curious about the president's visit. Plus, she got to watch Max and his band, Avenging Angels, play poolside without getting too close to him again. So, she'd had her sister, Elaine, over to her house to hang out with Carrie. She didn't want the girl to be alone right now, even though she'd taken care of herself pretty much from the age of nine years old, her mom being drunk the majority of her childhood. But Carrie was in a delicate state, and Elaine promised they'd paint nails and have some girly time, which Elaine was much better at than Safari.

She had turned in her response to the sexual harassment claim just before coming here. Basically, she had admitted saying the words, but her defense was that all the men said those same words all the time and nobody could possibly take them seriously. "Dickless wonder" was the number one go-to phrase that was always used when one of the officers was being a jerk or exhibiting less than manly-man behavior. For her to have said the words and then get singled out over them was beyond the pale, her answer said, and the police administration had only to poll the other detectives and beat cops about the use of the words inside the department to see that she was just one of many and there was nothing sexual and nothing harassing by the words. So, she felt good about her longevity on the job and couldn't see herself getting dinged over the harassment claim. Or so she hoped.

Safari accepted a passing glass of ginger ale and walked outside to the pool area. Avenging Angels were just setting up. They were following a mellower act, a cover band that did old country-rock songs, while the Angels did faster, harder rock. So it was coming to that point in the evening when things would start getting crazier than they already were. Even with the president here, some guests were stumbling drunk.

As Max uncoiled a cable for an amp, his gaze wandered around the pool area until it landed on Safari. When he winked at her, she gave him a small wave, then turned away. She didn't want him to think she was gawking. She decided to go back inside and pivoted on her foot and just then ran into a tall man coming out from the inside. They jostled each other as they collided, and Safari's drink spilled down his white shirt with the coral collar.

Safari apologized profusely. "I'm so sorry. I'm not even drunk."

The man grabbed a napkin from a passing waiter and wiped himself down. "No worries. It happens.

"Seriously," she said, "It's just ginger ale."

He chuckled. "I believe you." He wadded the napkin and threw it into the nearest trash bin and actually made the shot. They smiled at each other, and then he held out his hand. "I'm Thaddeus Murfee."

She shook his hand. "Safari Frye."

He shook his hand out and winked. "Quite the grip there."

Safari chuckled. "Yeah, I don't hold back."

"So..." said Thaddeus, are you a friend of Reggie's, the president's, or that young boy band here?"

"None of them, actually."

"Oh?"

Safari didn't really want to admit to a stranger that she was here to watch her ex-boyfriend's band play, so she flashed him her badge.

Thaddeus's eyebrows went up. "You're a detective?"

Safari nodded. "Yep, San Diego Police Department."

"Are you working today?"

Safari snorted. "When am I not working?"

"Fair enough." Thaddeus waved over a waiter and asked for two ginger ales. He handed one to Safari. "Here's to the good guys." And touched his glass to hers.

"So what's your story?" Safari asked him. The Angels were almost finished setting up and, soon enough, it would be too loud for conversation. And there was something about this man that made her want to get to know him. She'd never seen him before and doubted he was from around here. Even though his accent was neutral enough, he didn't scream SoCal.

"I'm a lawyer and here at Reggie's request." He took a sip. "Just helping him with some stuff for SkoolDaze."

"Huh. I wouldn't have pegged you for a lawyer. Got a card? Just to see?"

Thaddeus laughed and handed-over a business card. As the sun had dipped down and the shade they'd been standing in fled, his eyeglasses had darkened. "I reckon that's a good thing, me not passing for a lawyer."

"Me, too." She smiled at him to let him know she was just joking.

"I have a daughter about your age. She was a detective for the LAPD. You remind me of her. Not in looks—you guys are totally opposite in that she is tall and dark-haired—but in the way you stand, the way you talk. It makes me a bit homesick."

"Oh, yeah? I'd like to meet her someday, the dark-haired equivalent of myself," she smirked. "Where you from?"

"All over really, but currently my family is in Colorado. I'm just here on business. You got family, Safari?"

"Nah, I'm single, but I'm a Big Sister and fostering a young girl at the moment."

"Really? That's great to hear!"

"Yeah, I love kids."

"Me, too," said Thaddeus. "Me, too."

Chapter 12

As Thaddeus and Safari chatted companionably, the press was finishing up with the photoshoot. A young woman was called over from the bystanders and asked to answer a few questions by TV reporters as they jammed microphones in her face.

"Miss," said the beautiful young reporter from San Diego TV, "are you here tonight because you support the president?"

The woman, Joan McIntyre, almost rolled her eyes but stopped herself. She looked around nervously. "Yes—No—Yes, I support the president."

"How do his economic policies affect life here in California for young people such as yourself?"

Joan pursed her lips and thought hard before answering. Then, "My life is good. My friends' lives are good. We've all got high-paying jobs, most of us like our jobs, and most of us have health insurance. The cost of housing in California is the only thing that's bad. Of course, that's not the president's fault. It's been that way long before he got the job."

Another reporter, a traveling woman from CNN, managed to get her question asked. "Do you follow international news? The president's stance on the Middle East?"

"Um...not really. I think he's doing a great job, though. Nobody I know has gone off to war in a while."

The reporter smiled. She hesitated a moment too long, and a reporter from LA got his microphone front and center. "What is your name? Would you like to say hello to Mom and Dad?"

"Uh, Joan McIntyre. No hellos."

"Are you from La Jolla?"

"I live in the area."

"Are you married?"

"Single."

"All right, we'll turn our attention to this young man. What's your name?"

"Dusty Zamboa."

"Dusty, are you with the boy band?"

"I'm the drummer, but we're not a boy band, man. We're just a band."

The microphones went off in a different direction, and Joan stepped away. She took a deep breath and closed her eyes before going back inside the cabana where her tribe was partying with Boyz 'N Luv. Inside her purse was her father's pearl-handled pistol that she'd collected from the bathroom ceiling only minutes before. She was astonished and terrified to realize she had actually carried a gun to within five feet of the President of the United States just now.

She swallowed hard and forced her hands to stop shaking. She had come here tonight for the sole purpose of unseating Rita from the producer's chair in the latest Boyz'

CD and video. She'd had enough gin and meth that keeping her mind on that plan was becoming increasingly difficult. She had lost the thread of her plan anyway: how in the world was she going to get Rita to shoot Butchy? Was she going to have to do it herself and get the cops to blame Rita? What if she pulled the trigger but somehow got Rita's prints on the gun?

Suddenly, she could hear the breakers from the ocean not a hundred feet away, and they were roaring in her ears. She shook her head, frightened she had even brought the gun. Her heart was pounding with fear. How to ditch the gun? Then an idea formed in her mind from out of nowhere. She had ridden to the party with Rita in Rita's Jaguar. There it was, the perfect opening.

AN HOUR LATER, Butchy—with Addison still hanging all over him—announced he had to hit the head. He started in the direction of the men's changing rooms at the far end of the pool.

Dusty Zamboa followed Joan as she fell in behind Butchy. A kid of the streets in Rosarito, Dusty didn't quite trust Joan. Call it a gut instinct, or maybe it was the wild look in her eye, he couldn't verbalize it, but he was curious enough to see where she was going as she followed Butchy.

She was perhaps twenty feet behind Butchy and she was quite sure no one had seen her leave to follow. She didn't notice Dusty.

Then the night band, *Avenging Angels*, turned up its sound system. It launched into a sonic 120 dB version of the Stones' "Brown Sugar," and no one could hear what anyone was saying so the crowd had all turned to watch the band, feigning interest, most of them, before retreating to the quiet of the main house where conversations about money and power could continue.

Butchy gave Addison a quick kiss and a pat on the butt to send her to the women's changing rooms before Butchy entered the men's and ducked into the first john.

Joan boldly followed. She grabbed the gun out of her purse, pushed open the unlocked stall door, and stood behind the urinating superstar. She pointed the gun at the back of his head. At that exact moment, she realized if she shot Butchy, there would be no band to produce. The gig would be over. Rita would be arrested, and Joan might never get another chance to engineer a band of such popularity as Boyz 'N Luv. Her hesitation did her in.

Butchy swung around, spraying urine everywhere, and hit Joan with his balled-up fist. She rocked backward, flailing her arms. Dusty swooped into the changing room and charged Joan, and after a scramble, came up with the gun.

Joan turned and ran toward the door.

Chapter 13

The gun blasts were loud enough that the Avenging Angels band jerked to a halt. The lead guitarist had in one earphone that brought in the mix while the other ear was uncovered so he heard the gunshots and stopped in the middle of his sweeping pick. He stepped back from the mic, letting the song die on his lips, and, as he did, the rest of the band went silent as well.

There was a frenzy as people ran away from the vicinity of the gunshots. Phones were dialed to the extent that the 911 operator would later testify she received no less than seventeen calls in the space of four minutes.

Private security from Pelham's grounds rushed to the changing rooms at the other side of the pool from where the band was playing, the Secret Service communicated, and more people came running.

Joan, shot just left of midline in the back, had slumped to the floor, her body halfway out of the door so that it propped it open. Dusty was nowhere to be seen. Butchy had remained rooted to the spot, then he had passed out and toppled to the ground. Now the room was swarming with Secret Service agents, automatic weapons bristling, and private security was everywhere. Butchy was moaning and mumbling incoherently and then came the police.

Seconds later, Butchy was on the floor on his belly, spread-eagle, being handcuffed by the SDPD. "You shot her in the back!" cried one uniformed police officer. "And you're on TV!" But Butchy was still out for the count and wouldn't wake up until they'd hoisted him to his feet and slapped him across the face.

Butchy, for his part, was too frightened to speak, which was a good thing. Ordinarily, the police in such situations try to bait a subject into making unguarded statements, but Butchy was too frightened to respond to anything being said. He was propelled from behind to the door where he ran into a blizzard of photographers and TV crews.

Statements were taken by the police for the next several hours. No one saw anything. Except for one person, and he wasn't talking. He'd been walking to the toilets in the changing room himself when the shot rang out and the Secret Service had dragged him away. But before they did, he'd seen another man enter the changing room. But he said nothing about it. He admitted nothing because he didn't want his reelection statements overwhelmed by his becoming a witness to a shooting. So, when the Secret Service allowed the police detectives to ask their pointed question, "Did you see or hear or observe anything unusual tonight?" the president answered in the negative. He wasn't about to become a witness and, besides, from everything he heard, they had caught the shooter red-handed, who had even made an incriminating comment. At least that was the latest sit-rep the president had. They had their shooter. It was none of his concern, he rationalized. *Keep your mouth shut.*

One other thing tugged at his heart, however. The girl who'd been shot was the same girl who'd stood up for him at the impromptu press conference not ten minutes ago. She had extolled his virtues and told the world how happy California youth were with his presidency. Now she lay dead, and he wasn't going to step up and say anything. He didn't like that about himself but, hey, there was a whole lot a president didn't like about himself.

The failings were continuous on a daily basis, but politics at his level would allow for nothing less. He never made a decision that the other half of the country didn't like or loath him for. So he remained silent, seeking out the steady aura of the First Lady and allowing her to field questions the rest of the night, their old trick when he became too exhausted or run to the ground by probing interrogations from the press. He was finished and so he retreated, literally, to the sanctuary to the guest house of the mansion where he'd be hounded no more.

SAFARI FRYE WAS one of the first detectives inside the changing rooms. It was actually her handcuffs that had gone around the wrists of Butchy as he lay splayed out on the ground with her knee in his neck. Her cuffs, her collar. That's how it went in these cases. That's how it was decided which detective was going to run the case. Besides, she was senior on the location, a shift commander, and the other dicks who arrived deferred to her.

She was sitting in the backseat of her Ford Interceptor,

settling Butchy into the seatbelt, when a uniform approached her vehicle.

"The vic was just pronounced. One of the guests is a trauma doctor. He did what he could, but she died."

"Who was she?"

"A Joan McIntyre."

Safari turned to the young superstar. "Who was she to you, Butchy?"

"The engineer on our new album. I didn't know her name."

"You shot her?"

Terrified and extremely inexperienced, Butchy said yes, he had pulled the trigger.

"Why did you shoot her?" Safari casually asked. "She was running away from you."

"I—I was scared shitless. I didn't—I didn't— I want to talk to my dad, please."

"Is your dad here?"

"My dad is my agent. He should talk to you. That's what the TV shows say. That I should keep my mouth shut."

"Are you hiding something, Butchy?"

Butchy took the bait. "She came up behind me with her gun. I took it away, and she turned and ran. I—I— The gun went off, and I fell down. I don't know why it went off."

"All right. So you shot her, but you didn't mean to?"

"I guess so."

"But you were the one who pulled the trigger?"

"Yes."

"What if you hadn't pulled the trigger? Was she running for the door?"

"Yes."

"If you hadn't shot her—"

"If I didn't shoot her, she was going to get away. I didn't want her to get away."

"All right." Safari pulled her phone from her utility belt. "I'm going to record what you're telling me. Is that all right?"

"I don't care. I get recorded all day, and just about all night."

She set her phone to record and directed it at Butchy who was sitting back in his seat, his head leaned back on the rest. "Do you want to talk to a lawyer?"

He groaned. "No, I want to talk to my dad."

"Is your dad a lawyer?"

"No."

"Is what you're telling me free and voluntary?"

"I'm not free. I'm handcuffed. But I'm telling you the truth. I've got nothing to hide. No one can make me say anything I don't want to say."

"So it's free and voluntary?" pressed Safari.

"Sure, I have nothing to hide. She was going to shoot me."

"All right, you just sit back now. We have to take you downtown."

"Am I going to jail?"

"We're going to our downtown office to ask some questions and see about getting your dad to come in."

"All right, thanks."

"So you just sit back and try to relax. You're shaking. Are you cold?"

"No, I'm not cold. I'm scared."

"Sure, you are. Well, keep it together and you'll be just fine, Butchy."

"Okay, thank you, ma'am."

"Sure."

Chapter 14

The police began canvassing the partygoers, inside and outside the mansion. A set of detectives went to the guest house for the president and knocked on the door. The president's Chief of Staff answered, a quizzical look on his face. "Yes?"

Detective McKesson didn't bat an eye. "We'd like to talk to the president. We have information he was in the vicinity of the victim just before she was shot."

"The president is busy. He's on the phone with the Secretary of State at the moment. I'm sorry, but I cannot disturb him."

The detective put one foot inside the door and, just as he did, two Secret Service agents converged from the inside, blocking his way. "I'm sorry," said one, "but you'll have to wait in the hallway."

Detective McKesson wouldn't be deterred. "This is official police business. We have jurisdiction here. It's important we talk to the president without delay."

"You've been told the president is busy and cannot be

disturbed. You'll have to come back later. It would be best if you made an appointment by calling the White House switchboard."

The detective did not take a step back. He still had one foot inside the main door of the guest house. "Sir, with all due respect, we have jurisdiction here, and you were standing smack dab in the middle of a crime scene. I would strongly suggest you summon your superior officer to speak with me."

Suddenly, the Secret Service agent reached out, placed his hand on the chest of the detective, and pushed him into the hallway. He then slammed the door. Now the detective and his partner were standing in the hallway, looking at each other, when McKesson's partner said to him, "I'm calling for Safari. She'll tell us what to do." He removed his intercom from his belt, keyed the mic, and spoke slowly, "Detective Frye, we need you at Pelham's guesthouse where the president is staying."

Detective Frye squawked over the intercom, "I'm on my way. Wait one."

The detectives pressed their backs up against the wall and motioned for the uniformed officers to continue their canvass back at the main house. Within minutes, Safari appeared, shrugging into her cream sport coat as she came toward them.

"Lieutenant, ma'am, the president's people, on the other side of the door, won't let us speak with the president. We have information he had a view of the victim immediately before she was shot. We have further information that he may have seen what happened as he was approaching the changing room. He is an essential witness. But the Secret Service refused to allow us to speak with him. They told us to call the switchboard of the White House."

Safari's eyes narrowed. "Oh, they did?" She began pounding on the door.

It opened again. This time two Secret Service agents stood blocking the entrance. From behind them, the Chief of Staff said the president wouldn't be available that night, and the door began closing.

But before it shut entirely, Safari forced the toe of her steel-toed boot halfway inside. "Hold on. Why don't you gentlemen go grab your supervisor and bring him here to talk to me?"

The two agents' eyes met. Then one of them left. Less than a minute went by before a neatly dressed female agent pushed between the two men. "Yes?"

"You're the supervisor this evening?"

"I am. SA Norma Jean Riley."

"Agent Riley, I'm Detective Safari Frye. We need five minutes with the man. No more than that, and we'll leave you alone, I promise. But if we don't get five minutes, then I'll drop a hint to the media that the gentleman in there, the gentleman who's up for reelection, has refused to cooperate with the police in a murder investigation. A little bird told me he wouldn't like that. What do you think?"

"Five minutes? He can do five minutes. Can you come inside and wait while he finishes up in the office?"

"Yes, we can."

Chapter 15

Thaddeus Murfee was just leaving the driveway when the shot rang out. He didn't hear it and didn't see the flurry of activity behind him as he drove away. By the time he was back at his hotel, Butchy was on his way downtown in the backseat of Safari Frye's Ford.

At that same moment, Rita began making calls. First, she called Joan's roommates and told them to call Joan's mom and tell her there'd been an accident, to call the police. Next, she called Butchy's dad, with whom she was very familiar as the man often would attend recording sessions, particularly the nighttime sessions that would go until dawn. No way was he going to leave his son there unattended by a parent.

"Mr. Penstone," she said into her cell phone, "it's Rita, Butchy's producer. There's been an accident."

"Go on," said the father.

"Butchy's been arrested for shooting someone."

"*What?* Say that again?"

"I said Butchy is on his way to the San Diego Police Department. There's a lawyer I could send to meet him."

"Who?"

"A lawyer I met tonight. He could go meet Butchy until you get there. He seemed like the discreet type. Should I call him?"

"Definitely. Butchy needs someone with him."

"All right, I'm calling him now."

Rita called, explained the situation, and Thaddeus agreed to go to the police department downtown and babysit Butchy until a criminal lawyer could be arranged. It was an emergency, and he didn't mind doing it at all.

"By the way, Butchy is the nephew of Reginald Pelham. I know you were meeting with him, but you probably didn't know that Reggie is Butchy's uncle."

"You're right about that," said Thaddeus. "I didn't know. Nor do I know who Butchy is, and it doesn't matter. I'm going to do what I can to help him."

Thaddeus hung up, turned his rental, and headed at a high rate of speed toward the 5 freeway to downtown San Diego. Within minutes, he was southbound and following driving directions given to him by his iPhone.

Twenty minutes later, he pulled into police parking. He found the visitors' slots, parked the rental car, and headed inside.

Chapter 16

The president's Chief of Staff found a slot of time allowing Safari and her partner to "have a word" with the president. They were shown into his office inside the guesthouse and waited there in two overstuffed leather chairs while the great man was summoned. He walked in unannounced after only a few minutes. He was gnawing on an apple when he joined them. He backed up to the front of his desk and sat on the edge before making eye contact. Then he said, "What did I see before the shooting? Is that what you want to know? I saw nothing. Is that all you wanted, officers?"

Safari fielded it. "One of our officers was told by one of your agents that, as you were making your way to the pool changing rooms, you were almost to the door when there was the gunshot. We need to ask, sir, did you see anything? She collapsed with the door open so perhaps you might have seen inside the changing room as you approached?"

A huge bite of apple, a few moments of intense chewing, then, "I don't remember seeing anything. I can't be sure. The Secret Service is there to keep their eyes open so I don't have to. I was just going to the bathroom."

"The Secret Service was behind you, not in front. Why not?"

The president shrugged. "The Secret Service took hours to secure the place. We didn't expect much to happen. You know how it is in hindsight. Woulda, shoulda, coulda."

"I can't say, Mr. President," Safari replied. "But I hear you telling me you might have seen something as you walked toward the men's changing room so would you allow us to record your statement?"

"Definitely not. I don't give statements to the police and allow them to record me. I'm sure you understand."

"No, I don't understand. I thought presidents were never above the law. I thought presidents were the chief law enforcement officials of the entire country. And I thought you, Mr. President, would want to see justice done. I'm surprised at how difficult this all has been, to be frank."

"I'm a very busy man, Detective. And I'm about finished here."

He pushed away from the desk and stood fully upright. She guessed his height at maybe five-ten but he seemed six inches taller. She decided it was the Office of the President that lent him the additional six inches.

Suddenly, her anger overrode any intimidation. Suddenly, her own power returned. After all, they were both human, he no better than her. "Mr. President, if you're unwilling to allow us to record, I'm going to have to ask you to accompany me downtown and allow us to videotape your statement. That would be our standard protocol."

He smiled broadly and brushed her away with a flick of his hand. "Impossible. Presidents don't give statements, Miss… Miss…"

"Detective Frye. Everyone gives statements in La Jolla, sir. The law has no favorite sons in my jurisdiction. Please let your people know we'll be driving you downtown. We'll wait outside while you get ready."

"Now hold on! My schedule makes it quite impossible for me to undertake an unscheduled trip downtown. I'm running a country here, Ms. Frye. I'm sure you know that. By the way, what party are you?"

"No party. I don't matter enough to have a party, and besides my boss doesn't allow that. We're party-free in our shop, sir. Believe me, I have no ax to grind. I only want to get your statement and go home to bed. I'm tired and ready to close this case, truth be told."

"All right, please contact White House counsel, and we'll arrange a time and place for my statement. Until then, that's all we can do for now. Fair enough?"

She was tired. She could see that was as far as she was going to get, short of surrounding the house with police officers and shooting it out with the Secret Service. While that had a certain appeal, disgusted as she was just then, she knew it was ridiculous and so decided to back out gracefully. "Fair enough. We'll be in touch, sir."

Chapter 17

Thaddeus made his way into the police department and located the juvenile section. Butchy, he was told, was just then being processed into the juvie unit. He would probably have to wait for about an hour. Then his parent or guardian would have to be present before Thaddeus could speak with him.

"But I'm his lawyer," said Thaddeus to the clerk standing before him. "And I need to speak with my client without delay and definitely before any police officers ask him any questions. Can you guarantee me no one is interrogating my client?"

The woman, a sergeant at the police desk, said she couldn't guarantee anything. She turned away from the counter window and shuffled some papers around as if to point out to him she was too busy for his shenanigans.

"Now, hold on," Thaddeus abruptly shot out. "Do I have to go get a judge to sign an order to allow me to see my client without delay? Because I'm happy to do that, except the judges in this city are going to be very unhappy that you, Miss Sanchez"—he read on the badge on her shirt —"you are keeping me from my client. I'm sure any remarks you manage to get him to make will be excluded from his case. You certainly don't want that and you don't want me later telling your supervisor you were warned, but you ignored my requests, do you? You're on shaky ground here. Now, again, I request I be allowed to see my client in the next five minutes or I head for the judge's home. Which will it be?"

She lowered her head, punched at her phone, and spoke to someone on the other end of the line. Then she returned to the window. "Attorney conference room eleven. Down the hall on your right. Five minutes. Next!" she called over his shoulder.

Thaddeus stepped out of line and moved toward the hallway where, just then, a deputy in a liver-colored uniform opened the door and waved at him to follow her. He followed down the hall to room eleven, where he pushed the heavy oak door and went inside. It was dark, so he swiped his hand across the wall to find the light switch.

"We'll have him here in five minutes, Mr. Murfee," said the deputy after the lights blinked on. She then left the room.

Thaddeus placed his laptop on the steel table and slid a steel chair back so he could sit down. He sat and opened up a new document file, entered the headers, and waited. Then the door behind him opened, and he stood and turned, expecting to find Butchy there. Instead, it was a man with a deep tan, probably mid-40s, with piercing green eyes and graying hair. He extended his hand as he came into the room and said, "My name is Everett Penstone. I'm Butchy's father and his agent. What in the world has happened, Mr. Murfee?".

Thaddeus extended his hand, and they shook. "From what I was told, there was a shooting at Reggie Pelham's house, and Butchy has been arrested. I don't know who the victim was, and I don't know how Butchy was involved. They should have him here any minute."

"I talked to Reggie on the way over. You come highly recommended, Mr. Murfee, and he urged me to retain your services for the defense of my son. Are you able or even willing to work on Butchy's case?"

"Why don't we do this? Let me get a feel for what's happened here and then we can discuss all that."

Just then the door opened, and Butchy was ushered into the room with a female deputy on either side. Butchy was not handcuffed. He looked at his father and shook his head, and his father grimaced. But then he looked at Thaddeus and held out his hand to shake. Thaddeus took his hand, and they shook before the deputies moved Butchy into the chair at the end of the table across from him. His father then took the chair on the other side of Butchy so both were facing Thaddeus.

"I told you about going out to these places," said the father. There was a warning note in his voice, which was barely controlled. "You're risking everything we worked for with your partying, and I don't like it."

"Hang on a minute," Thaddeus said. "Before we get into accusations and blame, let me try to get a few basics nailed down. First of all, Butchy, what is your full name?"

The boy sat back in his chair, placing both hands on the seat at his sides. "My name is Booker. Everyone's called me Butchy since before I can remember."

"My name is Thaddeus Murfee, and I'm a lawyer here to help you. I was first called to help by Rita, and just a few minutes ago I had a few words with your dad, and it appears he wishes me to help you as well. However, at this point, I'm not sure I can. And the reason I say that is because I really don't know what's happened here and I don't know how I feel about you. I have to have good feelings about the people I defend, and I have to believe they're trying to get beyond whatever bad thing has happened to lead a decent life. Not all lawyers get to work this way. I'm one of the lucky ones who can afford to. So let's back up and start with why you're at the party tonight and who you went there with, if you please."

Butchy nodded. "The boys and I—"

Thaddeus interrupted, "The boys being…?"

"My squad, you know, all of us in Boyz 'N Luv—Jonny, Sammy, Dusty and I are staying at my Uncle Reggie's mansion while we are recording in La Jolla. He has a sweet place."

"How old are you Butchy?"

"Sixteen, but I don't have a driver's license yet. Been too busy with the Boyz to take the course and lessons. I own a Ferrari, but I don't get to drive it yet. Not legally."

"Okay, let me ask some questions that might appear to be unrelated. Give me your best answers without your dad helping. First, how much money did you make last year?"

"Our band earned four hundred and fifty million dollars. After taxes, I cleared fifty-five million. At least that's what Angie tells me. Angie is our CPA."

"And who is your manager?"

"My dad, Everett Penstone."

"If you had your druthers, would you rather have someone else be your agent and manager besides your dad?"

"No, I want my dad. He's been there all the way. He even bought me my first guitar when I was seven. He paid for lessons even when he couldn't afford them. I love my dad and want him right here with me."

"What about your mom? Are you close to her, too?"

"Yes, my mom and I are very close, probably even closer than me and my dad."

"I know you're only sixteen, but what do you want to do if the band ever breaks up or other opportunities present themselves?"

"I want to be in the movies. I've always wanted to be an actor. More than anything, I want my own movie. I think my Hollywood agent is working on that right now. Isn't that right, Dad?"

"Yes," said Penstone. "Isaac Abramson is Butchy's Hollywood agent. He has a script, and there is a director attached. Right now they're doing financing, and we've agreed to finance twenty-five percent with forty-nine percent on the back end. So far nobody wants it, but Butchy is the most popular kid in the United States right now. Someone's going to grab the deal, and then Butchy's got his movie."

"Butchy, who was shot tonight?"

"Joan McIntyre."

Thaddeus watched as tears flowed into the eyes of the young singer at the mention of Joan's name. The boy's shoulders shook, and he locked his hands together in front of him as in the manner of one praying. He pressed his forehead against his hands and moaned loudly. "I'm—I'm sorry. Oh, my God!"

"Butchy," said Thaddeus, "tell us how it happened."

"I—I don't know."

"Tell us what you remember as best you can. Did you argue with her?"

"No way. I was in the men's changing room at the pool

in the very first stall, man. All at once, I felt like there was someone standing behind me. I turned to look. Joan was standing there, pointing a gun at me. I damn near fainted. I grabbed the gun and turned it around and she began running. The next thing I know, the gun goes off. Joan is halfway through the door and lands on her belly, and I collapse on the floor. It was like all the air just went out of me, and as much as I wanted to help her, I couldn't even get up and get over to her.

"When I was lying on the floor, I must've passed out. The next thing I know, the room is full of police and people with badges and someone holding something under my nose that made my head jerk back. Then I hear someone say, 'Okay he's back now. Take him away.'"

"Smelling salts," Penstone senior said.

"My eyes open, and I'm looking at the ceiling. There's a fan going around, and I remember hearing music playing from somewhere. Someone says to me, 'Is this your gun?' And I just look at them. To be honest, Mr. Murfee, I didn't know what they were talking about. I knew I didn't have a gun. Then I see the face of the woman who brought me here. She's saying my name, over and over. And then I hear someone else say, 'He doesn't go by Booker. He goes by Butchy.' So then she starts saying, 'Butchy!' real loud, and I have to look at her. She's also the one who arrested me and brought me here. Nice lady at first, but then she put the cuffs on my wrists. They stand me up, and I see Joan lying face-down, except I don't realize it's Joan at first. Then I recognize her hair because in the studio we're all standing behind her at the console all the time and her hair is very distinct, that bright red with it shaved up the back. I say, 'What happened?' and the woman just looks at me and says, 'You shot her. Don't you remember?' To be honest, Mr.

Murfee, no, I didn't remember. The lady wasn't so nice after that. Her name is Safari, of all the dumb damn names to hang on someone. Then she brought me down here."

"And what happened down here?"

"They took me in the front and took my mug shot. They weighed me and put that doctor thing on my finger. They took fingerprints. The whole time they're doing all this, they've got this one guy in a uniform with a handheld mic who keeps asking me for a statement."

"Did you give a statement?"

"I don't think so. I mean, I answered all their questions, so there's that."

"What kind of questions did they ask?"

"Why I shot her, was I mad at her, was it my gun, did I bring the gun to the party, did I plan all this out ahead of time, what was my motive, and stuff like that."

Thaddeus nodded and made his notes on his laptop. "Well, no one can argue with you about where the gun came from. My guess is, the gun is going to have at least one fingerprint of Joan's somewhere. Which is proof that she handled the gun, too. The most difficult part of your case, Butchy, and Mr. Penstone, is the fact that she was shot in the back and from a distance. I believe someone said she was probably ten paces away from you when she was shot. That being the case, the district attorney will argue that Joan was fleeing when she was shot. This would mean that the defense of self-defense wouldn't be available in your case. And if that is true, then the district attorney gets to argue that it was an execution-style slaying."

"In which case," said Mr. Penstone, "he goes to prison for murder. Is that about the sum and substance of it?"

Thaddeus slowly nodded. "I'm afraid so, unless we can come up with another defense to the shooting."

Butchy cried out, "God, Mr. Murfee, please don't let me go to prison. They'll kill me in there."

"What other defenses are we looking at, Thaddeus?" asked his dad.

Thaddeus sat and thought for a full minute. It was early enough in the case that he didn't want to come right out and say he didn't see another clear defense to a murder charge, at least not based on the facts he knew so far. So he said, "I'm going to need some time to work that up. I need to know a lot more about the facts of the case as the police know them. With all due respect, let's hold that question in abeyance until we know more. Is that fair enough?"

Penstone shrugged. "I guess it will have to do." He looked to his son. "Butchy, you're just going to have to man up and live with this until Mr. Murfee can bring it to a happy conclusion for you. You're going to have to work closely with Mr. Murfee and do exactly what he says in order to get your best result. For the record, I agree that you would die in prison. You're young and almost pretty, and the men there will eat you alive. And I won't let that happen. I love you, son."

Butchy broke down in tears finally, as if he'd been holding it in for as long as he could, through the police car ride here, through his processing, and finally, when a few soft words were spoken to him, the dam broke.

His father hugged him in that rough manner of men but kept his hand on Butchy's back while he cried it out. After a few moments, Penstone said, "Thaddeus, what kind of money are we talking about here for me to retain your services?"

Thaddeus nodded. "I'm just going to ask you to pay my expenses throughout. As far as legal fees, the cost will be one million dollars for the complete defense. I want that one million dollars paid to a homeless shelter in San Diego. I'll be sending in the name of the shelter as soon as my daughter checks their legitimacy. You'll hear about this before the end of next week. For now, I think we've covered just about everything we can cover, except I want to caution Butchy to speak to no one about this case. In particular, Butchy, you should know that quite often the police and prosecution will give you a cellmate who really is working for them and who is trying to get a statement out of you that will help put you in prison. For this reason, it is essential you discuss this case with no one except me. Do not discuss it with your father, your mother, your best friend, your bandmates, your girlfriend, or anyone else. You understand what I'm saying?"

He hung his head. "I understand. My lips are sealed. I do want to ask one question. While this is going on in the court, will I have to be in jail?"

"It depends," said Thaddeus, "which is not the answer I'm sure you wanted to hear. It depends on whether the judge will allow us to make bail while the case is pending, and that depends on many things such as your association with the community, your contact with the community, your prior record, and things like that. I will make every effort to make sure you're out of this jail by tomorrow if possible. Bear in mind, however, that all of this is very unsettled right now. Your case is in a great state of flux and will be for the next little while. We're just going to have to do the best we can for you and leave it at that."

"Can I go home tonight with my dad?"

"Not tonight."

Butchy's face fell, and then he threw his head into his hands.

"Tomorrow you will have what's called the initial

appearance in court. I will make a motion that bail be set at that time. By this time tomorrow, it is my hope you will be out of jail and home with your family. Incidentally, if you are let out of jail, you will not be able to leave the state of California. I know your band tours, and I don't know if there is a tour presently scheduled, but if there is, you'll need to cancel until this case is over. While that might be a great financial hardship, there is no greater hardship than you getting tossed back into jail and your bond revoked should you leave the state."

"Don't leave the state. Got it. Can I still work with the band?"

"Sure. That doesn't change. But you also need the best PR firm in the world working with you right now. This case is going to cost you millions and millions of dollars in record sales. There's no way around it. So be ready."

"Lord," said Penstone, "that's right. I can't begin to imagine."

"Oh, you will," Thaddeus said. "All right, I'm going back to my hotel. We'll see each other again tomorrow in court. Good night, all."

"Good night," said Penstone and rose to shake Thaddeus's hand once again.

"Bye, Thaddeus," Butchy whispered.

Chapter 18

Moonbeam Russet made her way down to the beach that morning, predawn, as long tendrils of fog crept into the La Jolla topography from all directions. Moonbeam was fifteen, straight blond hair, and had the face of a cherub with just a dusting of freckles across her nose and cheeks.

As a member of the girls' cross-country team, she ran almost every day of the week. When she arrived at the water's edge, she spread her towel and began doing her warm-up exercises before her run. She was alone, carried no pepper spray, had no assault whistle, and was unarmed.

She was a straight-A honor student in school, played clarinet in the marching band, was working on a paper entitled "The Demise of Labor Unions Since 2000," yet still had time for her younger brothers and sisters, helping with their studies nightly. Moonbeam was still a young teen, at that age when they hadn't yet coupled up with a steady boyfriend or girlfriend. In her group, her six or seven girlfriends mingled with six or seven boys, variously, so that it couldn't be said there was a couple among them.

After her vigorous exercises, Moonbeam shrugged out of her sweatshirt, dropped it on her towel, and began jogging north along the beach. As she ran, she noticed that the streetlights along the sidewalk were still burning, one flickering as if the lightbulb was going out. For the most part, there were few other joggers around, and the early morning walkers hadn't yet arrived. The jog was one she made every morning and had for the previous three years. In fact, as she made her way along the sand, she mused how funny it would be if her footsteps in the sand became permanent from all the running she did there.

She was now abreast of the Pelham mansion, which jutted out onto the sand more than any other house along her route. It was a waypoint, so she checked her watch. She normally reached Pelham's around 3 $\frac{1}{2}$ minutes into the run every day. 3:45 said the elapsed time, so she picked up her pace.

Here came Robert Haas running toward her in his customary black latex top and bottom. She knew him by his profile, his canter, and his flaming red hair. As he neared her, the first rays of dawn broke through the fog. Robert was a senior now, the captain of the boys' cross-country team, and a good friend to Moonbeam. When her father abandoned the family two years before, Robert had begun bringing a bag of groceries by every Saturday afternoon after he got paid by his job at the grocery store. Moonbeam would never forget that and neither would her mother. They shouted hello at each other as they passed. Moonbeam felt good about seeing her friend again.

She checked her watch: 5:50. Now she could really let it

out after her first six minutes warming up. She increased her stride, and her feet began pounding the sand, leaving deeper footprints as she went along. Up ahead was Frenchy's Burgers, a green wooden structure low on the sand and from where Jim Frenchy and his brother sold hot dogs, burgers, fries, and onion rings to the beachgoers seven days a week. Drawing abreast of the structure, her view was momentarily blocked off to her right. Still, she pounded along.

Suddenly, from out of the shadows of the west side of the structure, there leaped a man Moonbeam hadn't seen until he jumped at her. She took one step to the side, but she was too late and too slow. He swung a baseball-sized rock from his waist up, connecting with the left side of her head and knocking her to her knees.

He then dragged Moonbeam back into the shadows. When his hand went to cover her mouth to keep her from screaming, she noticed that his right ring finger was cut off from the first joint, only a stub remaining. Although she struggled, he easily removed her latex running pants, under which she was nude.

For the next hour, Seagulls swept low and called out while joggers continued to rock on by and power walkers made their way along the water's edge. But no one noticed the crumpled form of Moonbeam Russet lying in the last remaining shadow of Frenchy's green building. According to her watch, she had left her towel one hour and twenty-two minutes earlier.

But according to her stilled heart, she would never care about that again.

A mile away, if that, the cooling engine of a Toyota Corolla ticked away. Stuffed beneath the front seat reposed a paper bag containing the running pants worn by Moonbeam Russet.

The Corolla's amber carpet was slightly damp beneath the paper bag. It wasn't the first time the amber carpet had gathered such evidence.

Nor would it be the last.

Chapter 19

At 9:55, Thaddeus was buzzed by the front desk of the La Valencia Hotel. Reggie Pelham was on his way upstairs for their appointment. Thaddeus was ready with his laptop and some preliminary research he'd retrieved last night after meeting with Butchy and his dad.

Pelham made his way inside, and they retreated to the office just off the living space. They took chairs at the desk and were now overlooking the beach and ocean just beyond. Thaddeus could make out a large family of seals just offshore, mothers teaching babies how to fish.

Pelham was wearing leather running shoes, five-hundred-dollar blue jeans, a white dress shirt open at the throat, and a thick gold chain from where suspended a small pendant with the word SkoolDaze in raised gold lettering. He wore a diamond-encrusted ring on his right middle finger. His left ring finger was bare, but there was a band of lighter skin the width of a wedding band now removed. He crossed his feet under the table and sat back, arms folded, in the manner of one preparing to watch a horserace.

In comparison, Thaddeus was wearing baggy shorts, flip-flops, and a T-shirt with a picture of a surfer. He wore no jewelry, and his clear-framed eyeglasses were perched on his forehead as he put the phone down after finishing off a drink order from room service. He looked at Pelham sadly. "I just heard about the girl on the beach. What a tragedy. Was it near your house?"

"They found her body about a half-mile from my house. She attended high school ten blocks from my house. I think my wife knows her mother from beach cleanup."

"So far I'm very unsettled about La Jolla. Two killings in two days," said Thaddeus. "Isn't this normally a pretty quiet little town?"

Pelham toyed with the neck chain. Then he shook his head. "I travel all over the world, Thaddeus, as you might know. I never feel as safe as I do when I'm at home in La Jolla. But, yes, these last forty-eight hours have us all shook up. First my nephew, Butchy, and now this girl from his class at high school."

"So Everett Penstone is your wife's brother, is that it?"

"Yes, and I must say Everett and I are much closer and on the same wavelength than Victoria and I ever were. He's down to earth, a good soldier, and the kinda guy you like to have covering your back. His sister, on the other hand, is flighty and neurotic. I could never trust her with a bank account or property of any value. The very idea of her shareholders' lawsuit trying to unseat me as CEO keeps me awake nights. SkoolDaze would cease to be were that to happen."

Their coffees arrived and a Danish for Pelham. As Pelham munched on his Danish, Thaddeus stirred fresh cream into his coffee. His thoughts were on the dead girl more than on Pelham's legal problems. And somewhere off on a radical tangent in his mind, he was thinking there must be some connection between the dead girl and Butchy's case, though for the life of him, he had no idea what that might be. The more he thought about it, the more his rational mind overrode his gut instinct, and he concluded any connection must be coincidental and didn't exist.

So he tried to move on from that, tried to apply his thought processes to Pelham's lawsuit, but was only half successful as thoughts of the dead girls, Joan and Moonbeam, pressed in on his mind from all sides. It was a sad time in La Jolla. He forced himself to address the case at hand.

"So what kind of assets are we talking about that Victoria is now suing about?"

"SkoolDaze R and D has developed new technologies in the form of algorithms and datasets for manipulating larger swaths of data than anyone has ever done before, using just a cell phone app. The technology will make cell phone banking applications look like first-grader finger paints by the time it makes its way into the mainstream. I think I told you previously I've taken about fifty-five million dollars under the table on these technologies. What I neglected to tell you was that the money has basically gone back into our home here in La Jolla, which is, of course, a community asset under California's community property law. So, Victoria, when the house is sold in the divorce, will receive her half of the share of the proceeds, anyway. Doesn't that nullify her lawsuit against me?"

"The problem with your thinking is the fact that other shareholders will also share in those profits from the sale of corporate assets. So while you might argue that Victoria is going to get her share regardless, her lawsuit is still supported by the fact that other shareholders will not profit in the same manner. Now, your CFO has provided me with a list of those assets as well as a breakdown on the basis and profits in each exchange. My office is in the process of guiding your CFO in reporting the sales on your books. The adjusting entries will reflect that the sales have only recently been completed in total, which will explain why the entries haven't been made until now. This is step one in your rehabilitation. I think we can apply the same rationale to the amended tax returns we're in the process of preparing to be filed with the IRS."

Pelham shook his head. "Victoria called me again last night. She wants to accelerate the divorce so that she can marry her French lover. Believe it or not, she then started asking me about the best way to protect her assets from the divorce against the new man in her life so that he can't bed and wed her and then run off with fifty percent of her net worth. Can you believe that?"

Thaddeus had to laugh. "Not really, but it's not that I haven't seen the same thing before. I have. Oh, what tangled webs we weave."

"Have you spoken with my divorce lawyer yet, Thaddeus?"

"No, and I don't expect to until I finish up adjusting entries and IRS amendments. I want to keep the timing straight so Victoria doesn't come rushing in and claim all these things were done in anticipation of the divorce trial. Let me finish up what I'm doing, and then I'll be more than happy to talk with your divorce counsel." Thaddeus refreshed his coffee, staring out the window at a group of a half-dozen seagulls squabbling over a potato chip bag. "It looks like I'm going to be defending Butchy. You have any ideas or comments for me there?"

"My nephew is a really great kid. He walked through

the golden door and has had the world fall in his lap but, amazingly, it hasn't turned him into a bad sort. Do I think he's the kind of kid who could purposely shoot someone in the back? Absolutely not. When he says he turned around from the urinal and Joan was pointing a gun in his face, I totally believe him. I've also nosed around a bit and found out that Joan's producer on the latest CD, Rita, had quite a crush on Butchy. I also hear Joan was in love with Rita, but not sure about that one unless she swung both ways. But possible." Pelham finished his Danish and wiped his fingers. "Jealousy? Ain't love grand?"

"Love is indeed grand, except when it isn't," said Thaddeus. "By the way, before I forget it, I've also been served a notice that Victoria's attorneys want to take your deposition in February. Please have your people get back to me about possible dates, keeping in mind the deposition will take about three hours. This is harassment, and they're using it to try to scare you into making a quick settlement, but we won't budge. In fact, as soon as you leave here, I'm going to file a notice of deposition on Victoria. Two can play the same game. I'm also thinking of setting the depositions on her lawyers in Paris, just to see what kind of encouragement they've been offering her in all this. From what I'm learning, Victoria doesn't seem to be a particularly motivated woman on her own, so I think she's being coached from the wings. It wouldn't surprise me, and I would love to be able to tell a jury all about where her ideas are actually coming from. I'm sure that until some lawyer explained to her what a shareholder suit was all about, she didn't have the foggiest notion. Anyway, it's getting close to eleven now, and I think I'm out of questions for you. I've still got a world of work today so maybe we should break this off now. What say you?"

"Makes sense to me. I'm growing more and more confident in what you're doing here for me, Thaddeus. I just want you to know how much I appreciate it."

"Not a problem. One other thing, following Butchy's initial appearance, I think I'm going to be looking for temporary office space here in La Jolla. With two litigated cases going on here, it only makes sense I have more of a presence in town. Just an FYI."

"That makes me happy to hear. Let me know if you need my help, and we can even arrange something in one of my buildings."

"Will do and thanks for the offer."

With that being said, Pelham excused himself and left the meeting.

* * *

The initial appearance was set for 1 p.m. When Thaddeus arrived at twelve forty-five, the deputies had already brought Butchy over from the jail. He and several other inmates were segregated from the courtroom crowd that was packed to bursting, all of them most likely here for Butchy, the superstar. The inmates were parked in the jury's box since there was no jury that day. Thaddeus came to the bar and made his way over to Butchy. He gave him a copy of the bail motion that he had filed the night before. The prosecutor, Marilyn Hansen, had already received a copy through the court's filing system, and so the government was apprised that Thaddeus would be moving for bail and immediate release.

Judge Homer Morrow took to the bench just before 1 p.m., plunked his reading glasses on his nose, and asked the clerk to call the first case. The clerk called another case, not Butchy's, the client and her attorney came forward, and the afternoon was off and running.

Thaddeus was seated behind counsel table and had a

good look at the courtroom and the prisoners in their orange jumpsuits. Word was out; the courtroom was filled with young girls in every other seat. Most were staring fixedly at Butchy. Some were even trying to snap photographs of their favorite singer with their cell phones. The clerk had earlier banned the use of cell phones in the courtroom, but that hadn't prevented Butchy's followers from trying, nonetheless.

Thirty minutes later, the clerk called *State of California versus Booker M. Penstone*. Thaddeus stood and walked confidently to the lectern, then turned while he waited for Butchy to join him there. As previously instructed by Thaddeus, his father joined him as well. The judge had the parties identify themselves and asked Butchy whether he had received a copy of the indictment, as he had now been indicted by the continuing grand jury. Thaddeus told the court that Butchy had indeed received the indictment and waived the reading of same.

Judge Morrow then said to Thaddeus, "Mr. Murfee, you've filed a motion to set conditions of release, which I have read and which counsel for the government has received. Please tell the court why you think this young man should be released on bail in this very serious matter."

Thaddeus nodded and launched in, "May it please the court that my client, the defendant Booker Penstone, is a very young person, undeveloped physically, and unable to defend himself against the type of prisoner he is going to run into while incarcerated. He is also a lifetime resident of San Diego, and his parents have been employed here all their working lives. They own a home in Ocean Beach, and there is extended family as well. Booker himself owns property in San Diego County. The only time he leaves the state of California is to tour with his band, which sometimes takes him not only across the country but around the world. Thus I am asking that the court not only release him on bail in a reasonable amount but also that he be allowed to leave the state of California and travel within the contiguous forty-eight states for the purpose of meeting contracted performances to maintain good business relations with the companies and people who have trusted Booker and his band. Your Honor, the facts of this case are also particularly compelling. If called to testify, the defendant would tell the court that just before the shooting, he was in a pool changing room, using the urinal, when he turned and saw a gun being pointed in his face by the decedent. He turned and wrestled the gun away from her. In great fear for his own life and, because he had never handled guns before and knew nothing about them, no one would be surprised that the gun discharged, shooting the decedent in the back. Thus, this was not a premeditated act, certainly does not rise to the level of murder in the first or second degree, and most likely will, at its worst, be found to be negligent homicide. At its best, Booker will be found not guilty and/or the charges dismissed by the court. For these reasons, it is the defendant's position that bail should be set in a reasonable amount and he be allowed to travel at will within the United States. Whatever the court orders, Booker will obey completely."

"Miss Hansen," said the judge, "I'm sure the government would like to be heard on this matter."

"Your Honor," said Marilyn Hansen, "the government is strongly opposed to any kind of bail in any amount. The evidence will show that the defendant, after the decedent had broken off any form of attack, continued pointing the gun at her as she was fleeing, and willingly and purposely shot her in the back, killing her. The evidence will show that he intended to shoot Joan McIntyre, and there had been previous bad blood between them. While Mr. Murfee may argue this was a case of a gun going off in the hands of a novice, the evidence will show the defendant, Booker Penstone, also owns several guns of his own, which he travels with and sometimes shoots at indoor firing ranges while on tour. We have several witnesses in this regard, and I will call them now before the court, if the court wishes, to make this very important point that, the defendant indeed was familiar with guns and knew exactly what he was doing when he pulled the trigger, intentionally killing Joan McIntyre."

The court said, "Mr. Murfee, what say you in regard to the defendant's experience with guns?"

"The defendant vigorously disputes and denies any previous knowledge of the use and handling of firearms and is frankly flabbergasted that the government would make such an allegation. His bandmates and road manager can testify that he never fires guns and that, in fact, he even abhors guns in line with the feelings of so many youths in the United States today, following the school shootings of the past several years. Again, the defendant asks for bail in a reasonable amount and that he be allowed to travel inside the United States."

"Counsel," said the judge, "the court is going to set bail in the sum of ten million dollars and restrict the defendant's travels to the boundary lines of the state of California. While the defendant has ongoing business affairs, so do a world of other people. Those defendants come before the court and are not allowed to leave the state of California while on bail. An exception will not be made in this defendant's case simply because he happens to be in show business and, judging from the audience in the courtroom this morning, very popular. Is there anything further?"

"I believe that's all on my motion to set conditions of release, your honor."

Looking at Butchy's father, Everett Penstone, the judge said, "Mr. Penstone, you are the natural father and guardian of Booker Penstone, is that correct, sir?"

"Yes, sir," said Penstone, "I'm Booker's father."

"And you, sir, hired Mr. Murfee to represent your son? Is that correct?"

"Well, yes, your honor."

"And you're satisfied with the services here today?"

"Yes, Your Honor."

"Very well, there's nothing further at this time. This case is adjourned."

Penstone told Butchy they would be at the jail at 5 o'clock to pick him up.

In the crush of reporters and young admirers, Butchy was spirited away by the deputies back to the jail where he would undergo processing out. Thaddeus returned to La Valencia and had a late lunch, then began making calls.

He decided to hire a security service to stick like glue to Butchy and make sure he complied with all conditions of release: no association with criminals, no drugs, no alcohol, no weapons, no leaving the State of California, obey all laws, and on and on. Thaddeus wanted to be sure there were no shortfalls that would wind his client back in jail. He had been dead serious—Butchy wouldn't survive in jail.

Not with the customers they had there.

Chapter 20

Detective Safari Frye needed a cut and color. And she wanted to treat Carrie, do something for the girl that might make her feel a bit better. Sometimes you needed to start with the outside and work your way inside.

The place to go for that service in La Jolla was Surfs Hairstyle Salon along Prospect Street, just one block from the beach. Inside were slinky black and silver furnishings, the stylists in their beach town outfits, and the brew of Colombian coffee for the taking. She was greeted by Nanci with an *i*, who asked if she could get her anything while she waited. Safari demurred. She plopped down in a leather and chrome sling chair, and Carrie sat down next to her. The young girl immediately opened the latest issue of *La Jolla*, a glossy magazine brimming with slick ads and models younger than Safari could ever remember being. They'd only been there a few minutes when her stylist came for her, a thirtyish woman named Beverly, this time with a *y*.

Safari offered Carrie to go first, but she declined, to read the rest of the magazine, so Safari got up and followed Beverly to the farthest chair in the back on the right hand side of the salon.

"What are we thinking about today?" asked Beverly. Beverly had been Safari's stylist for years and they'd come to a sort of distant friendship.

Beverly finger combed Safari's hair, lifting and letting it fall loosely back into place. The exercise made Safari realize how badly she needed a cut.

Safari's forehead furrowed. "Something easy. I like to jump out of bed in the morning, take a shower, grab a Danish and some coffee, and hit the road. I don't have time for styling, blow drying, or any other crap. My hair is the least of my problems in the morning. Other times, I'll be riding around with the windows down in my car, and I need a cut that stays in place when I jump out.

"I'm thinking shorter, so we can either do a sort of bob or pixie cut. You look beautiful with your long style, but you're talking utility. Natural and short is going to serve you best."

Beverly pointed out a couple styles that she thought would look good on Safari out of a hair design magazine, but Safari just wasn't sure. "You're the professional. What do you think?"

"Well, even a bob will take some time to care for and I think you'd look super cute in a pixie style cut." As Beverly talked, she played with Safari's hair, moving it this way and that. "You already have the bangs so let's just cut it short up the back, like this one here." She pointed at the magazine in Safari's lap. "But you're talking about eight inches of hair off."

"Let's do it," said Safari. "I'm ready."

Beverly readied the color for the highlights and returned shortly. While she brushed on the color and then folded the hair into aluminum foils, Safari kept up the chatter, "You guys have re-furnished the place since I was here last. Did somebody buy out Marceline? New owners?"

"No, Marci still owns the place. But she's partnered now with two gay guys who own other salons up and down the coast. They're trying for what they call the unified look, and this must be it."

Beverly let the foils set for fifteen minutes then led Safari over to the washbasin. She clipped a towel around her neck and then had her lean her head. As she washed, she talked, "Kent's wife was in. You remember Noel?"

"Of course, I remember her. I saw her last night. She had a little too much to drink, but that's a whole other story, and what's new? Never mind, forget I said that. It's catty. Anyway, why mention her?"

"No reason, but she did mention you were in trouble down at the office."

"Jesus, this town knows about everyone else's business. Besides, I'm not in trouble. The chief just took issue with something I said about another dick."

Beverly knew she was on to something. "God, girl, don't leave me hanging here. What did you say?"

Safari threw caution to the wind. "I called Eugene Michaels a dickless wonder. Now they've brought me up on sexual harassment charges. You understand this is absolutely confidential and goes no further than this chair, right?"

"Girl, don't even bother. Everything you say here is confidential. So what brought that on anyway?"

"It was about working conditions and hours. Real detectives don't work forty hour weeks; there's no such thing. Anyway, I needed Michael to work late one night and he wouldn't do it."

"Why not?"

"He said he had to help set up for his wife's bridge party."

"Oh, Jesus, you have got to be kidding. I know his wife. She doesn't come here. Her hair looks like a ten-dollar hack job, and she just doesn't seem to give a damn. I mean, she's probably a nice person and all, but she really needs to think twice about where she's getting her hair done. But I didn't know they were married. I thought they were boyfriend-girlfriend."

Safari shrugged. "I don't know. All I know is that he told me his wife needed his help. Maybe there's a girlfriend *and* a wife. I really don't know and don't care. Anyway, he went to Adamson and filed sexual harassment charges against me for calling him a dickless wonder. Can you believe that?"

"So what's going to happen? Your job isn't being threatened, is it?"

"That's why I'm here. I need to look good for Friday."

"What's Friday?" asked Beverly.

"Chief Adamson and a civilian and an Administrative Law Judge are going to decide whether I should be found guilty of the sexual harassment charges or not. The whole thing is bogus because men call each other dickless wonders all the time, and a hell of a lot worse, but let a woman do it, and suddenly it's World War Three. I think they have to do it, otherwise Michael would raise a stink in the papers. At least I think that's what they're afraid of. I'm really not worried. I think I'll be found innocent in about two minutes. All they need to do is poll the other detectives to find out how we really talk. Anything goes. There's nothing that can't be said, and nobody rats anybody out. Michaels has no friends left because of what he did. I hate to think what might happen if he ever needs backup and his partner isn't around. But that's for another day."

"I was gonna say, he needs to be thinking about his own safety. The whole thing sounds stupid to me. Does he have a lawyer?"

"I don't know yet. If he does, he'll be at the hearing Friday and probably try to drill me a new one."

"Okay, sit up now and let me towel you dry."

Safari did as instructed and surrendered to the towel being rubbed vigorously around her head. She was then moved back to the styling chair.

A half-hour later, the two women were surrounded by ringlets of hair on the floor. Most of it, though, clung to the cutting cloth fastened around Safari's neck. So far, they had discussed the weather, people they knew in common, and the upcoming surf competition. Then Beverly moved in. "What do you know so far about Moonbeam?"

Safari's posture tightened. The case was hers. "I can't really talk about that right now. It's my case."

"I mean, the poor girl, I can't even begin to imagine how someone could do something like that. Are there any suspects?"

Safari grimaced. "Beverly, you know better. You've known me for five years, and you know I can't talk about active cases. Besides, if there were any suspects, I couldn't say anything anyway."

"So there aren't any suspects yet? That's what it sounds like."

"Come on, girl, enough already."

"Some of us were talking, and someone said they

weren't going to the beach anymore, not without a big crowd around. Is that where we're at now?"

Safari said, "I'll give you the same answer I give everybody. You always want to be careful about your surroundings and know who's around you at all times. It's 2019. This is no longer your parents' world. And it's definitely not the world where you grew up."

"It's just so sad. If I had kids, I'd be horrified at letting them go to the beach alone. So you guys think it's someone from La Jolla or maybe somebody passing through?"

Safari sighed audibly. "Beverly, how dumb do you think I am? I've had the best lawyers in Southern California try to get secrets out of me who were a hell of a lot smarter than me and you put together. So far, I'm batting one hundred percent. Let's change the subject."

They continued, talking about the shooting at Reginald Pelham's, the boy band, and Butchy Penrose. But it wound up the same as the Moonbeam conversation. Beverly wanted names, dates, and facts, all of which Safari was unwilling to supply. The conversation then petered out and abruptly ended with the haircut.

Beverly spun her around in her chair, and what a difference! Safari's naturally blond hair was now a bit brighter with the highlights, but it was the cut that was so drastic. Where she'd had long hair, it was now short up the back and around her ears. But she had to admit, it wouldn't take much effort to take care of. Just would need to get it cut more often. She was okay with that.

Safari then waited while Carrie got her hair done. The teen left her own hair long and just got a trim and some highlights.

After Carrie finished up, they paid their tab and stepped outside. "Glorious," said Safari. "SoCal forever!"

They crossed Prospect Street and climbed inside her Ford interceptor. She pressed the starter, and the powerful eight-cylinder engine jumped to life.

She squealed her tires in front of Surfs almost as if she were fleeing the area.

An idea had come to her.

Chapter 21

The plate glass walls of the southwest corner, first floor, of Reginald Pelham's home, were retractable. Pelham stood by the entrance to the room and held down the rocker button until the walls were fully pulled back. The fresh morning air, mingled with the fresh morning sunshine, put a smile on his face despite the problems he was encountering with his estranged wife, Victoria. His manservant, Jonesy, was fluffing the pillows on the L-shaped couch. "I'm telling you, Jonesy," said Pelham, "the woman has definitely sprung a leak. She's nuttier even than when she was living here with me."

Jonesy didn't answer. He had learned long ago it was totally unsafe to take part in the arguments constantly raging between the Pelhams. "Take sides at your own risk," he told the other workers. It was good advice. The husband-and-wife team could be embroiled in a knockdown-drag-out fight to the finish at 10 a.m. and by 2 p.m. be locked inside their bedroom with a *Do Not Disturb* sign on the door.

Pelham sat down on the vertical leg of the L, facing the

beach. There was sand not ten feet from where he sat, and any moment now there would be beach walkers and joggers glancing sideways into his room as they passed by. Some of them would stop and stroll over and strike up a conversation with him. He never avoided these folks and was only too happy to invite them inside if they asked to use the restroom or wanted water to drink. Always the host, Reginald Pelham was well-liked around town and was known for being a pretty down-to-earth guy who might show up at the market driving a Chevy pickup ten years old just as happily as if he were driving his brand-new Maserati.

His cell phone buzzed in his pocket, and he answered, "Hello Victoria, I expect you're calling to tell me about your latest lawsuit against me?"

Her voice was as clear coming from Paris as it would've been coming from the next room. "Reggie, I heard about the shooting at *our* house. You have any idea what this kind of thing can do to property values? Do I need to get a restraining order against you so that you don't waste the value of our common assets?"

"Please, calm down. We have no control over what our guests do at a house party. And speaking of waste, Merlin just sent me a copy of your American Express bill. Do you realize you're spending sixty-five-thousand dollars a month on room and board in Paris?"

"Darling, let's just say living with you introduced me to the finer things in life, and I'm unwilling to give them up now. Incidentally, now that you mention it, my lawyers will be asking your lawyers for your American Express bill for the same time period. You know what? I'm willing to bet a dollar to a donut that your bill is at least ten times higher than my bill. Are you willing to take my bet?"

"I wouldn't really give a damn except I'm also paying

for the upkeep of that ne'er-do-well boyfriend of yours, Pierre."

"His name is Francis Vichy, and you damn well know that. You'd also be well advised never to forget it, because as soon as we can, we're going to get married and Francis will become one of your larger shareholders along with me. I can already tell you he hates everything about you and agrees you shouldn't be running SkoolDaze given how crazy you've become. And who was the young miss who got shot Saturday night in my home, anyway? Is that someone you were banging?"

Reggie said, "Joan McIntyre was a sound engineer for Butchy's band. I'd never met her before. The whole thing is shrouded in mystery, but the cops tell me they're on the verge of getting to the bottom of it. I'm sure you'll be able to call them by the middle of next week and have all your questions answered, Victoria."

"Well, you'll be happy to know I'm not actually calling just to bust your balls," she said. "I need ten million dollars in my account by Friday. Francis has an idea for a business that's actually begging to be funded. In fact, you might even be interested in putting some of your own money into it once you hear what it is."

"I can hardly wait to hear what your master of commerce has in mind."

"Everyone over here hates the Brits for leaving the EU. Francis is going to market the hell out of a new motto, 'Brexit Don't Break It.' Catchy? He can see it on a whole line of coffee mugs, T-shirts, baseball caps, balloons for the kids, and every other type of product with a message. I think it's pure genius, don't you?"

"That's it? 'Brexit Don't break It' is about as far removed from something that's going to catch on with people as cancer in rats. First of all, it's too long, and second of all Brexit is a British topic, not a European one. Tell Francis to keep looking. I wouldn't put a dime in something that stupid."

"Just because you don't get it doesn't mean it's not a hit. Be sure the money's in my account by Friday so we can create product for sale."

Pelham watched a man and woman about his and Vicki's age stroll by on the beach. He didn't know them, knew nothing about them, but at that moment would've traded places to have his wife back, things good between them, and be taking a walk on the beach with her. It made him sad, having her away and in the arms of another man. He really loved his wife. But he also knew that no man could ever hold her. She was a free spirit who would be forever dancing from lamp to lamp in search of the ultimate fix. There really was nothing more to say. He simply had made a bad choice in the first place twenty years ago. Pelham considered himself a lucky man because they'd never had children, always too busy with this business to start a family. On the other hand, he mused, maybe children would've been the exact thing Vicki needed to keep her home. Well, he'd never know now. That ship had sailed.

He said, "I'll have the money in your account before five o'clock today. I really do wish the two of you the best of luck, and I hope this is the product Francis has been looking for."

"You can be a dear sometimes, Reggie. This is one of those times. But don't think I'm going to back off my shareholder suit just because you're sending me money. Ain't gonna happen. Tra la, Reggie, I'm off. Goodbye."

"Goodbye, Victoria, and good luck."

Pelham sat back and swiped his hand across his eyes. It

came away damp, and he sat there shaking his head and gazing out at the Pacific Ocean. The whole thing made no sense. He had thought she was happy with him when she said she was going to Paris for a week to shop the fall line. Then two weeks turned into four and four into eight and now this. A lover, a divorce, and a lawsuit. All in the same year.

"Jonesy, let's close the windows," he called to his manservant. The walls began swooshing shut as Jonesy depressed the rocker button at the entrance to the room. "While you're there, let's close the blinds as well. Maybe I can get in a quick nap before heading back downstairs to the office."

Pelham leaned back and shut his eyes. He hadn't slept well last night. Any sleep would be welcome, even if it were just fifteen minutes.

Victoria had sounded almost human, and she had kindled in him a hope he might be able to settle their differences without dragging the entire mass of their lives through court.

It was but a little hope, but it was hope.

He consciously regulated and slowed his breathing and, minutes later, was asleep, soundly, for the first time in three days.

Chapter 22

Rita Reynolds, sitting at the mixing console in Sunset Studios, never heard the maintenance room door when it opened into the talent room. She was hunched over the console in the control room, listening to a Boyz 'N Luv track through the Neumann speakers, and the room, in a manner of speaking, was rocking. She was alone so she had locked herself inside. The entire studio was dark except where Rita was sitting, and the only light was from the LEDs of the console.

The control room was 10 x 20 feet. It was separated from the talent room by a thick double-pane glass, soundproof, eight feet long. The control room shimmered in the LED light and, had Rita been paying attention, she would've noticed in the talent room the dull glint of silver as the figure drew a gun from a waistband holster. The figure then began creeping toward the door that separated the control zone from the talent room. Just as he laid a hand on the door handle, a door on the far side of the talent room, the maintenance room door, flew open and the chief maintenance worker, Eduardo Martinez, pushed his wheeled trash barrel ahead of him into the room. He snapped on the overhead lights just as the figure entered into the control room, the pneumatic door mechanism closing it behind.

The figure held up the gun to Rita and said, "Not a word."

Rita's head snapped up, and she saw the gun. The figure was wearing a hoodie and a dark neck gator decorated with a large skull up over his mouth and nose that muffled their voice. She recoiled in horror and then passed out in fright, her head falling atop a bank of Neve buttons and dials.

The figure then went to work. A tourniquet of rubber tubing was tied taut around Rita's left wrist. Pruning shears were then extracted from his right rear pocket where some men carry their wallets. He applied the shears to the right ring finger of the unconscious producer, and with an abrupt snap of the handles, the finger was separated from the hand.

Rita shot upright with a start and screamed in pain as the figure hovered behind her, placing the separated finger inside a hoodie pocket. But the pain was too much, and Rita passed out again.

On the other side of the glass wall, Eduardo Martinez, who had fired up the industrial-strength vacuum cleaner, heard none of this assault. He continued running the roller of the vacuum in the area where the talent gathered around the main mic boom, an area that was always pasty with cigarette ash and spilled drink refreshments.

It was just as the man was about to remove Rita's leggings that Martinez decided the talent room was clean enough and he'd move onto the control room through the connecting door. He unlatched the door and pushed it open with the nose of the vacuum.

The hooded figure was out the back alley door in a second and stepped out into the alleyway behind the studio and into his Toyota Corolla. The figure then disappeared into the early evening light and was gone.

Back inside the control room, moments later, Martinez found Rita unconscious and dialed 911, the vacuum still humming in the background.

Five minutes later, the EMTs arrived and came bursting through the back door of the studio. They applied a proper tourniquet as well as a field bandage.

Rita came around and began answering questions as she was prepared for transport to the hospital. The burly blond-headed EMT asked her, "Who did this to you?"

"A man wearing a black hoodie. He had a gun. What the fuck!"

"The police are on the way. In fact, I hear them coming up the alley right now. They will get two questions, then we'll be on our way."

A black police officer and a female with corporal stripes rushed into the room. The female took one look at Rita and rushed back outside, running for the sidewalk at the end of the alley. She knew she was too late but was determined to take a look both ways just in case.

Her partner immediately sized up the situation. He said to Rita, "Who did this?" Again, she said that it was a man wearing a hoodie who brandished a silver gun. The police officer then asked the EMTs the extent of the injury. The reply was that a finger had been snipped away from the hand. The officer then asked whether the finger had been located and was told it had not.

The police officer asked Rita whether she had seen the person before.

"There was something about him that was familiar, but

I'm not sure. I might've seen him hanging around with the band before."

"What band would that be?"

"Boys 'N Luv. A group that I produce. Our engineer was murdered Saturday night at the Pelham party. You've probably heard about it." Rita looked down at her heavily bandaged hand and again fainted. The EMTs lifted her onto the gurney and rolled her outside to the waiting ambulance where she was lifted and pushed inside. The driver closed the doors behind her, and the EMT riding in the back gave her a shot for pain. In a burst of heavy exhaust from the transport's diesels, the ambulance lumbered for the end of the alley where it rounded the corner and was gone.

Left behind, the police officers searched the control room for the missing finger. Ten minutes later, Detective Safari Frye arrived on the scene. She also accessed the control room from the alleyway, asked questions, and was brought up to speed by the uniformed officers. She advised them the case would be hers as a collateral inquiry to the death of Joan McIntyre. She requested a crime scene team, who arrived within fifteen minutes. As they began taking photographs, she tracked down the closed-circuit TV in the studio proper. Safari, satisfied the investigation was proceeding in a proper fashion, then left the scene, intending to go to the hospital and speak with Rita there.

Safari located Rita in the emergency room where she was being treated for the amputation. In between nurses and physicians, Safari was able to ask a few questions while Rita lay supine on the examining table in a curtained area. Morphine was onboard and the patient was drowsy but able to answer questions.

"Was it someone you knew?"

Rita shook her head, saying, "You're the tenth person

who has asked me that tonight and, I swear to you, he was all covered up. I couldn't see anything and it was dark."

"I'm going to switch on my microphone and ask you to describe what you can remember."

"All right."

"Was he Caucasian?"

"I couldn't tell. His eyes were dark but shaded by the hoodie."

"Did you get a sense of his age?"

"Like I said, it was very dark in the control room and, with the hoodie, there wasn't much you could tell. I don't even know what color his hair was or if he even had hair."

"Did he say anything to you?"

"I don't think so. I was passed out during most of it, except just after he cut off my finger when I came to and screamed. Then I passed out again."

"Who are your enemies?"

"In truth? The *work* I do is quiet and removed from the world, and my only real contacts are an engineer or two. Out of all these people, I don't have any enemies. I haven't pissed off anyone in traffic, and I haven't broken up with a boyfriend in over a year."

"Think hard about this—is anyone jealous of you?"

She hesitated before answering, "I have done something I don't ordinarily do. I slept with a member of the band. I don't know who knows that, and it only happened twice. But he doesn't have any girlfriends because his parents really didn't allow it at his age."

"Do you know his parents?"

"I've met his father, who is also his manager. He seems like a pretty down-to-earth guy."

"What about the young man himself? Would he have done something like this?"

"Do you mean was it him?"

"I'm asking whether it might've been him and you didn't recognize him."

"I'm sure it wasn't him. Butchy's just a kid. He would never do something like this. It's just not how he is."

"Did he say anything?"

"No."

"Then how do you know it wasn't Butchy."

"Butchy and I have a thing. He wouldn't do this."

"I'm not convinced."

"Well, that's your problem then."

Safari pressed on. "This next question might seem kind of off-the-wall, but I'm going to ask it anyway. In your mind, as you lie there, do you feel or see any connection between what happened tonight and the murder of Joan McIntyre?"

Rita slipped away but heard the question through a fog. She fought her way back and tried to give a good answer as the cop was really trying to help her. "That's a hard one. Can I think about that and get back to you?"

"Definitely, yes. Also, do you think there is any significance why he would cut off one of your fingers? Do you need it for work?"

"Now that is bizarre to think about. I'm going to need time with that one, too."

"The reason I ask is I just got the autopsy report on Joan McIntyre. What happened to you tonight has me ready to call in reinforcements. It seems that Joan's right hand was also disfigured. Her ring finger had been severed from her hand and was not found at the scene."

"You've got to be shitting me."

"No, I'm not. But it's also a break for Butchy in a way. It doesn't clear him absolutely. But Butchy passed out. The fact that it wasn't Butchy who mangled her hand is some indication of innocence. At least I'm certain that's how his lawyer, Thaddeus Murfee, will view it."

"I think I'm going to be sick."

At her words, a nurse moved forward with a plastic bowl and lay it upon Rita's chest.

"I'll leave you alone now. Thank you for answering my questions."

"I think I need armed protection. I'm going to hire a bodyguard for the next little while."

"You know, I don't blame you. I say go for it."

"I'm going to close my eyes now."

"Thank you for your time, and I'm sorry this happened."

Chapter 23

Rex Seager joined his partner, FBI Special Agent Jim Nesmith, and together they drove to the Denny's just off the freeway in Ocean Beach. Safari Frye was already there waiting at a quiet booth back by the restrooms when they walked in. They joined her there and ordered coffee. When it arrived and everyone had tempered a cup to their liking, Safari went first.

"I think we've got another Hillside Strangler on our hands, gentlemen. Clever, cunning, and careful."

"The 3C Killer," said Rex Seager, naming him on the spot.

"Works for me," she said. "So, the 3C killer likes ring fingers. I don't know why, but he's cut off three of them now."

"And he likes females," said Jim Nesmith, a recent CPA grad and even more recent FBI Academy grad. He was on the tall side with wide shoulders and a fit physique. Nesmith played league basketball and drove the lane no matter who stood between him and the basket. Rex Seager thought the world of his young partner and, even more so, valued the youngster's mindfulness and logic. Seager himself was known as a logician and forensic scientist, so the two of them were a bright match.

"That's right," Safari agreed, "he does like females. He's killed two of them in La Jolla and made an attempt on a third."

"Hold it," Agent Seager said. "It sounds like you're concluding that 3C fired the bullet that killed Joan rather than the boy band kid?"

"Thaddeus Murfee is trying to sell the theory. I'm restating it for what it is. If Butchy fired the fatal shot, then maybe we rethink the serial killer aspect and don't run with it. But if we give the marksmanship to 3C, then we're getting somewhere. I would prefer to be getting somewhere even on less-than-perfect knowledge about who-did-what. Otherwise, we're getting nowhere because we don't recognize the serial killer in our midst until it's too late, and he strikes again. That's why tomorrow I want to set up a bait and switch on the drummer, Dusty Zamboa. This is a person of interest to the PD. Maybe not to the FBI, you haven't told me. But I'm interested, and I'm wanting your buy-in on a little bait and switch tomorrow."

"How's it work?" asked Seager.

"I want to give the drummer a golden opportunity to kill a beautiful young surfer. The girl I have is twenty-two-years-old, lives in La Jolla, and reeks of SoCal. She's also an acting student. She's our bait. After Zamboa ogles her, and she disappears around the bend of the beach, I'm bringing in the switch part of the bait and switch. She's Corporal Nancy Hamm of the San Diego PD Business Frauds bureau. She and SoCal could double for each other in the movies—that's how good they are."

More coffee arrived. Seager lifted the carafe and poured. The men dosed their second cups and waited for Safari to continue. She took cream only, speaking as she dribbled one-half of the small silver pitcher's contents into her mug. "I'll have cops playing volleyball. There's a net right next to where I'm setting up the band's photograph shoot. You two will be tossing a football around on the other side of the shoot. If Little Drummer Boy tries to sneak off, he's going to have one of us following in his tracks."

"You really think he's stupid enough to try something in broad daylight with a beach full of people around?" asked Nesmith, the recent grad. His voice sounded incredulous, and he was frowning. "Because I don't get it. I don't think he'd dare act with an audience around like that."

"That's where you're wrong," Safari said, "if the Joan McIntyre shooting is his work. That happened with an entire contingent of Secret Service agents just outside by the pool. I don't know how he could get any more daring than that. Yes, I think we can plant a lure tomorrow and snare him. Besides, what have we got to lose?"

Rex Seager smiled. "Now there's the kind of logic I like. The old 'what do we have to lose' logic. When all else fails, punt the ball. I'm ready, Safari. Let's put it out there and see what happens."

"I'm right there with you since you put it that way," said Nesmith. "If we end up landing a whale, I would love that. So would my jacket." He meant the "jacket" of his personnel file. Landing a serial killer was still big stuff in the Agency, even though it had been done many times before.

Chapter 24

What the media didn't know was that the girl on the beach, the high-school runner named Moonbeam, had been disfigured, too. Her right ring finger was missing from the first joint on.

Safari thumbed her own ring finger. Murfee was going to have a field day with this. She had no option but to call him with an update. She wasn't the type of cop who played Hide the Ball. What she knew at this point, he would know, too.

She sucked in a long breath, then dialed his hotel. "Thaddeus Murfee? Safari Frye here."

"Hey, detective. What's up?"

"We need to talk. Can I swing by your hotel?"

"Sure, coffee shop okay?"

"See you there in fifteen."

"You're on."

Café La Rue at La Valencia hotel offered California-French dining at Paris prices. The croissants the lawyer and detective ordered were hot and buttery, the coffee a steaming pour-over. Safari popped a bite into her mouth as soon as the waitress served. Thaddeus was more deliberate, allowing time for it to cool first. Then he would sample. He wondered if the same could be said of their approaches to investigation of criminal cases, him slow and patient, her quick to arrest.

After Safari filled him in on Moonbeam's autopsy report and the attempt on Rita's life, Thaddeus waited a beat before he responded. He took a sip of coffee. "I'm troubled to hear about Rita. Was she able to get a look at the person who attacked her?"

Safari shook her head. "You'll be glad to know, first off, that the guy was much bigger than Butchy. Rita also says she knows Butchy, and he's just not the type of kid who would do something like this. So, two points for your side."

"Points aside, I'm just relieved that it wasn't much worse. After you called, I also checked in with Butchy, who's been home with his parents all day today since his grandmother is visiting from New York. The alibi is airtight. Please understand, Safari, that I see this whole development in a favorable light for Butchy. There's someone out there who, as far as we can tell, has it in for young women. I'm talking Moonbeam at the beach, Joan at Pelham's house, and now Rita at Sunset Sound Studio. I think I can argue successfully to a jury that you have a psychologically deranged actor on your hands. I think I can argue successfully that this has entered the realm of a serial killer."

She tossed her head in disagreement. "You might be able to make those arguments and successfully, Thaddeus. But the fact remains, Butchy fired a gun at Joan. After he fired the gun, she was found dead not twenty feet away from him."

"That's right, but let's not forget her finger had also

been severed from her hand. When the police found Butchy, he was unconscious on the floor or just barely coming to. It's very clear it wasn't Butchy who mangled her hand."

"That's very likely. But the fact remains, Butchy fired the gun that killed Joan."

"Aha, which begs the question, did anyone else also fire the gun after Butchy had fainted? I think there's room to make that argument now."

"I think your guy goes straight to prison should you make that argument. It's very weak and specious. I'd hate to be your client in that courtroom if you try to run that one by the jury. People around here are very sophisticated in these matters. We don't get dumb juries who believe whatever they're told by slick defense lawyers."

"Who said anything about dumb juries?" Thaddeus asked. Her words had ruffled him, and he was heating up. "A smart jury suits me just fine."

"With your skewed perspective? I guess not, friend."

He bore in, "Truth be told, it's going to take a very sophisticated jury to understand the timing required for Butchy to faint, another person to take the gun and shoot Joan, amputate her finger, and meld into the crowd before the police arrived." But even as he said it, he realized how ridiculous it sounded. How 'specious,' as Safari had put it.

"Thaddeus, when you put it like that, your scenario sounds all but impossible. While I never try to help defense lawyers, I hope you're not done looking and investigating yet." She smiled as she said this, lightly shaking her head, almost in amusement.

He was right there with her; the approach would be a very difficult, if not impossible, story to get jury buy-in. But, as a matter of fact, his investigation *had* only just begun.

"While we're just batting things back and forth," he

said, "I'm wondering what steps the San Diego PD is taking to protect the public from whoever is doing this. You must be under a ton of pressure to produce results on Moonbeam and Rita. Any suspects in mind?"

"We have some ideas and names that we're running down. I'm sure you'll know when we know that we've turned over the right rock."

Safari was no longer wolfing down her ham and cheese croissant. In fact, it lay half eaten, forgotten. A thoughtful look was fixed on her face when she asked, "What about you, Thaddeus? Do you have any names that you're running down?"

"Actually, I do, and when I've made a few more inquiries, if they pan out, I'm going to be more than willing to share my investigation with you, Safari. Like you, I'd rather play these things out in the open than lay snares and traps for my opponent. While my client is always number one, it seems to me we both have a public duty not to withhold information that might possibly lead to solving these crimes. I can promise you that if I turn up a viable lead, you'll be the second one to know."

"Thank you," she said. "I've been snooping around, and I've been told by a police official in Flagstaff that you are a man of your word. Which, in fact, is why I came to you this evening, because you are trustworthy and won't be holding a press conference as soon as I've left tonight."

"No, there'll be no press conferences. I don't try my cases on TV or in the newspapers."

Safari stood and extended her hand to shake. Thaddeus reached, and they shook hands. Safari shrugged. "Until then," she said with a smile.

"Yes," he said, "until then."

After she was gone, Thaddeus lingered in the café. He

poured himself more coffee and then, suddenly ravenous, ordered a cheeseburger with avocado. After all, he thought with a smile, it was Southern California, and everything came with avocado in some form or other.

He was also aware that sitting two tables away, along the restaurant's hallway wall, was an unshaven man with dark eyes who just might've been listening to his conversation with Safari. Which was the real reason Thaddeus hadn't immediately gone back upstairs to his room and ordered room service. He was lingering to see what he could make of the man.

After several minutes more, he realized it was a standoff. The dark stranger was waiting for Thaddeus to leave the restaurant. *All right*, thought Thaddeus, *I'll make the first move*. He held up a hand, and the waitress brought his ticket. He gave her the room number, initialed the page, added on a gratuity of 25%, and left the restaurant. He didn't, however, go right back to his room. Instead, he went to the end of the hallway, turned left, and went through the double doors out to the swimming pool area.

The shadows were long, and the night lights twinkled around the pool and along the walkways. The warm air of the Santa Ana kissed the poolside area, making for a pleasant atmosphere. The stars were just appearing in the early night sky; it was a very peaceful moment.

He was wearing penny loafers without socks, khaki cargo shorts, and a T-shirt with a pocket. He kicked off the shoes and selected a poolside recliner where he could sit and appear to be doing nothing. He watched out the corners of his eyes for the dark stranger to appear in the area, but so far there was nothing. Children were playing and squealing with joy in the shallow end. Couples and families ordered drinks and desserts, but still no stranger.

Thaddeus couldn't shake the feeling that he was being watched. But he didn't want to be so obvious as to turn around and check who was behind him. The point was, Thaddeus didn't want the stranger to know he was onto him.

A pool waiter approached to inquire whether Thaddeus would like to place an order from the bar. Thaddeus said he would like a glass of sun tea with a twist of lemon. The waiter smiled and turned away.

Thaddeus shut his eyes and drew a deep breath. He'd spoken with Christine, his wife, that morning, and all was well at home in Durango. He'd had to tell her that this trip was going to extend, that he still was not satisfied with the posture of the defense in Butchy's case. She had asked him if he wanted her to join him to help. Christine was a very accomplished trial lawyer in her own right, and he always preferred having her in the fray with him. But this time he told her no, just stay put. It was the type of case that was going to require a ton of questions and dead ends before he found what he was looking for. Plus, they had both agreed when they moved from Flagstaff to Durango that they needed to put the kids first. All of their kids needed both parents, and so Christine would stay there with them. Even though they missed each other horribly, they left it at that. He would give her a call if he got stuck.

Five minutes later, the waiter appeared with Thaddeus's iced tea. It was placed upon a cork coaster on the glass tabletop beside him. He took a long swallow, and then, as he moved the glass away from his mouth, he realized that the man had come out of nowhere to take the recliner beside him.

"So what leads do you have, counselor?" asked the man.

Thaddeus's head swung around. "You're talking to me?"

"Yes, I am," said the man, and in one smooth motion, he opened a wallet and displayed the unmistakable badge of the FBI. It was the same man Thaddeus had observed in the restaurant, and his first thought was: why on earth would the FBI be eavesdropping on a conversation between a local detective and a defense lawyer? He intended to find out.

"You were in the restaurant when I was speaking with a local detective. Why were you listening to us?"

"Let's just say the FBI are feeling our way into this mess at this point. Let's just say, also, that I'm here to recruit you. I need to know what you know when you know it. There's more to what's going on right now than just your client's defense case."

"I'm listening. How about we start with your name?"

"Rex Seager. FBI, San Diego."

"Thaddeus Murfee. Durango, now La Jolla. But you already know that."

"Thaddeus, we have reason to believe the two La Jolla murders are connected to a string of murders between here and Portland. It could be our man has already moved on, and I'm a day late and a dollar short. It could also be he hasn't finished here yet, in which case you and I need to buddy up."

"Sorry," said Thaddeus, "but I think you've got me mixed up with the police department. I'm investigating a case, and what I learn, I don't plan to share with anyone." With the exception of Safari Frye, he admitted to himself.

"Oh, but I think you will, Mr. Murfee, after you understand that the FBI and Secret Service share information continuously. You may or may not know that after your client fired the gun at Joan McIntyre, the first agency on the scene was the Secret Service. The Secret Service found a piece of evidence that just might exonerate Butchy Penrose. But because the Secret Service is not a law enforcement agency, that bit of evidence may or may not be turned over to the local PD. In other words, sir, there's a chance you will never locate the evidence that could set your client free. Now you know. You should also know that if you go running to the judge to seek an order to produce that evidence, that this conversation tonight will be denied and you'll be left looking foolish."

Thaddeus slowly nodded. "And what do I have that would make you come forward and tell me all this?"

"You have access to a member of the boy band, the drummer, Dusty Zamboa. It's a boy band, but he's a bit older. At this point in time, the drummer is a person of interest. I can't say more. Bottom line, we're taking a hard look at him, and you could be very helpful."

"What's it cost me to play?"

"We're going to throw a piece of bait out on the beach tomorrow. We'd like you to help Zamboa find his way out there. Given the opportunity to act, we'd like to see what he does."

"I'll have to think about this," said Thaddeus. "Call my room at seven in the morning."

With that, Thaddeus stood, slipped his shoes on his feet, and headed for the elevators and his room. He had calls to make and no time to waste.

Fifteen minutes later, he was speaking with his daughter, Turquoise, an ex-Los Angeles Police Department detective. He explained what he needed. She said she would get back to him within the hour.

He then called Butchy. He used the excuse that he wanted some photographs depicting Butchy in a typical beach party with his band. They were to meet him at ten a.m. on the beach. He would have a photographer present. Butchy quickly agreed. They would meet him there, he promised.

Thaddeus texted Turquoise. She was returning with preliminary information.

He realized how deep the boy band waters might run. If his hunch was right, huge sums of money would dry up, and teen hearts would break.

Tomorrow could change everything.

Chapter 25

Victoria Pelham arrived in San Diego from Paris wearing expensive brown slacks, a pleated white shirt, and a beret. Choos clad her feet, and leather luggage followed close behind her through the airport out to the waiting limo always at her disposal in SoCal. She climbed in back, asked her bodyguard for a gin and tonic, and removed her shoes while they traveled the short thirty minutes north to La Jolla. She would be staying at the Pelham home—in her own suite, consisting of bedroom, dressing room, and den.

"Reggie can just go to hell," she told Marion, the maid who answered the door. "We have nothing to say to each other, so don't tell him I've arrived."

The next day, she appeared in court with her lawyer, prepared to convince the judge that a temporary restraining order should be entered against Reginald Pelham to rein him in and assure that he didn't waste or sell more marital or SkoolDaze assets. They were both one and the same in the community property state of California.

The judge was Margaret Mary O'Reilly, who ascended to the bench when her predecessor was shot down in the last in-court shooting of a judge before weapons were banned from courthouses. It almost went without saying that she had passed judgment from the bench most of her eighty years. In fact, she, Margaret Mary, could no longer remember when she hadn't been a judge. It must have been a long time ago, she recounted for the amusement of her great-grandchildren. But not to worry, Judge O'Reilly was sharp as a tack and was never shy about dropping the hammer on wayward husbands summoned onto her domestic relations turf.

Reginald Pelham walked with a swagger into the courtroom, accompanied by Thaddeus Murfee, ready for a no-holds-barred knockdown, drag-out, pitched battle with his wife. She was attempting to control what measures he might wish to take with his baby SkoolDaze, and because of this she was the enemy who must be destroyed no matter the cost.

Thaddeus had warned Pelham that his wife was a fifty-percent owner of SkoolDaze. He had reminded Pelham that Victoria also owned one-half of every piece of furniture, every vehicle, boat, airplane, and home appearing on the marital community's list of assets so nicely appended to Victoria's motion. Oh, and she was also jointly liable, of course, for all community indebtedness, which, as a legal and equitable manner, ensured her formidable power before the court to look out for herself equally with Reggie.

Judge O'Reilly called the court to order, and Victoria Pelham stood and was sworn before taking the witness chair. Once seated, she began giving testimony.

Said her attorney, Walter Barnham IV of Beverly Hills, "You're living in Paris with a friend?"

Victoria's eyes flashed. "More than a friend, Mr. Barnham. I've made no effort to hide my current relationship. Unlike my husband, whose many relationships will never be fully known to this court."

Asked Barnham, "And you have knowledge of his romantic comings and goings as well as the financial expenditures he makes to please his stable of conquests?"

"I do have knowledge. Your office and investigators have obtained every last scrap of paper and electronic entry of every financial transaction by my husband or his lieges over the last twenty-four months. He hasn't made a move we don't know about."

Thaddeus was somewhat taken aback by this comment. Pelham hadn't told him he was being watched. In fact, just the opposite. Pelham figured he was operating completely outside the knowledge of his wife since she was so far removed and living in Europe. It occurred to Thaddeus just then that, based on Victoria's knowledge of his financial affairs, the afternoon might be much longer than the "thirty minutes or so" his client had predicted the hearing might last. Yes, there had been requests for documents and interrogatories exchanged, but that was an ongoing process and neither Thaddeus nor Pelham imagined, based on the volume of documents dumped on Vicki's lawyers, that her forensic team had made much headway against the sheer volume of the document dump. Now Thaddeus was beginning to realize his client might have sorely underestimated the adversary's grasp of the company's—and Reginald's—finances. Thaddeus, so newly on the case, was afraid he was about to learn the hard way just how much the Mrs. in fact knew.

"Starting with the removal of company assets. Are you

aware of any sale of SkoolDaze assets outside the normal course of business?"

"Like behind-the-scenes sales?" she asked.

"Yes."

"He has sold no less than one-hundred-and-four software programs and algorithms developed by *our* company and has kept the money one-hundred percent in his own pocket. Offshore, I'm saying."

"Can you give us an example?"

"Oh, sure. He sold three software routines to Ahmed Accountants out of Dubai, software routines capable of managing electronic assets without human intervention. Some call these software pieces high-speed trading vehicles. I know this for a fact because one of the parties involved was someone my team had planted. Reggie, my husband, walked right into it and received an EFT to his bank in Grand Cayman in the amount of eighty-six-million dollars and change. I can tell the court about at least a dozen others if necessary."

"Not necessary," said Judge O'Reilly. "The court understands the problem."

"What's she mean by 'problem'?" whispered Reginald to Thaddeus.

Thaddeus whispered back, "It means the judge has just characterized the first of your transactions she's heard about as a problem. That's not good. Now pipe down and let me listen please."

Barnham continued, "And then there are gifts and expenditures for the pleasure of multiple young women, correct?"

"Oh, yes," said Victoria, crossing and uncrossing her Jimmy Choos. "He spent ninety-five-thousand dollars on a necklace from Tiffany's and gifted it to an eighteen-year-old premed student attending UCSD. I mean, really, Reg? Was the two weeks you spent holed up with her last Christmas in Aspen really worth a diamond-encrusted necklace that I would be proud to own myself?"

"Don't answer," Thaddeus instructed his client, who he could feel, sitting beside him, swelling up to take the bait and make an in-court comment in return, a comment that would almost certainly injure his case. "Your Honor, I would ask that you instruct the witness to keep her questions off the record and between counsel and herself. My client isn't on trial here and certainly isn't being cross-examined by the witness just now."

"Sorry, Mr. Murfee," said Judge O'Reilly, "but your client and his get-em-up cowboy practices *are* on trial here today. As for the questions, the court instructs the witness to save her questions for such time as she and the respondent might speak between themselves. Would my mental image of a quiet dinner between the parties where they settle their differences be too hopeful? I wonder. Counsel will continue. The court is making its notes."

"What other expenditures are you aware of, Mrs. Pelham?" asked Barnham of Beverly Hills.

"I know that he pledged twenty-five-thousand dollars a month to Jane Goodall's Chimp Eden in Africa. Reggie has a thing for chimpanzees. Maybe it's because they have about the same IQ as his human female companions? I'm sure I don't know. But $25K—there you are, documented on exhibit eighteen."

Thaddeus blanched. It appeared Mrs. Pelham even had exhibit numbers committed to memory. This was serious and getting more serious with each question and response.

"What else?"

"My husband sold one-hundred-and-fifteen-thousand

shares of SkoolDaze common stock and was supposed to split the proceeds of that sale with me. So far he hasn't, and every time I ask, he says he's put me on an allowance in Paris and he's deducting my living expenses from my share of the sale. He says he's doing it to protect me." She sniffed as one sniffs who's been offended by their spouse.

"Your Honor," Barnham said, addressing Judge O'Reilly, "I can continue for the next several hours with similar complaints against the respondent, but all of these same matters are contained in the petitioner's application for temporary restraining order. My going over them in court today seems somewhat repetitious."

"Agree," said Thaddeus.

"The court agrees as well. Consider the TRO granted. Mr. Pelham, all future financial transactions by you, made not in the ordinary course of business and exceeding ten-thousand dollars, will require pre-approval from your wife's counsel and, if you're unable to agree, then the matter will be presented by stipulation for the court to approve or disapprove. Such presentations better be damn few and far between, I would caution the parties, because the court isn't in existence to referee family squabbles over money. In other words, I don't want to see even one such incident where the parties cannot agree on a proposed expenditure and, if I do, then I will be leveling contempt findings against the guilty party. Mrs. Pelham, you are likewise restrained by the TRO just like your husband. As to the alleged one-sided incidents in the petition, the court considers those proven. Mrs. Pelham is awarded one-half of all such sales and transfers, payable immediately. Anything further, gentlemen?"

"No and thank you," said Barnham.

"Nothing," said Thaddeus. He had momentarily thought of arguing the truthfulness, or at least the accuracy, of the wife's claims but then thought better of it. The truth was, Pelham had been found out and he owed the money. No sense in pissing off the judge by disputing those claims when only minor headway might be made and, on the opposite side of the coin, the wife might have missed certain transactions that might be brought out on the husband's cross-examination by Barnham IV should Reggie take the stand to make his defense. So Thaddeus let it slide.

"DIDN'T you tell me there was nothing to her accusations?" asked Thaddeus once the client and attorney were driving north to La Jolla from San Diego on the five freeway. "That sounded to me like more than nothing, Reggie."

Reggie Pelham shook his head and tugged at his necktie with two fingers. He managed to pull free the knot and unbutton the top button of his shirt. "I had no idea I'd been invaded by prying eyes. I had no idea I was under surveillance by Vicki's version of the CIA. Holy shit!"

"Well, I hate to say it, but a reckoning has arrived. I'm going to need a listing of all transactions you've been a party to that aren't included among those she's listed in her petition for restraining order. I know there's more she's missed. I need to know about those."

"How do I proceed now?" Pelham asked. "Do I really have to get court approval every time I want to honor my lady friends with gifts appropriate to their wiles, their charms?"

"You were there, Reggie. You heard the judge. Courts enter these *in terrorem* clauses in their orders to encourage the parties to settle quickly. I would encourage you likewise. Let's set our sights on settlement now. You would be well-advised to do this. In fact, if you don't, you're going to drop a bundle on legal fees, and your lady friends are going to go without and you're going to probably end up on the wrong end of a citation to show cause—tantamount to going to jail, in plain terms. I'm going to prepare and provide a full accounting of all marital assets. I'm going to need your detailed help. This is probably going to keep me here in La Jolla at least two more weeks but we really need to get this done and done right. Judge O'Reilly isn't someone you want to stonewall. It could get very nasty in her court very fast. For openers, I need such a list by Friday of this week. Any problem with that?"

"No, no problem. What about valuations, though?"

"We'll just employ the best forensic accountants and licensed appraisers, realtors, brokers, and dealers. Top-drawer, unquestionable credentials all the way. We don't want to go back to court to argue the value of a stock listed on the New York Stock Exchange, if you follow me."

"Of course not."

"I've seen it happen. Pure disaster. It won't happen here. Self-describing asset values are no contest then, agreed?"

Reginald sighed. He was being asked to agree that face values such as stock, bank accounts, CDs, brokerage accounts, and all the rest of it would be freely given and admitted. There would be no games with those things. "Fine," he at last said without conviction.

Thaddeus smiled. "I'm on your side, Reggie. When it's time to fight, I'll tell you. Agreed?"

"Agreed."

"Good, then. I'll proceed."

Chapter 26

Her name was Helen MacInnes and she loved her California lifestyle. A Chicago transplant, she had gone from four seasons to two seasons: Perfect and Wonderful. Today she was earning her keep in her chosen profession of actress. Which was always a good experience. Except this role was different. Her only part was a walk-on—a walk along, really, where she walked along the expanse of beach at the bottom of Vallecitos Road and then north for about one hundred yards where she would disappear behind a public bathroom/shower facility and then be seen no more.

Helen first dug her toes in the sand at 10:22 a.m. on a Saturday morning, about one hour after the weekend sun lovers had started to take all the parking spots in the entire area. They'd come, traipsing east to west with their families, their coolers in tow, lots of kids walking ahead with inner tubes around the extended bellies and plenty of infants in strollers with the sun shields up and in place. Everyone smelled of sunblock, at least the smart ones did. And Helen watched them coming as she began her stroll just at water's edge.

She was dressed more skimpily than she might otherwise for the beach, her fulsome body filling out the low-slung bikini pants and top. She jiggled when she walked—that had been one of the requirements of the detective who hired her, the detective named Safari. She was to walk with an exaggerated roll of her hips as well. She'd been told she was the bait in a deadly game of cat-and-mouse, and she'd been told she would be under close surveillance every step of the way. At no point would an undercover police officer be more than thirty or forty feet away, posing at different points along the way as swimmers, surfers with their boards planted in the sand, and even those masquerading with families.

A hundred feet into her walk, she came to a spot where umbrella video lights were arrayed around a small band of very young guys playing their instruments and drum box. She knew the group, or at least her younger sister did, although she couldn't quite place their name. Boyz-something, but wasn't sure since they had arrived on the music scene after she had moved on musically.

The band was playing a tune she couldn't avoid on the radio. It played on several radio stations through her Kenwood car stereo system, invited or not. She didn't know the name of the song they were playing but then, as she drew abreast, she realized they weren't actually playing and making music but were lip-syncing the song.

The scene was setup to look like your typical underage drinkers' beach party, complete with a false keg of beer and girls much younger than Helen lurking around the boys as they "played." Helen had been instructed to slow her walk as she passed by the band, which she did. She'd also been told to try to make eye contact with the drummer and let her gaze linger there, which she also managed to do. Then she tossed off a half-smile and turned her head away, continuing her slow, rolling stroll up the beach.

SAFARI HAD TAKEN up her position at the beginning of the walk along La Vereda Street. She paralleled Helen as Helen walked the beach. Safari took care to dodge distracted traffic and bicyclists and inline skaters along the beach-access road. Plugged into her right ear was a wireless, operated with a lavalier mic under her T-shirt. She pushed a baby carriage that shielded from passersby an M16 assault rifle in case it turned out the serial killer was heavily armed or consisted of more than one man.

Waiting at the traffic light at Calle Frescota Avenue, Safari heard her earphone crackle.

A voice said, "Dick One, Beachcomber here, over."

"Dick One," she replied, "over."

"I have Snake Hips in sight and am following along the break wall."

"Roger that. Any sign of Little Drummer Boy?"

"Passed by his stage sixty seconds now. Remains drumming."

"Were you able to see if he looked at Snake Hips?"

"Unknown, Dick One. Facing wrong way to see."

"Copy that. Anyone else on the air see? Dick One, over."

"Starfish copy. It seemed he looked from my view. I still have eyes, over."

"Stay put, Starfish, over. Anyone else have Snake Hips?"

"Angel Fish, copy. I'm with the nuns, and they're walking the beach."

"In their habits, over?"

"Roger that. In their habits, guns on board."

"Roger that, Angel Fish. Dick One out."

No other traffic came on the line after Safari signed off. Nor should they, not unless Snake Hips, Helen MacInnes, was followed or accosted or threatened in any manner. Were she followed, the entire net would close and the threat would be remediated. She walked another fifty paces, dodging skaters and beach cruisers every other step.

Just then, Safari's earpiece crackled.

"Dick One, this is Audience. Little Drummer Boy has just exited the stage and is walking toward Frescota. He's dressed in Khaki cargo shorts, red T-shirt, and silver sunglasses. He's in a hurry, over."

"Roger that, Audience. Dick One will double back. Star Fish stay with Snake Hips. Maximum distance ten meters. Copy that?"

"Copy. Star Fish out."

"Angel Fish walk toward the stage. Beachcomber, get on Little Drummer Boy. Dick One in front, Beachcomber behind. We've got FBI across the street in unmarked vehicles. All eyes for any other subject who might try to follow Snake Hips. Dick One, over."

"Roger that, Dick One. Angel Fish out."

DUSTY ZAMBOA–LITTLE Drummer Boy—hurried up to the lifeguard station with its bathroom and shower complex just off to the side. He'd never needed to pee so badly. He had told Butchy as much before leaving the video shoot.

When he returned outside, he didn't see Beachcomber waiting beneath the lifeguard tower, vaping. But he smelled his presence. The fragrance was of Granddaddy Purp to Zamboa's practiced nose. No pot smelled alike to the connoisseur, which Zamboa fancied himself to be and maybe he was, because at twenty he'd been using since his twelfth birthday when his older brother dialed him in. He had been a daily, almost hourly, vaper ever since. Now he turned away from the vape and headed toward the sidewalk that paralleled the beach on Camino del Oro.

He was to meet his dealer two intersections up at Paseo del Ocaso. Off he went, not in any particular hurry, for the band was on break while the shoot director went over the next segment to be shot with the musical director. The other band members were in the band trailer, probably talking to a female or two hustled up that morning.

Zamboa hoofed it up to the light and waited for the green. He shifted nervously from foot to foot. His eyes darted everywhere, as would the eyes of any kid about to score vape cartridges, but he failed to notice the lady on the other side of the intersection, the lady with the baby carriage, the lady known in her earpiece as Dick One. As he crossed the street, she turned away and seemed to be addressing a problem with the carriage's left rear wheel. Her back was to him as he hurried past.

Safari immediately came upright and began following, cursing herself for allowing him to get ahead of her. Now she had Beachcomber on her tail. Without moving her mouth, she told Beachcomber to close it up and get on up ahead of Little Drummer Boy. Beachcomber in his jogging shorts, NB shoes, and half top ran past Safari and then passed Little Drummer Boy. Zamboa didn't seem to notice at all. Now Beachcomber was in the lead so he slowed to walk at a good clip, holding his arms above his head as one in need of full lung expansion, a deep breath.

Eyes were on Zamboa at this point from all four sides, including the FBI in reserve along the other side of the street.

Safari was certain they had him cold.

The FBI was certain they had him cold.

Dusty Zamboa was jonesing for a hit off the vape pipe, oblivious to the eyes that now measured his every step.

DUSTY ZAMBOA CONTINUED his trek up to Paseo del Ocaso. He arrived five minutes before the meetup with his pot dealer. A simple enough meeting; marijuana was legal in California, but Dusty was below the legal age. Another nine months, and he'd be good to go inside any marijuana outlet, but for now it was verboten. So he waited, unaware he was surrounded on four sides by city police, county sheriffs, state police, and FBI.

At eleven minutes after, a street person everyone knew as Whisper crossed the street and sidled up to Zamboa. He clutched a small brown bag that said *Fast N' Friendly* on the side. Zamboa passed the man a crisp new hundred-dollar bill then sweetened it with another twenty, just to keep up the man's interest in providing future service. From the sidelines, FBI cameras whirred and clicked as the hand-to-hand transaction completed. Wordlessly, the two men separated. Zamboa spun on his heel and headed back west toward the beach, retracing his steps. Midway along the first block, he stopped and swapped cartridges in his vape pipe. Fumes flared out of his mouth and nostrils as he took his tenth hit of the day. Time to rock-and-roll, he told himself. He held his arms out level from his body and imagined he was flying. The truth lay in there somewhere between the imaginary cockpit and the imaginary tail section of the imaginary airplane. He swayed from center the rest of the way along the sidewalk. The airplane wobbled on its longitudinal axis.

But never had a flightless airplane had so many pictures taken of a transfer between a minor and a dope dealer. None of them would prosecute; nobody on the scene, no police agency, gave a damn that Zamboa was underage. It happened at least a million times a day in California, and no one really cared anymore, least of all the cops.

Zamboa reached the bandstand in his imaginary airplane and took his seat upon the beat box while waiting for the shoot to resume. He looked intelligent and well-scrubbed—the exact look a member of a boy band needed to project if he were to pass a mother's screening. But inside, inside his brain where the wiring schematic was embodied, his synapses were firing randomly to the call and behest of Granddaddy Purp, Northern California's finest pot ever.

At least Dusty Zamboa liked it.

He imagined himself a young man who wouldn't hurt anyone or anything, who would remove bugs from dwellings and place them carefully on the ground outside like the Buddhists did. Dusty, a man who revered and treasured life and all growing things.

Especially California purple bud.

Safari Frye had her answer: wrong guy. As did the FBI have its answer. A serial killer—they were still thinking serial —was still at large. Helen MacInnes continued her leisurely walk up the beach, rolling her hips and wondering if Jack the Ripper were two steps behind. When, at the end of her trek, she was handed her sweatpants and T-shirt and she pulled things on and arranged her flip-flops, she was told that she could go. "I get to keep the two-hundred bucks just for one walk?" she asked, incredulous. She was told the money was hers to keep and thanked for her help. She was reminded she had signed a non-disclosure and she couldn't discuss her activity with anyone. She said she knew all about that, and the coppers had nothing to worry about. Her mouth was zippered.

Chapter 27

Victoria Pelham lazed in her bathtub in her wing of the mansion, eyes closed, imagining Francis Vichy's hands caressing her with soapy water. Memories of a warm bath and fragrant oils on Rue des Plaintains in Paris washed over her, and she shivered with happiness. Reggie didn't know yet, but on the day the divorce became final, Vicki would trade vows with Francis in Monte Carlo before disappearing to the baccarat tables with the twenty-two-million dollars she had retrieved from Reggie's schemes and dealings after court on Friday. She laughed and sipped her French tea, a chamomile sprung from the daisy flower and favored since the Middle Ages. There wasn't anything French she didn't love. She squeezed the soapy water from her washcloth, folded it twice, and affixed it over her eyes before inhaling and dozing almost at once.

Scrunch.

Victoria Pelham's eyes popped open beneath the damp washcloth. She'd heard something. Or maybe not. Maybe it was the splash of the spigot dripping into her bath. *But that couldn't be it*, she thought. It sounded like a footstep. The sound a flip-flop made when it scrunched on a smooth concrete finish. "Scrunch scrunch!" the sound again. She listened harder this time. Bath time was always a favorite of hers, a time of peace and renewal. Bath time had never been a time of fearsome noises.

Until now.

She slid the washcloth from her eyes and leaned forward in the tub. Had she heard the sound again? She couldn't say one way or the other. But whatever it was, the sound was unnerving. Maybe it was time to climb out of the tub and do her skin with product. Sunblock was huge in La Jolla. The equatorial sun was hell on white transparent skin such as Vicki's. Her dermatologist, the Botox Man, warned her every visit that she needed sunblock every time she went out. "Make it your first layer," he insisted. "Then do the cosmetics. But a layer of protection first and always."

She complied. Very rarely did she venture out without sunblock. So, yes, she'd climb off and towel dry and go to her dressing table and reload the sunblock onto her skin. Doctor's orders. She'd seen the malignancy pictures. God forbid. Those poor people. Could you imagine letting yourself go long enough that a deadly mole had time to kill you? Who wouldn't go to the doctor first?

Scrunch.

Oh, my God. Someone—someone in flip-flops—was nearby. Perhaps in her bedroom, maybe her dressing room. Both had Spanish tile floors, red tiles, smooth and cool year round.

"Vicki," said a muffled voice. "Vicki, I want to try your mascara. It's urgent."

Goose bumps erupted, covering every inch of her body.

She yanked a towel from a bar and wrapped it around her torso. It must be one of the workers Reggie often ordered up to do work around the house. That would be a simple, and happy, explanation for the sound of a familiar man's voice just outside her bathroom. But just for safety's sake, she slid open a drawer in the bathroom cabinet and withdrew a nail file. It was metal, though not all that long. Still, it was better than nothing. If he were an intruder, maybe she'd get a shot at piercing his throat with the nail file as he choked the life from her with his bare hands. Her thoughts were coursing through her mind, a torrent of words and feelings as she considered whether she would answer the voice that needed to talk.

"Who's there?" she said, making every effort to sound strong. Strong, she hoped, but tepid, she admitted. She tried again. "Goddammit, who's there?"

Bold enough. Tough talk.

She waited. Then he said, "I am your future."

"Not my future. My future's in Paris."

Now that sounded dumb. Victoria shook her head and rolled her eyes. *Simpleton.*

"I'm dialing the police. I have them on speed dial. I suggest you turn right around and leave."

"I cannot go away empty-handed. I need mascara."

This couldn't be happening. What in the world? "What do you want me to give you?"

"It's too late to give. You went too far with Reggie this time."

"Tell him I'll give his money back." She was panting with fear, her heart racing, her pulse thumping in her neck.

"It's too late to give money back," said the voice. "He says keep the money."

She gasped and looked down at her withered finger

pads, drawn into striations from the bath water. *Wrinkled from wet*, she thought.

She forced herself to stop shaking, and think. She tried a different tack. "The police are on the way. You stayed too long and left me no choice!" she shouted.

"Please come into the bedroom, Vicki. I have something to show you."

She stepped back and flung the door shut with a bang. Towels on the backside of the door slithered to the floor. She turned the lock. There, safe now.

Then she heard a kick, down low on the outside of the door, a loud thump. But flip-flops don't make thumps. So it wasn't flip-flops she'd heard. Unless there were two men.

"I hear sirens," Vicki lied. "They're coming now," she cried at the closed door.

Another thump, and the door splintered, flung from its hinges. A booted foot, a leg, appeared inside the bathroom where the door had been. Vicki shut her eyes and slashed air with her nail file. A hand seized her wrist in mid-air and squeezed so hard she had to drop the file. She felt the towel slide to the floor. Nude, alone, and afraid to look.

A fire erupted across her belly, a wide swatch, and her right hand flew to the area. It was wet and getting wetter and she felt an intestine squeeze out between her fingers. Then came more of it. Her hand was full of warm, wet sausages. At least they felt like sausages, the kind Reggie once liked on Saturday nights when they had breakfast at night.

Don't think of Reggie! Run, you fool! She staggered and fell back against the door behind her. It was closed but swung open onto her den. But there was another door beyond that one, a door leading to the hall and downstairs. If only—

Another slash, two inches higher, more fire. And still,

she couldn't get herself to open her eyes, as if seeing it made it real. Now, she had to use both hands to press her belly in, the blood gushing like a waterfall over her fingers.

I am serrated, she thought. *I have become someone dying. This cannot be happening. I don't want to die. I'm too young. Reggie hates me. I thought it was funny before. I was enjoying... I am dying.*

She released her innards with her right hand and reached around behind. Frantically she twisted the doorknob, but her blood-soaked hand couldn't find purchase. She finally turned to grasp with both hands, but the man caught her shoulders from behind, pulling her backward as she struggled to move forward through the door.

A fire erupted across her throat. She had been cut. Her tongue was receding back down into her throat. She lifted her hand and touched the serrated edges of the new wound running ear to ear.

Then she fell forward. She dropped to her knees, now on all fours when a rough boot kicked her in the side and she went sprawling headlong, face-down in a guttural whimper that was meant as a cry for mercy but instead never formed in her useless voice box.

Her fingers gripped the braided rug beneath her upper body. She remembered its green and red and pink fibers from long ago when she had sat upon that rug and excitedly tried on new baby seal winter boots. "Look," she had said to herself, "I have zippered a seal around my leg."

If only.

Then she relaxed and let it come. Let it have its way with her, bleed her out, relax her struggles, entice her soul to leave, to abandon the dying flesh it had once enjoyed. Those were her final thoughts.

And then she died.

Chapter 28

The entire scene by the door was photographed and vacuumed and dusted and DNA samples cut and snipped. Only then did the detectives swarm the den and bathroom.

Safari stopped at the open doorway to the bathroom. "Wow."

"What are you seeing?" asked Griffiths.

"No footprints. A partial palm print on the vanity. Do you know what? He placed his left hand on the vanity and his right hand on the den doorknob and swung himself through the bathroom. So he'd leave no footprints. We know he did this because of the ecchymoses along her side where she's been kicked. We'll see what the M.E. says."

Safari said these things to the man known earlier that day as Beachcomber. His real name was Ned Griffiths, and he was a two-year detective who sometimes partnered with Safari in the field, like today.

Griffiths, standing inside the den and peering back into the bathroom, shook his head. "Amazing how you know.

But how did he attack her in the bathroom and leave no prints in the blood? Oh, the door. That's right."

"That's right. He kicked it off its hinges, then stood on it. No prints on the door, Evelyn dusted. Forget everything I just said, Ned. I'm just thinking out loud here. Has anybody found Mr. Pelham yet?"

"He's returning from L.A., someone said."

"Who found her?" asked Safari of the first uniform on the scene.

The young officer replied, "The cook. She called her for drinks. No answer, so she came up here to talk to her."

"What's her name?"

"Miss Gaynor."

"First name?"

"Misty. Misty Gaynor."

"You're serious?"

"Yes, serious."

"Okay. Send her into the den. We'll start interviews in the den."

Safari went downstairs to the den, off the family room. She took over Reggie's desk, clearing a spot for her laptop, phone, and yellow tablet. Soon, she was joined by the young woman who identified herself as Misty Gaynor. She was mid-thirties, short, dark hair tied back in a bun, and most likely Filipino descent.

Safari told her to sit in the seat across from the desk and then began. "I'm told you're the one who found the body. Where were you all afternoon?"

"Vikki—Mrs. Pelham—didn't want any lunch. But she wanted fresh greens for a salad tonight. So she sent me to the farmers' market. I left for there about noon. Busiest time of day and traffic was bad, so it took me a half hour to get there and find parking."

"What did you do there?"

"Bought a hundred dollars' worth of organic produce and cheese and some local bath potions I thought she might like. Vikki loved her bath fragrances and soaps and oils. Then I went to Starbucks for a frap, long line, then back home. Altogether, I was gone about two hours."

"What time did you get back home?"

"Actually about three. I was gone quite a while."

"What did you do when you returned?"

"Started making up a salad. I like to make it and then let it chill. It flavors better. Some people would disagree. But I've got my methods. So I made the salad and then called Vikki to ask about tea. Each time there was no answer. Finally, I went upstairs and—"

She broke out in long, mournful sobs. Every time she tried to continue recounting what had happened, her emotions took over and she couldn't speak. This continued several times. Safari sent an officer for water, but that didn't help either. It was just going to be a matter of waiting for her to come around. Safari tried to ease the woman back into it by discussing weather, local musicians and artists, beach happenings, and the rest of life in a small town. Then she came back to the topic at hand.

"Can you tell me what you saw when you went upstairs?"

"First was the blood. It was everywhere. On the walls in the bathroom, on the floor. I was afraid to go through the bathroom to look for her. I stopped and dialed nine-one-one instead."

"Did you ever see her?"

"I could see her bare legs through the bathroom. She wasn't moving, wasn't making any sounds. I called and called but she never answered, of course. So I just waited in her bedroom for the police. I also called my boyfriend and told him."

"Who's that?"

"John Harold Johnstone. He's a mason in Oceanside. He should be here soon."

"Did you disturb anything in the bathroom or den?"

"No."

"Did you enter the bathroom?"

"No."

"Or go around the other way and enter her den?"

"No. I watch CSI. I didn't want to contaminate the scene."

"Misty, who did this to Vicki?"

"I don't know. I've asked myself that a thousand times. Everybody loved Vicki."

"Did you ever see her fighting with Reggie?"

"No."

"Or hear them fighting?"

"No. They left each other alone. They went their separate ways and have for years. They treated each other politely. They ate together...sometimes. And even attended each other's parties now and then. Nobody could ever convince me Reggie had anything to do with Vicki's death."

"Okay, fair enough. Then who do you think might have done this? Your wildest guess?"

"I would have to guess someone broke in looking for money or jewels. Someone was looking for something to steal, and Vicki caught them. So they murdered her so they wouldn't get caught. That's what I think happened."

"Just someone broke in and did this?"

"Yes."

"What if I tell you the police have searched the entire

inside and outside of the house, and there's no sign of forced entry?"

"I don't care. They got in somehow. Maybe Vicki herself let them in, I don't know."

"When you left for the farmers' market, who was in the house at that time?"

"Vicki. And maybe Kohlrabi."

"Who's Kohlrabi?"

"Her yoga instructor. He hasn't been here in a long time, but he came this morning. She probably called him because she's been gone."

"Tell me about Kohlrabi."

"He's from India and does yoga and TM."

"Transcendental meditation?"

"Yes, TM. He's very gentle from what I've seen. He wouldn't hurt a fly."

"Would he hurt Vicki? If he wanted to steal something?"

"No, he's even written books he sells on Amazon. He's very wealthy, I hear."

"Who told you that, Misty?"

Misty leaned away from the table. "I don't know. I must've gotten it somewhere."

Safari made a note and then resumed. "Was there anyone else in the house when you went to the farmers' market?"

"No. I would've known. I'm in the kitchen where I see and hear everything, if you know what I mean."

"What about Jonesy, Reggie's manservant?"

"Oh, Jonesy. I forgot about him. He might have been here. He's so quiet it's spooky. Always lurking, that guy."

"Might Jonesy murder Vicki?"

"Jonesy's gay. Gay guys don't kill people. They decorate."

Safari ignored the comment. She continued without regard, "Did you ever see Jonesy and Vicki interact? Did they get along?"

"He was Vicki's shoulder to cry on. They were always whispering back and forth. I don't know about what. Jonesy works for Reggie, but he's very partial to Vicki. You can just tell."

"Where is Jonesy now?"

"He was in the kitchen making calls on the extension there. I think he was talking to Reggie at one point."

"I'm going to end this now. Would you send Jonesy in to talk to me?"

"I will."

"And thank you for helping us today."

"You catch whoever did this and burn them good. That's all I care about," she said on a cracked sob.

"We'll do that. Thank you, Misty."

She sniffed. "I'll send Jonesy."

"S'long."

After Misty left the den, Safari stood and stretched. She walked the perimeter of the room, randomly checking volumes on the shelves and paintings on the walls. She was still looking and stretching when Jonesy walked in.

"Hamilton Jones," said a paunchy, elfin man of about sixty. Safari sized him up in a second and knew someone his size and build could never overwhelm Vicki with a knife. He was wearing a rich suit with a pale blue shirt and green and red necktie. His shoes were brightly polished, and he shot his cuffs as he stood waiting before Safari.

"Safari Frye," said the detective, extending her hand. They shook and then took seats at the desk.

"Terrible, just terrible," said the slight man. He'd been crying, his eyes still watery and his nose runny as he kept dabbing with an embroidered handkerchief.

"It is terrible. Thank you for taking a few minutes to speak with me," said Safari. "This won't take long. I'm basically just trying to find out who came into the house today. Especially who was in the house when Vicki was attacked."

"I was here in my room, listening to Rachmaninoff."

"Classicist, are you?"

"I enjoy divine music. He's the greatest of the great."

"So you didn't hear anything unusual, I take it?"

"Nothing at all. I don't play my music all that loud, either, out of deference to my employer and his house. I live here and, while that's an honor, it comes with grave responsibilities. I take great pains."

"You're English? Is that the accent I'm hearing?"

"Forty-five years ago, yes. I guess some things such as accents stay with us, like our noses."

"Maybe so. What part of England?"

"Sussex. Born and raised."

"Came to the States when you were in your teens?"

"Fifteen years old. My father was American. He retired here. So mum and I obviously came, too."

"Mr. Jones, who was in the house this afternoon?"

"Me, Vicki, and Misty. Mr. Pelham was in Los Angeles. He's been gone since before daybreak."

"How do you know he went to LA."

Jonesy spread his hands. "Because that's where he said he was going."

"And you believed him?"

"Are you serious? Of course, I believed him. Who wouldn't?"

"Mr. Jones, who would want Vicki Pelham dead?"

"Goodness, isn't that all the question of the day? Let's see. I can think of no one stateside. Maybe someone in France? But her partner there does hair, so that doesn't make for all that many enemies."

"Did Vicki have a trade or profession?"

"Vicky was an influencer on Instagram and YouTube. Her weakness was clothes. And shoes. And bags and hats. People followed her. Vicki's YouTube channel has over two-hundred-thousand subscribers. Very successful. Maybe someone saw her in a video and got the idea to rob her? Could that be it?"

Safari made her notes. "It certainly is as good as any other theory at this point. Now look, Mr. Jones, I fully expect your loyalties lie with Mr. Pelham. I get that. But justice needs you to set that aside just for a moment while you tell me, describe for me, the relationship between Reggie and Vicki Pelham. Aside from the fact they were separated, when they came together again, did they get along?"

"He loved her. He lived for her phone calls. He hated Francis Vichy, her lover. But he never quit loving Victoria. He would have died defending her had he been here today."

"He was in Los Angeles you say? Are you positive about that?"

This time, Jonesy was ready. "Let's just say he dressed for Los Angeles. Where he actually went, I'm sure I wasn't along. So it would be conjecture by me."

"What did he like about Vicki?"

"Most of all? He loved to hear her laugh. He loved how caring she could be, way back when. Before he—before he—"

Safari asked, "Before he what?"

"Before he ran her off. They were happy until SkoolDaze began eating him alive. SkoolDaze sucked him dry. She got lonely and went to Paris. It's an old story. Confidentially? He was warned. I warned him myself that no woman would put up with two years of no meals together, separate sleeping times, little to no conversations. He became consumed with his brainchild as it came alive and skyrocketed in popularity. He let it take him away. Goodness, now I've said too much, I'm afraid."

"Who was in the house today?"

"Me, Misty Gaynor, Vicki and, much earlier, Mr. Pelham himself. There might have been two or three drop-offs—dry cleaning, food deliveries, that kind of thing."

"How would someone get inside the house and get to Vicki without anyone hearing?"

"Goodness, that is the question, now, isn't it? I'm sure I don't have that answer, detective. But I'll do this. I'll think about it, and if I think of anything, I'll let you know."

She swiped a business card from her jacket pocket and passed it across the desk. Jonesy grabbed it up and put it into his shirt pocket, patting it shut.

"Call me if anything comes to mind," she said.

"So I shall," said Jonesy with a curt nod. "Let me think about it."

"Yes, please do. Is Mr. Pelham back yet? Send him in if he's here, please."

"Will do, Detective."

Chapter 29

Driving home from LA, Reggie Pelham fielded the call from Jonesy. Hands free, he said, "Go Jonesy. I'm passing Carlsbad and we're bumper-to-bumper."

"Yes, I hated to call while you're driving. I'm afraid there's been a tragedy, Mr. Pelham. Vicki has been murdered. I'm so sorry, I'm—"

"Too much traffic noise, Jonesy. Please say again."

"I said, Vicki's been murdered. Someone attacked her with a knife. The police are here. Should I call your lawyer?"

His hands froze on the wooden steering wheel. His jaw was set hard as stone, and his eyes were clouding with tears. It was all he could do to hold on and keep driving. Stopping, pulling off, was the last thing he needed. Right now, before he let go of his feelings, he needed a lawyer.

"Call Thaddeus Murfee. Tell him I must see him before I go home," he bit off the words. He allowed the first tears to pass through his eyes but quickly recovered, clearing his vision with two fingers. He swallowed hard, determined to plunge ahead.

"Will do."

More tears and more dabbing, this time with a Starbucks napkin he found in his console. He loved Vicki, and the news sent him into shock. He realized with a start that he shouldn't be driving at all. But still he drove south.

Five minutes later, Pelham's phone again vibrated.

"Thaddeus, thank you for calling."

"Mr. Jones called me. Very upset. I think Vicki's been murdered. We must meet before you go home, so come directly to my hotel. The desk will know you're coming."

"On my way."

THADDEUS ENDED the phone call and punched the number for room service. He'd have coffee waiting when Pelham arrived. Plus, he needed a good jolt right now, especially after the terrible news about Vicki. He had no use for the woman's case against Pelham, but he understood it was just a case about money and had nothing to do with the fact both husband and wife might be pretty damn good people apart from it all. He had no axes to grind, and he was terribly sorry to hear the news. Then, as he waited on the coffee to arrive, he settled into thinking about Pelham's exposure.

The cops would be everywhere asking questions. Mr. Jones had explained the murder evidently occurred within Vicki's suite of rooms, probably in her bathroom. Thaddeus didn't know the layout, of course, and so couldn't ask pertinent questions. But he did feel a great responsibility to Pelham to prep him for the inevitable police questions. At this point, taking the high road and refusing to speak with the police might be the legally savvy thing to do, but it wouldn't win him any friends inside the detective corps. In fact, it would serve to anger them if he clammed up. It would alienate them, and right now that was the last thing he wanted. After all, they had no suspect, and Pelham had been gone himself, so they had no connection between wife and husband at the time of the murder. Jonesy had placed it just after noon or thereabouts and told him Pelham had been in Beverly Hills since that morning. He said he had told the police detective the same thing. She had asked him about it twice. Thaddeus would have to sandpaper Pelham on this answer. Maybe he'd made a cell call and the call could be traced to a nearby LA cell phone tower. Maybe some other connection or video of him in a restaurant or hotel or office complex—there was always something in the Age of No Privacy. The coffee arrived, and he allowed the server to prepare the table beside the window overlooking the pool.

Pelham arrived looking drained of color and very frightened. His hands curled and uncurled and his eye twitched. The pressure was on; Thaddeus couldn't blame the man. "Come in, Reggie. Let's get some coffee in you and talk about this thing for a few minutes before we take you home."

"Take me home?"

"I'm going with. You're going to need to talk to the detectives, and I want to be there when you do."

"I'd appreciate that. I've been thinking it wouldn't look good for me to refuse to answer their questions. I've got nothing to hide."

Thaddeus blanched. "Those are the most dangerous words any lawyer ever hears. 'I've got nothing to hide.' In fact, the police require very little to turn their sights on anyone. The law enforcement mindset requires a suspect. Nine out of ten crimes are solved the same day they happen. So you can't blame the police for needing to point a quick finger. They're swamped, and they want to close files. But you also don't want to give them a reason to think of you as anyone except a bereaved husband. So, here's my first point. Your separation from Vicki was all her idea. You loved her desperately and wanted her home with you. You want her in your life."

"Nothing untrue there. It broke my heart every day to wake up and find her gone. I love her desperately."

"Of course, you do. So let's look at all the ways you've been expressing that love. First, you've made sufficient money available to her, even to carry on her lifestyle with her Paris flame."

"That's one-hundred percent true. If she needed anything, she could just write a check. She always knew that. She always did it, too. No problem there."

"Second, you've called her repeatedly and tried to talk her into coming home."

"My cell phone will prove that I've called her just about every day. And yes, I was begging her to come home. I love my wife, Thaddeus. There was never anyone else for me."

"Which brings me to our third point," said Thaddeus. "You didn't chippy around on her."

"What's that mean?"

"You didn't have other women around."

"No, I didn't have them around. But I never lacked for female companionship. I've always had my followers."

Thaddeus nodded. "So when the subject comes up, I want you to tell the detective there have been times when you've been terribly lonely and heartbroken and have tried being with another woman to lessen the pain of losing Vicki. But say, along with it, that the other woman thing never worked and it was never the same as having your wife with you."

"Which is totally true. Everything else was a letdown. There's been no satisfaction. There's been no infatuation. No lasting desire. Maybe a stiff dick every now and then, but that's only because I'm a healthy male with male desires and lusts. None of it meant anything."

"Let's leave out the word 'lust.' The last thing I want the police to think is that you're a man capable of lusting. You can desire but you can't lust. Don't go there, please."

"Got it."

"Last point, Vicki was on Instagram and YouTube as an influencer. She showed off expensive dresses and jewelry and shoes and all that. It only makes sense that someone would target her and come after the diamonds she flaunted. It makes her a perfect target in a jury's mind, should this go that far. And for your sake, I sincerely hope it does not. But the influencer thing opens the door to motive from someone outside the marriage. It's a very happy connection between your wife and the world's underbelly. Happy for you, not so much for her. At least that's what I'm guessing has happened here. It only makes sense."

An hour later, they walked into the den at Pelham's house and agreed Reggie would answer any and all questions.

"No limit on what I can ask?" Safari said to Thaddeus. "I know he's in horrible pain over this."

"He wants to do it," said Thaddeus of the client sitting beside him. "Painful as it might be, he wants the police on the right track from the outset."

She turned to Reggie. "What leads might you have for us, Mr. Pelham, now that your lawyer has brought it up?"

Reggie had steeled himself. He was sitting upright on the client side of his own desk, his face tight and his look unemotional. He intended to keep the feelings at bay and not allow himself to do or say something he might regret. "I've been thinking about it on the drive home. Vicki's Instagram/YouTube habit. She was on public access social media talking about jewelry and expensive clothes several times a week. Wouldn't you agree this might draw unwanted attention from undesirables?"

Safari ignored that the husband was trying to make her the one to answer questions. She was way down the road on that kind of ploy and felt somewhat put off he had even tried. It said something about him that he'd gone there. "Social media is something that anyone who cares about his or her family's safety should avoid like the plague," Safari said. "So why Vicki? Surely, she knew better."

"Why? Because Vicki actually believed she deserved to be an influencer. Flavor a sense of entitlement with a few million bucks and you've got unwanted attention too often. I think it got my wife killed." As he said this, the tears began flowing, and he wiped his eyes with a tissue on his desk. It was genuine and heartfelt. No one doubted that.

So far so good, thought Thaddeus. *Let's just keep it at this level with this degree of commonsense about bad guys and social media. It's a good place to be.*

"What about you, Mr. Pelham? What was your weakness? You said your wife might have had a sense of entitlement. Did that same bug ever bite you?"

"Probably it did. It's easy to get a little too puffed up from great financial success. If I'm not careful, I can start to believe the glowing *Forbes* article about me or the complimentary *Wall Street Journal* bio. I work at keeping my head down and my ears closed to that kind of stuff. Vicki, on the other hand, believed her own press. I know this for a fact. Why else did she up and move to Paris on the predicate of assessing coming fashion trends for her Instagram and YouTube viewers? She honestly believed they cared about her. She honestly felt safe with all the world watching. I never did, so I never sought out that kind of exposure. I think it's what got my wife killed, detective. I don't think your case is a complicated one when it comes to motive. She flaunted her jewels and clothes, and someone evil was watching. There's your case."

"Well, thank you for summing up my work, Mr. Pelham. I only wish my world was really that simple. But, unfortunately, it's not. Everyone is a suspect to a detective with my seven years. Everyone gets examined. Including you. So, while I appreciate how helpful you want to be, please don't be surprised if I show up at your office in the future wanting to speak with you again. That wouldn't be a problem were it to happen, Mr. Murfee, would it?"

Thaddeus forced a wide smile. "Of course not. Reggie Pelham intends to cooperate one-hundred-percent with all police requests. If you need him, just call me and I'll arrange ASAP."

"Oh, I have to go through you now?"

"It's just the way I work. I'll want to be with my client during any and all questioning. We all have our exposure in these cases, Detective. Why, did you think I would declare my own client fair game to you? But all cooperation will be forthcoming. That much, I can promise. Is there anything else today?"

"Mr. Pelham, did you murder your wife?"

"I did not."

"Did you hire someone to murder her?"

"No."

"Did you give money or something of value to someone to see her dead?"

"Of course not."

"Where were you today at noon and the hour or two after?"

"Los Angeles."

"What proof do you have of that."

"I called Vicki from LA. It will be geo-located to a Beverly Hills cell phone tower. It will also show up on her cell phone recent calls."

"You called her why?"

"To tell her I loved her and I missed her. I do this just about every day."

Safari sighed and shuffled the papers before her on the desk. "You've discussed this statement with your lawyer?"

"I have."

"What did he tell you to say?"

"He told me to tell the truth."

"Why, was he worried you might not tell the truth?"

"No, he was worried the police might try to trip me up and get me to say something that wasn't true."

She shook her head. "Haven't we all seen this Q and A before?"

"It's scripted since vaudeville days, I'm sure," Thaddeus said with a broad grin.

"You gentlemen are pushing all the right buttons. That's all for now."

"Thank you," said Thaddeus. "Here's my card. Call if you need more."

"I will," said Safari. "All right, let's call it a day. I'm starving."

"I know a great place with fresh tilapia," said Thaddeus to the detective. "And I'm buying."

"Is that a bribe?"

"Absolutely."

"Then let's go."

THEY LINGERED OVER OPEN-FLAME SEAFOOD, sun tea, and steamed veggies as they pushed back and forth on the Butchy Penrose case. For the moment, at least, Reggie Pelham was off the radar and parked on the fringes of what got said and what got avoided on purpose so the evening meal was a comfortable one.

Safari told Thaddeus about her time as a patrol officer, how she made it to detective, and then just happened to mention the discrimination complaint she was facing tomorrow.

"I called another detective a dickless wonder," she told Thaddeus. "I was angry and over the line, for sure."

"What was the injury?" Thaddeus asked.

She realized it was probably the first time anyone had looked at the event in that light. "The injury? His injury? I guess his feelings were hurt. Maybe embarrassment. I know I'm embarrassed about what I said in the light of day, away from the constant uproar of working violent crimes. That work takes a toll. I became hardened. I became inured to many feelings about what I'm seeing. My sense of appropriate behavior with my own squad got cross-wired. We cross the line of decency and polite language, all of us. Seeing infants who've been murdered over crying for breast milk does that to a person. Calling someone a dickless wonder… We all say it, and much, much worse. We are working the sewer, and our language reflects that. These aren't excuses, but they are explanations. Bottom line? You had to have been there."

"Which is one thing in your favor. The people hearing the case have all been there, correct?"

"Well, not all of them. I've learned my case will be heard by a deputy chief of police, a civilian administrative law judge, and a local pastor. The police chief has definitely heard the language I used. The ALJ will be proceeding by the book. The pastor? I don't know. Maybe full-blown anti-discrimination, or maybe the other end of the spectrum, the kind that forgives people their shortcomings. It's always the luck of the draw in these things."

"Do you have a lawyer?"

"The police union has provided me with a cardboard cutout of a lawyer. This guy is always busy when I call, and the one time I got into see him, he was certain he could 'cut a deal.' That was his main thrust. He wanted to cut a deal. Without regard to whether I was guilty of anything or not. Just do a deal and close the file. He's a guy who gets paid by the file, not by the hour, so I'm just a number to him. A number to be processed and brushed off. Good riddance to me."

"That isn't good, Safari. You need an advocate this time out."

"Hey," she said over spumoni, "what if you show up with me? What if you represent me? Can that happen?"

"It can, but since I'm defending Butchy and you're involved in his prosecution, it wouldn't look right. Believe me, I would do it, but I've had the State Bar Association of Arizona down my throat recently, and I can't go anywhere near bar complaints again. Not with my Colorado license."

"What if I handed off the Butchy case to another dick? Would that remove any barrier to you sitting in with me?"

Thaddeus looked contemplative as he sipped his coffee. "Hmmm. Maybe it would. Let me do a little reading on it when I get back to the room, and I'll call you with an answer. How late are you up?"

"Seriously? I'm scared, Thaddeus. I probably won't sleep at all tonight."

"And the hearing is tomorrow morning? What time?"

"Nine a.m. City Council sub-committee room nineteen downtown."

"Could I catch a ride with you? We could use the time to talk."

"Of course. I can pick you up at eight."

"I'll call you later tonight. Let me look around at some ethics' rules and also some discrimination cases so I can see if I can even help you if the ethics aren't a barrier. It will be around eleven o'clock when I call."

"Fair enough. I'll definitely be up and waiting to hear. My God, thank you, Thaddeus. You have no idea how much this means to me."

"One other thing," he said with a note of caution in his voice. "How does this affect your investigation of the Vicki Pelham murder? Are you thinking my client Reggie Pelham is a possible suspect?"

"Not at this point, no. In all honesty, that might change down the road. But as we sit here tonight, I don't have an ax to grind with him. None."

"Fair enough. We're green lights and one-ways then. I'll get back to my room and fire up my computer."

He paid for their meals and her drinks and off he went to the La Valencia Hotel.

TWO HOURS LATER, he called Safari. He was in. They spoke for another forty-five minutes at a more granular level, and Thaddeus came away with names and phone numbers and ranks. He then hung up and began making calls to other SDPD detectives. Some were members of Safari's squad, some weren't. To a man—and woman—they all agreed to show up tomorrow morning and testify on behalf of Safari. All of them said the same thing: the whole complaint and investigation and prosecution was a boondoggle. Words and insults like the one Safari used were just a daily part of police life. How it got legs and became a thing in her case, no one knew. But there you were. It was real, and it was dangerous to Safari's career. So her support agreed to show up.

Chapter 30

When Safari picked him up at the hotel, her first words to Thaddeus were, "I've removed myself from the Vicki Pelham case. Now you definitely have no conflict, present or future, in representing me today." Thaddeus was glad to hear it and relieved. That possible conflict was the one stickler that had him tossing and turning all night. Now it was resolved and his confidence level jumped. They parked in police parking and went inside the city hall building at 202 West C Street. She knew the way; Thaddeus followed with his briefcase and laptop. He knew the facts and knew the case law. He was ready.

Reed Thurgood, representing SDPD's Police Standards and Ethics, was the first to arrive at the hearing room. He was a thin man with thick lips, a comb-over hairdo, and wearing a neatly pressed suit and a heavily starched white shirt. *Mister Clean*, Thaddeus thought when he saw the man, *the keeper of the department's conscience. At least in his own eyes.*

They shook hands, but it was clear to Thaddeus that

Thurgood had no real interest in meeting him or in discussing a possible resolution to the case before the hearing began. He had the anointed glow of a man on a mission, a man who knew his cause to be right, the keeper of the good and just. With the brushoff and prickly distance surrounding Thurgood, Thaddeus sized him right up. He'd been up against a hundred Thurgoods over the years. Pierce the shell and own the man. There was that, for openers.

The judges, a tribunal consisting of a deputy chief of police, a civilian administrative law judge, and a local pastor, noisily entered the room and took seats ordinarily held down by city council members. They seemed to be in good spirits—a good sign—as they shook hands with the police officials and detectives and addressed Thaddeus as "counsel," even though he wasn't licensed to practice law in California. Administrative rules, adopted locally, allowed him to appear as the representative for any party appearing before the tribunal. This, he had checked last night on the city attorney's website. He was good to go.

Thurgood went first. He called Eugene Michaels, the complainant, as his first witness. Detective Michaels was a hulk of a man whose bulging biceps totally filled out the sleeves of his sport coat and whose ample butt caused the hem of the coat to separate at the top of his almost-visible crack from behind. Thaddeus took all this in and shook his head. He watched while the witness was sworn in by the ALJ and seated in the witness chair. Then they began.

Thurgood, remaining seated, asked the witness to identify himself and give his badge number and address, which Eugene Michaels promptly provided.

"You are acquainted with Detective Safari Frye, are you not?"

"I am."

"And you filed a complaint against her alleging sexual harassment?"

"I did."

"Was your complaint in reference to a single incident or a series of continuing incidents of sexual harassment?"

"Single incident. But I knew if I let it slide, there would be more. That's why I filed."

"Does she have a history of continuing sexual harassments directed at her detective squad?"

"She does."

"Describe those, please."

The witness leaned back and drew a deep breath. "Well, she calls her men names. Dickless wonders, limp dicks, pussy-whipped, stuff like that."

"How often do you hear her use these terms?"

"Constantly. She rides the troops constantly and uses this language."

"What did she call you, Mr. Michaels?"

"Dickless wonder."

"Are you dickless?"

"No, sir."

"But you are a wonder?"

"Some people think so. I do my job, and I apprehend criminals."

"You are aware that just a one-time incident can be sexual harassment?"

"I am."

"Is that why you're here?"

"It is."

"That is all."

Thaddeus was surprised when the questioning abruptly ended. But then it was his turn to cross-examine the witness, so he began. "Mr. Michaels, describe how you felt when Safari called you a dickless wonder."

"Stupid. Reamed out."

"Did you deserve it?"

"Maybe, I don't know."

"What happened to make her say it?"

"We were working the Argonne case. I couldn't stay late for stakeout. So she got pissed and called me the name. Sorry, but I had promised my wife I'd be home early."

"Is 'dickless wonder' a phrase you hear often in the detective corps?"

"Yes."

"What about pussy-whipped?"

"Yes."

"What about limp dick?"

"Yes, we hear all these things."

"Isn't it true the detectives and police officers constantly refer to each other with these terms?"

"Oh, hell yes."

"Yet, nobody is really dickless, limp, or whipped, am I right?"

"It's just figures of speech."

"Knowing this, why did you file this complaint?"

"My wife told me to."

"So maybe you are a bit pussy-whipped?"

"Objection!"

"Withdrawn," said Thaddeus. "I withdraw the question. Sorry, sir."

"No problem," said Detective Michaels. "I know what you meant. This whole thing sounds ridiculous in the light of day. I'm sorry I filed."

At which point, the judges then asked the witness

whether he wished to withdraw his complaint, and he said he did.

Hearing concluded.

"OOPS," said Thaddeus as they stepped through the city building's exit. "Forgot my briefcase. I'll be right back."

Safari went on through the double doors and stopped, waiting for Thaddeus to return. As she waited, she noticed not twenty paces away, pulled up at the curb, a man standing at the trunk of his car with the trunk wide open. Then she recognized the man: Kenneth Chesley. How the hell had he made one-million bail?

It wasn't coincidence. She immediately knew he was waiting for her.

Safari reached to her IWB holster. She gripped the gun but didn't draw it out of her holster. Her gaze was fixed on Chesley. The man was standing where the sidewalk curbed onto the street. He appeared to be rummaging for automobile tools, such that Safari's next impression might have been he had a flat and was looking for a jack.

Still, she gripped her gun as she walked forward. Suddenly, he turned and dropped into a combat shooting posture. Several nearby police officers responded by ducking down and drawing their own weapons. Then they were pointing all guns at the man with the pistol. He didn't flinch, just kept his gun trained on Safari.

What came next happened in a flash, less than a second. Afraid for the detective's life, one of the closing officers drilled Chesley with a gunshot to the shoulder. Before he collapsed, Chesley managed to squeeze off one round. It spun through the air, catching Safari at her left side, just above her hip. The bullet knifed though the soft hip flesh, connected with the spinal canal, and severed the detective's spinal cord at the L4 level. She immediately went down in a bundle. "Carrie," she muttered, "I'm sorry."

Coming through the exit door with his briefcase in hand, Thaddeus sized up what was happening and immediately fell on top of Safari, shielding her with his body to protect against any follow-up shots. But the advancing police already had the shooter face-down on the sidewalk, spread eagled even though he was crying out from the pain of the bullet that had entered his shoulder. The pain was excruciating, but he gathered himself, shouting toward Safari, "She was going to shoot me! Her gun's on the sidewalk!" When he said this, a booted foot dropped on his head, mashing his face hard against the sidewalk. Then Chesley passed out from pain.

Meanwhile, Thaddeus had lost it and was moving directly toward the pinned man, intending to tear him limb-to-limb. A police officer tried to intervene but Thaddeus pushed him aside, whereupon two more officers managed to wrestle him to the ground and subdue him. "No," he cried out, "let me at him!"

"He's lost it," said one officer to the others.

Thaddeus hadn't lost it, but he hated to see injustice happen in any form. He was a lawyer through and through, but the scum—the man who had shot Safari—deserved their own justice.

But then...one thing the shooter had said was true: Safari's service weapon was lying in plain view on the sidewalk where the CSI team would later find it and photograph it.

Safari was lying flat on her back, staring straight into the noonday sun. She knew peace. A scary peace, the silent type, the calm after the storm. She knew she should be in terrible pain but, in truth, she felt nothing because the bullet had terminated all feeling from the wound site south on her body. Paralyzed and unable to move anything from the navel down, she lay patiently, listening to the voices around her. She turned her head just in time to see Thaddeus taken down, and then she waited for the EMTs and the ambulance she heard drawing nearer by the second. Then there were figures around her, examining her without moving her and, sometime later, loading her onto a backboard, then onto a gurney, and then rolling her still form into the ambulance.

Somehow, Thaddeus had convinced them he was Safari's lawyer and got to accompany her to the hospital. A police detective who knew Safari loaded Thaddeus into his vehicle and began following the ambulance away from the zone of police and official vehicles toward the hospital just two miles distant.

Safari was rushed into the hospital, her ID wallet and badge spread open on her chest lest anyone doubt who they were dealing with and the priority. A team of neurosurgeons and neurologists was quickly assembled and the films, tests, and discussions all began rolling at once.

Thirty minutes later, it was decided. They would dress the flesh wound, which turned out to be easily treated with sutures and antibiotics since the shot had entered and exited. Then they would stop. As with all cases of a transected spinal cord, there was very little else to be done but wait and see.

By evening time, she was alert and resting. However, she was in abject horror at the damage done. She couldn't move her legs, couldn't move her hips, and was already urinating only with the help of a catheter. Her other functions and abilities were yet being tested.

Thaddeus was able to see her at seven o'clock that night. He had been waiting just down the hall in the visitors' staging area ever since she'd arrived. He had been on his cell phone, as he would later tell her, with just about everyone he knew. He had learned, among other things, that the shooter was, in fact, Kenneth Chesley, who had been arrested and charged with attempted murder. But there was a strong caution. Someone had hired Lewis James Atwater for Chesley, the most accomplished and experienced criminal defense lawyer in Southern California. Here was a man who demanded one-million-dollars before he'd even come visit you in jail. Still, someone—who could say who?—had ponied up the one-million. Atwater had already visited Chesley in jail.

Phone lines were lit up late into the night at the offices of the District Attorney as prosecutions were discussed and argued and discussed again. Conflicts between Safari and the prosecution's office were discussed because she had, on the one hand, drawn her service weapon, and the possibility of a self-defense case versus an assault by an officer was rippling along. The long and short of it was that the District Attorney wanted to avoid even the appearance of impropriety given the staggering leverage and talents of LJ Atwater. By 10 p.m., it was decided the DA's office couldn't be too careful and the Attorney General should be called in.

Safari's detective partner, Ned Griffiths, related these matters to Safari at 11 p.m. She immediately alerted. No, she told her partner, tell the DA there was one man she wanted prosecuting Chesley, and that one man was Thaddeus Murfee. "Any man," she said through the haze of the drugs they were pumping into her, "who would cover me with his body, ready to take a bullet for me, is the man I want prosecuting my case. No one else has my okay. Get it done."

After midnight, the District Attorney himself came to the hospital and found Thaddeus still awake and drinking coffee as he kept his vigil. The DA cut right to the chase. Would Thaddeus prosecute the case? Thaddeus, remembering Chesley's boast that he could do whatever he wanted and there wasn't "a fucking thing" anyone could do about it, made his decision in a split second.

"I need a desk, a computer, and an investigator. Then I need to be left alone."

"Thank you, Mr. Murfee," said the DA.

"I'll be there at eight in the morning. Have the coffee on."

"The initial appearance will be at nine o'clock in the criminal court."

"I'll be ready. There will be no bail this time."

"Excellent, we'll have your *pro hac vice* motion ready to handle this one case in court. Welcome aboard, Thaddeus."

"One more thing. Turquoise Murfee is the name of my investigator. You will swear her in and authorize her to carry concealed."

"Done. Turquoise Murfee's paperwork will begin processing first thing in the a.m."

"Good. She'll be joining me by noon."

Chapter 31

LJ Atwater came into court wearing an expensive Italian suit with a scarlet pocket square and scarlet tie. His entourage consisted of a bag man for the roll-around briefcases and a backup attorney who would take notes and pass comments and arguments to Atwater. A third individual was a jury consultant who came into the case early to gauge media and spectator reaction to various approaches and postulates of Atwater himself. Finally, he had his PR wing in tow, the woman with pink hair who would prepare the press release and shoot the after-court video for dissemination to the media outlets of Southern and Central California. *No Stone Unturned* was the promise printed on all the master's business cards and letterhead. LJ Atwater also called himself the "King of Not Guilty" to anyone who would listen.

Thaddeus, sitting with his investigating officer at the prosecution table, took all this in with a curious eye. While Thaddeus had known no small success himself at defending cases in criminal court, he had, frankly, never seen a machine such as Atwater's as it geared up to do battle. On the one hand, he was impressed with the action; on the other hand, he was confident he would ride roughshod over the King's best efforts.

His investigating officer was Turquoise Murfee, his own daughter, who had flown in from Durango. Turquoise had been sworn-in as a special investigating officer attached to the San Diego County District Attorney's Office. As such, she was issued a police detective's shield and was authorized to carry a concealed weapon. Her involvement in the case had turned out to be Thaddeus's only condition for him to get involved. Turquoise was wearing a simple black dress, knee-length, and a black jacket and turquoise necklace. She wore a gun on her hip and was wired for immediate radio contact with the SDPD's dispatcher. All was ready to proceed.

Judge Hillary M. Kenyon took the bench with a flourish and poked her reading glasses into place. Her gaze swept across the packed courtroom as she puckered her lips, a critical look passing across her face. "Is that it?" she asked Atwater.

"LJ Atwater for the defense, Your Honor. If your comment is in reference to my staff, it's the same staff that always accompanies me when I attend court on behalf of the next falsely accused. In this case, I am representing Kenneth Chesley, who is fortunate to be alive and with us after being targeted by Detective Safari Frye, who had it in for him."

"Counsel, let's hold all that for the jury. Please step forward with your client."

Four deputies accompanied Kenneth Chesley in an

orange jumpsuit to the lectern in front of the judge. Atwater pushed his way between them until he was standing shoulder-to-shoulder with his client. Thaddeus Murfee came forward and stood apart from the others. He had no idea what was coming, but he was ready for anything.

"Mr. Murfee, you are appearing as a special prosecutor, I'm told?"

"I am, Your Honor. I'm appearing for the State in its prosecution of this defendant. My *pro hac vice* motion has been allowed and the order signed by you early this morning."

"Very well, let's begin." Judge Kenyon addressed the defendant. "State your name for the record."

"Kenneth Chesley."

"Mr. Chesley, are you aware of the charges filed against you today?"

Before his client could answer, Atwater interjected for him, "He is aware, Judge, and we deny each and every sentence and allegation in the complaint. We further allege the defense of self-defense. The detective in this case was serving as the guardian for a certain child who was wrongly claiming Mr. Chesley had injured her with a cigarette. The evidence will show it was the child's mother who caused that injury. The evidence will also show that the detective, in a fit of pique, was handling her service weapon in a manner intended to intimidate my client and even brandished her weapon as if intending to shoot and kill him. Unfortunately for her, he fired first after being intimidated, and she was injured. Or claims she was injured. Accordingly, the defendant is ready to plead not guilty and demand a jury trial."

"We can combine the arraignment and initial appearance. Is that what you're asking for, Mr. Atwater?"

"It is. Defendant pleads not guilty to these bogus

charges and requests bail set in a reasonable amount. Reasonable meaning five-thousand dollars or less."

"Mr. Murfee, would you like to be heard on the issue of bail?"

Thaddeus jumped right in. "I'm certain the court will agree that a defendant who was already free on bail in another murder case and who then shot a detective should be denied bail. Hell, he should never walk free again, when you come down to it, given his lack of remorse and willingness to shoot and kill with abandon. Judge, how many more citizens have to be injured or murdered by Kenneth Chesley before the judicial system says 'Enough!' The state respectfully requests that bail be denied."

"Bail is denied, gentlemen. The defendant's plea of not guilty is accepted. The clerk will set a trial date of…"

"November second at nine o'clock a.m.," filled in the court clerk.

Judge Kenyon continued, "Very well. I expect discovery to proceed in an orderly manner that follows all the rules. Woe to the party who disrespects those rules and causes this case to return to my court on some trumped up motion to require discovery responses or alleging lack of cooperation. I take discovery very seriously and expect liberal application of the rules. That is all. We're in recess. Gentlemen, I'd like to see you in my chambers, stat!"

Thaddeus and Atwater followed the judge out of the courtroom to gather with her in her office and, presumably, get blasted for the morning's display of overreaching and attempting to try the case in the media.

They were correct in their presumptions. Judge Kenyon, after unzipping her robe and waiting for the court reporter to set up, wasted no time.

"Mr. Atwater, if you ever again use my court as a microphone for your theories of the case, you will find yourself being held in contempt and fined or possibly introduced to my jail. Mr. Murfee, I expected more from you in your approach to bail. Please remember that, differently from your previous appearances as counsel for defendants, you're now seeking to see justice done for all citizens. Limit your remarks and arguments accordingly. Are we both understanding what I'm telling you?"

"Your Honor," Atwater began, but she held up a stern hand.

"Sir, do you understand, yes or no?"

"Yes. But Judge—"

"No, 'but judges.' You've had your moment in my court and much more. Be still now. Mr. Murfee, do you understand my admonition to you?"

"Yes, Your Honor."

"Mr. Atwater's flamboyance will seek to bait you into creating error for appeal. I caution you not to allow that to happen."

"Yes, Your Honor."

"Very well. Now both of you get the hell out of my office and don't come back until the day of trial. No discovery shenanigans."

Atwater caught up to Thaddeus in the hallway that led back to the courtroom. "Mr. Murfee, I'd like to take the deposition of Safari Frye."

Thaddeus spun on his heel. "Oh, you've got this mixed up with a civil case, sir. There are no depositions in criminal cases. Thanks for asking." He turned and began walking away.

Atwater called after him, "Very well, I shall file my first discovery motion with the court."

"File away."

"The judge won't like it."

"Won't like it away."

"She'll be angry."

"Angry away."

That night on News at 7, Thaddeus and Turquoise watched from Thaddeus's hotel room while Atwater appeared on TV.

"Today in court, my client's rights were denied. We wanted to take the deposition of the police officer who was taking aim to shoot my client and kill him, but the prosecution wouldn't allow it. This is the worst kind of deprivation of civil rights. The Constitution makes it very clear that all American citizens should get to face their accusers but, now, thanks to the special prosecutor, Mr. Chesley doesn't get to ask the detective why she was seeking to murder him on the sidewalk that day. In all my years of practicing law—"

"Blah, blah, blah," said Thaddeus as he muted the sound on the TV.

Turquoise rolled her eyes. "Wow, just wow."

"I know. This is going to be a hell of a ride with this guy."

"He never quits." Turquoise shifted on the end of the bed, one knee bent, and faced her father. "Dad, why are you doing this?"

Thaddeus sat up in his chair. "Why? Because a friend of mine was shot. I'm going to see Chesley in hell before I quit. The only difference is, I'm not going to announce it. I'm just going to do it."

"Fair enough." Turquoise nodded but looked thoughtful. "I'll be right beside you."

"Now let's go see Safari and see what kind of day she

had. I want to bring her up to speed on the first court appearance today."

"Let me grab my sweater, and I'm right with you."

"I'll grab the rental and pick you up in the circle drive at the front door."

Chapter 32

"So far," Thaddeus told his team on Monday morning, "we know Chesley burned Carrie, strangled Maryjane, and shot Safari. I've got my suspicions about Vicki Pelham's murder, but that's just a suspicion, no evidence. At least so far."

His team now consisted of himself, Turquoise, Demi Manal, a paralegal, and Stone Imanski, who worked as a typist and paralegal and part-time investigator, depending on where he was most needed. All the team was appointed from the DA's office except for Turquoise. As of yet, there was no backup attorney, which was normal with the DA's office in cases like Chesley's where the notoriety was high and the defense opportunistic like Atwater's group. But his team satisfied Thaddeus. He felt he had everything he needed to score a conviction.

"I'm going to list out what we have on Safari's case," said paralegal Demi Manal. "First off, we have Chesley. We can look to impeach him if he testifies. We can offer evidence of the strangulation of Carrie's mom as a prior bad act to show he acted in accord with his will toward violence."

"Carrie's mom?" asked Stone Imanski.

"Maryjane Dillon," Thaddeus told him. "This office has a case pending against Chesley for murdering her. Steve Hermann is prosecuting that case, I believe. Stone, you go ahead and get the details from Steve and then prepare a line of questions we can use in court to show a prior bad act. Have your research attached to those questions, near the top of the page, so I'll have my arguments ready when the defense objects to me asking those questions about Maryjane."

"Got it," said Stone. "I'll do the same for prior convictions, too, in case he's pled guilty before so we can use a prior conviction to impeach."

"Good enough," Thaddeus said. "Demi, let's have you begin putting together jury instructions for Safari's shooting. I especially want you to look for enhancement instructions so we can try to enhance his sentence based on depravity or severity of the injury, those kinds of things. We can talk more as you get into it."

"Roger, boss," Demi said with a smile. "I like your style already, Mr. Murfee."

"Well, thanks. Turquoise will locate all video of the shooting. It was just outside of a public building so there should be cameras everywhere. From the video we can find, we'll go after license numbers of nearby vehicles and try to locate drivers or bystanders who might've witnessed the shooting. We've already asked for a list of police officers in the area who might've witnessed. So far, we have two patrolmen, one of them being the man who shot Chesley in the shoulder. Others will be known soon. Turquoise will then take their statements, and I'll sit in on the eyeball witnesses.

I want to hear for myself how certain they are, who will make the best witnesses, and so forth. By the time this case goes to trial, I want no wiggle room left for Atwater. This time, we're going to trial, no pleas with reduced sentences, so just know that what you're working on here is for keeps. We have a paralyzed police detective, and this one's balls to the wall. Any questions?"

"Do I have a ride yet?" Turquoise asked her father.

"I'll get a car assigned to you," Stone said. "No problem there."

"All right. I'm going to take Turquoise with me and go get Safari's statement. The detectives working it up are Denise Staggler and Vernon Maxim. I have their initial reports, but I've purposely asked them to allow me to do Safari's interview so it comes out like I want. We're off to do that now. Let's meet back here at three and see where we are."

"Right," said Turquoise.

"Will do," said Demi.

"Roger that," said Stone.

Thaddeus and Turquoise went downstairs to police parking and climbed inside Thaddeus's rental. Safari had been moved to Alvarado Hospital and was being treated there by San Diego Spinal Physicians, a group out of San Diego. Its members were Harvard, Baylor, and Mayo Clinic so the SDPD felt she was in the best possible hands.

They went north on the five freeway, north on 163, then east on the eight, exiting at College, where they broke off their discussion of the case as the hospital loomed. Turquoise was driving and wheeled it into a slot just beyond the ER entrance, and they went inside.

She was sleeping when they entered her room, but lightly, because she opened her eyes and smiled.

"Hey," she whispered to Thaddeus, "I heard you were my main man now."

"I couldn't say no," he replied. "Thanks for asking for me. This young lady is Turquoise Murfee, my investigator who also happens to be my daughter. Turquoise, this is Safari Frye. You both remind me of each other in so many ways."

They nodded and smiled and traded hellos. Thaddeus and Turquoise took the two chairs on the hall side of the bed. Thaddeus would ask questions and would make notes. There would be no recording as they didn't want to turn over a recorded statement to Atwater that he might be able to use in court to impeach Safari if her court testimony differed even the slightest from a hospital statement. There would be no hospital statement, then, which is also why Thaddeus had asked the case detectives, Denise Staggler and Vernon Maxim, to hold off on taking a statement. All the balls were in the air, and there wouldn't be a misstep.

"Do you feel up to going over a few things with me?" Thaddeus asked.

She managed a small smile. "I was wondering when this would happen. Fire away, Mr. District Attorney."

Thaddeus smiled. So it was—District Attorney. The reverse side of the coin for him. It wasn't the first time it had happened in his career, but it was the most important, possibly, and definitely the most difficult.

"Can we begin by you taking us through what happened when you walked outside the city hall building?"

"Well, you were with me but you forgot your briefcase and immediately turned around to go back inside and collect it. You left. At almost that exact instant, I spotted Chesley at the back of his car. It was obviously no coincidence. I knew he must have followed us there and had been waiting for us to return back outside. He was probably maneuvering his car all that time to get a parking spot right outside the exit we'd just come through. So I reached to my gun holster."

"That's an inside-the-waistband holster?" asked Turquoise.

"IWB, yes. I just gripped the handle. I didn't draw it out. But I had my eyes on the asshole the whole time. Our eyes locked up. He looked like he was taking stuff in and out of the trunk of his car. It looked innocent, but I knew it wasn't. He was there to shoot me, and I had no doubt of that."

"But why there?" asked Turquoise. "He must've known there were police vehicles and cops every ten feet."

"I've thought about that. The only thing I can think is that he figured there would be the usual chaos along a busy street crammed with pedestrians, people coming and going from city hall. It was easier than trying to get close to me in my home parking or whatever."

"Makes sense," Thaddeus agreed with a nod. "So what were you thinking when you put your hand on your gun? We know what you saw. Tell us what was in your mind."

"Honestly, I felt like the worst was going to happen. I knew there would be shots fired. I was looking for a field of fire that didn't include passersby. I didn't want to inadvertently shoot a cop or a civilian."

"You knew it was coming."

"I knew that any second he'd come up out of his trunk with a gun instead of the jumper cables and tire jack he appeared to be wrestling around with. I remember praying it wasn't an automatic weapon that would spray me with bullets. I knew I'd never survive that. Then I made the decision to shoot him first."

"You were still gripping your gun?"

"Still gripping my gun. In the blink of an eye, he then dropped into a combat shooting position. I saw cops hitting the ground all around. Then they were drawing their guns. They were all pointing at the guy. But he didn't back off, didn't even flinch, just kept aiming at me. Then someone cracked off a shot that hit him in the shoulder. As he was going down, he pulled his trigger while looking me right in the eyes. One shot, and I'm crumpling, then on my back on the sidewalk. If there hadn't been other officers around, he could have easily walked up and finished me off. I'd even lost my own gun."

"At what point did you lose your gun?"

"As I went down. His shot hit me like I'd been hit by a car."

"It was a .45," Turquoise told her. "No wonder it felt like you were hit by a car."

"Yes. There was no discussion in my head. I just went down and must've blacked out for a moment or two because I can't really remember hitting the ground. Next thing I know, I'm lying there on my back looking up at this beautiful San Diego noon sky. The sun is out, birds are singing, and I cannot move. 'Fuck that!' I remember thinking. Then I must've passed out again. Next thing I know I'm being rolled into an ambulance, and I think I see Thaddeus following alongside my gurney. Then the doors closed, and I was alone with an EMT working on my IV."

"What do you know about the bullet wound?" Thaddeus asked.

"I know it entered my hip from the left and passed through my spinal cord. I'm completely transected. No chance of ever walking again. The docs and nurses and PT's come in here and start talking rehab, but I just laugh.

There's no rehab for this one. I just wave them off and tell them to go down the hall to the next room. I know my own future, kids."

"It sounds like you do," Thaddeus said with a sorrowful tone. "I'm so sorry I couldn't protect you. I just missed the whole thing."

"Really? What did you see, Thaddeus?"

"Just when I came outside again you were already down and I ran to you, only a couple of steps. I tried covering you with my own body, nothing heroic, of course. The shooter was already face down on the sidewalk with about eighty cops around him."

"There could've been other shooters. It was a brave thing you did, dropping over me like that."

"You would've done the same for me. I knew that."

"What about other statements you've given," Turquoise asked. "Is there any other statement floating around that we need to be on the lookout for?"

"Get the police reports and see what those guys have written down. Make sure they say exactly what I'm telling you here so Atwater can't find inconsistencies in the statements and reports. I don't want inconsistencies. They always confuse a jury when a good defense lawyer has inconsistencies. He'll drive that home and give his guy a chance at going free because of them. So nail it down. I'm tired now. Are we about finished?"

"We are," Thaddeus said. He stood up and began putting his laptop away. Turquoise did the same with her iPad. He leaned down and gave the detective a gentle, brotherly hug while Turquoise took her hand and squeezed. "So sorry," Thaddeus said.

Safari saw the tears in his eyes and knew. She was in the best possible hands.

"One other thing, Safari. And this goes without saying. Atwater will try to send investigators into your room. Make sure you give no more statements to anyone, especially not to strangers and especially, *especially*, not to hospital personnel as they always get it wrong, and we don't want stupid shit coming into court that some physical therapist puts in a report and claims you told him. Just say no."

She made a zippered mouth sign then closed her eyes.

Then they were gone.

Chapter 33

Atwater sent a letter to Thaddeus. He wanted to take the statement of Safari Frye. Thaddeus wrote right back, reminding the lawyer that there was no law requiring Safari or any other witness in a criminal case to speak with defense counsel. He went on to refuse the interview, though he knew what would be coming next.

Sure enough, sixteen days later, Atwater filed a motion to preclude Safari from testifying at trial. He told the court that the so-called victim refused to speak to him, Atwater, and he was thus barred from adequately preparing his defense of Chesley. The motion was set for hearing in one week.

Ordinarily, such a motion would have been summarily denied without a hearing since victims are never required to speak to defendants or their lawyers or investigators but, in this case, Atwater went one step further. He alleged, in his motion, that the victim had been instructed by Thaddeus Murfee not to speak to Atwater and thus Thaddeus Murfee was engaged in "obstruction of justice and circumventing the rules of discovery at California Penal Code, Section 1054-1054.10." Thanks to the additional language of obstruction, the motion was set for hearing before Judge Hillary M. Kenyon.

On the morning of the hearing, Thaddeus appeared in court with Turquoise, while Atwater came bouncing into court with his entourage again, consisting of bag man, backup counsel, jury consultant, and PR person. A TV crew from two local TV stations was also in attendance, alerted by LJ Atwater that the prosecution was hiding witnesses from the defendant and that this time the "District Attorney has crossed the line of all fairness and good faith." His PR arm had obviously been hard at work, thought Thaddeus, upon viewing the TV crews setting up.

It was Atwater's motion, so he went first.

"Your Honor, a very serious development has come to my attention. My investigators have attempted to take the statement of the so-called victim in this case, Safari Frye. The court will remember that Ms. Frye is the police officer who drew her gun to shoot my client when, alas for her, he was faster on the draw and shot her before she could shoot him. Of course, her aides, the other police officers on the scene, did manage to shoot him before he shot her, so they almost carried out the assassination of my client. Only his quick thinking saved his life and brings him before us today.

"My investigator, Sam Morningstar, attempted to arrange an interview with Ms. Frye—with the prosecuting attorney present—but she refused. We tried a second time, this time soliciting the help of Mr. Murfee in gaining access to the so-called victim, but he refused. I'm prepared to put Mr. Morningstar on the stand to testify that he was told by Safari Frye that Thaddeus Murfee instructed her not to speak to me or to my investigators. While, of course, a victim has no duty to speak with me or my investigator, when the prosecutor specifically tells her not to give us a statement, then the prosecutor has overstepped and is engaging in preventing a witness from testifying.

"Under California Penal Code Section 136.1, it is a crime to knowingly prevent a witness or the victim of a crime from testifying in court. In our case, Mr. Murfee's instructions to not speak to me results in keeping her full story from coming out in court because the statement I expect to obtain will be quite different from the testimony Mr. Murfee will introduce at trial. Mr. Murfee's offense should be reported by the court to the attorney general as a continuing crime, and the victim should be ordered by the court to speak to me. I can produce testimony regarding these matters, or the court can accept the verified statements of Mr. Morningstar attached to my motion. Thank you, Judge."

Judge Kenyon looked across to Thaddeus Murfee. "Does the State wish to be heard on the motion?"

"Yes, Your Honor. I will avow to the court that neither I nor any of my staff have ever told Detective Frye she isn't to speak to the defendant or his agents. However, Detective Frye knows the rules in question and knows she isn't required to speak to anyone. That has evidently been her choice, and so she shouldn't be ordered now to do any such thing as speak to LJ Atwater or his perjurious assistants. I say 'perjurious' because it is perjury to say I had anything to do with any of this. The defense counsel and his investigator are advised that my office will be looking closely at this perjury, and I will be sending an investigator to speak to the defendant's Morningstar to see what proof he has of backing up his statements against me. If he has no evidence, then I will recommend he be prosecuted for perjury.

Defense counsel would do well to cease coming into court with these lies and false accusations. The motion should be summarily denied."

Atwater was instantly on his feet. "We can prove Mr. Murfee instructed his client not to speak to us because we have her recorded statement telling Mr. Morningstar that Mr. Murfee told her not to speak to us. I am sending the recording to Mr. Murfee as soon as court is over. I will likewise provide the court with the wav file as soon as we're done here. It is her voice, and she is very clear in her statement."

Now Thaddeus had no answer. He suspected, however, that if they did have a comment by Safari that said what they claimed, they probably caught her while she was drugged in the hospital and willing to say anything.

"Your Honor," Thaddeus said, "I would ask the court to continue this hearing in order to give me a chance to speak to my client and play for her the defendant's recorded statement."

"Mr. Murfee," said Judge Kenyon, "I have warned you not to bring these fights into my courtroom. I will listen to Mr. Atwater's recording and, if your client is heard to be saying these things, I will dismiss the case and set the defendant free with his bail money returned. We're done here. We're in recess."

The judge stormed from the courtroom. Atwater was already in front of the TV cameras, explaining that the state had been caught preventing a witness from telling the whole truth about the case. He was also claiming victory.

When Thaddeus and Turquoise passed by, Atwater turned, smiled, and winked.

"Now you know, counselor," said Atwater into the

camera. "You're in a dogfight with LJ Atwater. You just lost that fight. Enjoy the rest of your day."

Thaddeus was already headed for Scripps Hospital.

There was a case to try to save.

THADDEUS PLAYED the recording for Safari at her bedside:

Investigator: Do I have your permission to record our conversation?

Safari: Yes

Investigator: You're speaking from Scripps Hospital?

Safari: Yes

Investigator: What is your condition?

Safari: Fine, but I'm paralyzed from the waist down.

Investigator: At the time you were shot, were you drawing your gun?

Safari: I think so. I don't remember for sure.

Investigator: But you at least had your hand on your gun?

Safari: Yes, I had my hand on my gun.

Investigator: Did you intend to shoot Mr. Chesley?

Safari: I don't remember. They said my memory might get better with time.

Investigator: Who said that?

Safari: My rehab doctor and therapists all said it.

Investigator: But you do remember touching your gun?

Safari: Yes, I was touching it.

Investigator: And you might even have been removing it from its holster?

Safari: I might have been.

Investigator: Did you see Mr. Chesley get shot?

Safari: I think so.

Investigator: Did you draw your gun then?

Safari: I don't remember.

Investigator: Well, your gun was found beside you on the sidewalk. So evidently you took it out of your holster, right?

Safari: I must have. It wouldn't fall out. It has a safety strap to hold it in the holster.

Investigator: So you unfastened that strap to remove it?

Safari: I don't remember. I guess I did.

Investigator: This recording is with your full knowledge and consent?

Safari: Yes. Thaddeus Murfee said not to talk to you, but I don't see why not. I feel fine.

Investigator: Mr. Murfee told you not to talk to me?

Safari: He said I wasn't up to it yet. I was taking too many drugs to make sense.

Investigator: And he told you not to talk to me?

Safari: He said I should refuse your request. So I hope you don't try to use this in court. You're not, are you?

Investigator: Probably we will, yes. Do I have your permission to use it in court?

Safari: No, Mr. Murfee said not to give a statement for court. Or anything else. I'm confused. Can I talk to him and call you back?

Investigator: You can if you'd like.

Safari: All right, I'm going to see if it's okay now to talk to you for court. Please let me do that before you use it, okay?

Investigator: I can't agree to that. I'm sorry.

Safari: You don't have my permission then. I'm hanging up now.

. . .

THE INQUISITION ENDED at that point. Thaddeus looked up from the recording transcript. He looked into Safari's eyes. "This recording is dated six days after the shooting. Were you still on medication then?"

"Hell, yes, Thaddeus. I'm still on medication now. There's lots of pain."

"Were you under the influence of pain meds when you gave the statement?"

"Of course. That's why I couldn't remember much of what he asked."

"I thought you said it was because you had memory loss."

"They say my memory problems are directly related to my meds. They say everyone has memory problems who takes meds like these."

"My God," said Turquoise. "The guy made it sound like you remembered just about everything. He weaseled it around."

"He did," Thaddeus agreed. "It will have a strong impact on the jury. We've got to keep this out of evidence. Can you help me get together your nursing notes so we can see what kind of meds you were on and how much?"

Safari said, "I'm sure I can. I'll ask and have a uniform bring them to you."

"Fair enough. I'll file an amended response to the motion to preclude your testimony after I've seen the nursing notes."

"Thank you, Thaddeus."

IT WAS HALF-PAST one when the nursing notes arrived downtown at the DA's office. Thaddeus and Turquoise immediately began reading. Gabapentin and morphine were her primary pain control medications at or near the time of Atwater's investigator's call to Safari. They made calls to Safari's treating doctors and learned common side effects of morphine and gabapentin included cogitation, drowsiness, and difficulty thinking. Were these deficits the same aspects of Safari's condition when interviewed by Morningstar? The argument could certainly be made. And would be made.

Thaddeus had Demi draw up a reply to Atwater's motion that included within it a counter-motion to preclude the use of Safari's recorded statement at trial. The argument went that Safari was under the influence of narcotics and other drugs at the time of giving the statement and her mental ability, her cognition, was impaired. Would the judge buy it? Thaddeus confirmed with her primary doctor that he would testify at the hearing.

His name was Richard Xavier Spencer, and he was a medical doctor out of Duke with a neurosurgical specialty at UCLA. Post-doctoral work had included more of the same. Thaddeus called him to the witness stand the next week in an attempt to quash the use of Safari's recorded statement.

"Doctor Spencer, have you read and listened to the recorded statement of your patient, Safari Frye?"

"I have."

"Do you have an opinion of her mental state at the time she gave that statement, based on the drugs she was being administered at the time?"

"I do have an opinion."

"Would you please tell Judge Kenyon your opinion?"

"Objection," Atwater said. "The doctor doesn't know

firsthand what drugs she was given that day. Only the attending nurse would know what she actually took."

"Counsel?" the judge said to Thaddeus. "Response?"

"Judge, the doctor didn't administer the drugs; he prescribed them. Which puts him more clearly in the position of one who would know the victim's mental state than her treating nurse."

"Gentlemen, the court tends to agree with the prosecution. This is a bench hearing, and I want to hear what the doctor says. I'll give it the weight it's entitled to and no more. Please proceed."

"Again, Doctor, do you have an opinion of Safari Frye's mental state due to the drugs she was taking at the time she gave that telephonic interview?"

"Her mental state would have been severely impacted. She wasn't herself. She would have been impaired, so it wouldn't be fair to use her words in court."

Thaddeus stopped and fiddled with his papers, letting the doctor's words fully register with Judge Kenyon.

"So for this reason, the medications she was taking, you believe it would be unfair to hold her to those words?"

"Based on the medications, to some extent. But even more, based on her injury. This patient was also suffering PTSD and probably still is. Her memory would be impaired; her thoughts would be scrambled."

Thaddeus knew if he went after it a third time there would be an objection that would be sustained and that would let the wind out of his sails, so he quit.

"Nothing further, Your Honor."

The judge looked to LJ Atwater. "Counsel? Cross-examination?"

Atwater took his place at the lectern and shuffled his papers for several moments. Then, "Doctor, isn't it true you were censured by the California Medical Association for testimony you gave in the case of *State vs. Packer*?"

The blood drained from the doctor's otherwise ruddy face. "I was censored, but I can explain."

"And isn't it true that case was overturned on appeal because the State Medical Association censured you?"

"Yes."

"In that case, you told a sitting jury that the woman accused of smothering her baby was suffering from PTSD because the child was born of a rape, correct?"

"That's correct."

"Yet, the state then brought in the woman's sister, who was present in the room at conception, who testified that it wasn't a rape, that it was a two-on-one sexual adventure, correct?"

"Correct. But I—"

"So your testimony was thrown out, correct?"

"Correct."

"So you've previously given courtroom testimony that freed a woman only to have the court later find you had ignored the fact there was another consenting female present at conception, correct?"

Meekly now, "Correct."

"So how can we be expected to believe you today?"

"This time I'm telling— No, today it is the truth. I know it to be the truth."

"Because you were there and know Detective Frye was the victim rather than the perp? Aren't you just assuming that fact?"

"I guess we all are—"

"So, if the court is to believe you, the court has to accept the presumption you're making about the facts, correct?"

"Correct."

"But that presumption is actually a question for the jury, correct?"

"Correct."

"So wouldn't it only be fair to allow the jury to hear all the testimony and then decide how much weight to give your testimony rather than keep Ms. Frye's testimony from the jury like you and Mr. Murfee are trying to pull off here?"

"It would be fair for the jury to decide, yes."

"I'm glad you think so, doctor. Your Honor, the state's counter-motion to exclude the detective's statement to my investigator should be denied."

"Counsel for the state?"

"No more questions. But the motion should be allowed. The doctor knows all the facts."

"How is that so, Mr. Murfee?" the judge asked. "None of us knows all the facts yet. Your counter-motion is denied. The telephonic statement of Ms. Frye will be allowed into evidence. You're fortunate, Mr. Murfee, that the court isn't going to hold you in contempt for attempting to silence a witness, as well. You had told her not to speak to the defendant or his lawyer. That better not happen again in this case, or you'll wind up behind bars."

Thaddeus could hear the media behind him shuffling to get out into the hallway and setup for the victory sound bites to come from Atwater. He cringed and sat down, defeated.

Turquoise nudged him. "It's only a battle, not the war," she whispered.

Then they were in recess and packing up to leave the courtroom.

"Mr. Murfee," said Atwater, "I'd now like to take the

statements of all your investigators, including the detectives assigned to the case. I assume that won't be a problem?"

"These are statements you can take if they agree to talk to you. You ask them, not me," Thaddeus said.

"Tsk, tsk," said Atwater. "You are a slow learner, sir."

"I like it that way," said Thaddeus.

"Of course, you do, dear boy. Bye for now, Mr. Murfee. I'll be calling."

But Thaddeus had already turned away, ignoring the guy.

Atwater never quit coming. This case was going to take everything the special prosecutor had to give.

It was time to double his efforts.

Chapter 34

The wheelchair was the worst part. It wanted to become part of her, but she was resisting. She couldn't envision herself tagged to a piece of steel and rubber the rest of her life. But it insisted, and she finally started to yield. She had no other choice. It was either accept the spoked wheels or remain in bed or chair-bound.

She started by learning slowly, navigating through doorways, around tables, up to the kitchen sink and—now what? She couldn't reach to turn the taps. So she brought workmen in to make accommodations. Chairs were obtained to match the height of the wheelchair, same with her bed. Luckily, she had a ground-floor apartment, or that would have been another obstacle to tackle. As it was, she'd sold the Harley to her ex-partner, Ned Griffiths. He had always admired her bike, so she sold it to him for a good deal. Hell, he'd backed her up enough in the last couple of years, it was the least she could do.

It was a new world. For both her and Carrie.

And how did Safari feel about it all? She was hurt, more

than anything. Hurt that someone had wanted to take away the use of her legs, the use of her bowel and bladder function. Everywhere she turned, there were tubes and a bag. Emptying, cleaning, observing one's waste production functions. At times she was unable to express the rage she felt, the pain welling up inside her chest and bringing tears to her eyes. She tried to explain, long-distance, to her mom in North Hollywood, her childhood home where her younger twin sisters were still in school and didn't have words for her except to express their sorrow for her. She tried to accept her dad's kind words from Richmond where he toiled in the Ford assembly plant and the same from her brother in Rockford.

She considered herself fortunate there had been no current boyfriend, no breakup to suffer through because they couldn't adjust to her new horror-filled life. The thought brought tears to her eyes as she once again thought about Max, the love of her life.

Chapter 35

"What can I do to help?" Thaddeus asked her the day before the trial was set to begin. They were sitting at the kitchen table at her apartment, a cup of coffee in front of both of them. "Are there special accommodations needed in the courtroom? In the courthouse itself?"

"There are wheelchair stalls in the ladies' restroom—I've read the ADA laws. All public buildings must accommodate losers like me."

"Please, you're anything but a loser," he pleaded with her. "You're a hero to the rest of us. The world is now your servant."

She gave him a querulous look. "Really, Thaddeus? Have you seen the mess they make of your automobile with the hand-controlled operating mechanisms? There went any style I may've once had." She laughed, but it sounded empty to Thaddeus.

"Just kidding about that. Thank God they have what they have, actually. And everyone has been so good and nice to me. There's been so much help. But at the end of the day, I'm the one who empties my bag at night so I don't overflow and wake up with wet, brown sheets. I hate my life, if you must know. This whole trial has become meaningless in my mind.

"I've moved on, Thaddeus. I've left behind the world of good guys after bad guys. Now there are just faces on the sidewalks and in the elevators, who don't see me. Do I sound like I feel sorry for myself? Well, I do. Anybody in my circumstances would feel sorry for themselves. My shrink says it's natural, but I'll eventually overcome it. Well, I'm waiting for that. I'm sorry, Thaddeus. Please forgive me. I'll grow."

"Never give it a second thought. I'm only here to put the bastard who did this behind bars so it never happens to anyone again. Right now, he is behind bars, too, where he'll stay the rest of his life. Just bear with me while I ask for your help in convicting him. I'll need you to testify, to help me tell the story the jury needs to hear. After that, I won't make any further demands on your time or energy. Deal?"

"Deal."

They shook hands then.

"So here's our case, just so you know. First up is Detective Maxim to give the twenty-thousand-foot overview of the case. Then I'll put Turquoise on the stand to talk about videos and other real evidence. Rian O'Bannion will testify third about how he shot Chesley and what he saw just before he pulled the trigger. After that will come your doctor, Dr. Spencer, to testify about the injury you suffered. Just as a matter of proving the significance of the injury so that I can meet the burden of proof, and so that later on, I can argue aggravating factors at sentencing. My last witness will be you, Safari. I'll ask you to go back over the shooting, and then I'll bring you into present day and your struggles. This will be done, again, for aggravating factors. I'm sure you understand. There will also be an evidence tech or two, especially CSIs to go over the physical evidence collected at the scene. There's also one other line of presentation I'm working on, but I won't get your hopes up with that until I'm sure where I stand. Are we clear?"

"Clear as glass."

"If there's any other evidence or testimony you wish me to present, please speak up."

"What about Atwater? What can we expect from the great—his own words—LJ Atwater?"

"Well, he's found some video evidence of his own, so there's that. Will he have Chesley testify? He really can't present a defense without him. So we'll have a chance to impeach the bastard. That's the bit of surprise I might be working up."

"Don't hold me in suspense, Thaddeus. What do you have up your sleeve?"

"Well, it has to do with the Vicki Pelham murder."

"You're thinking Kenneth Chesley?"

"Let me wait on that, please."

"Of course. I'll try not to pester you.'"

"No bother. I just hate to get hopes up prematurely."

"I understand. I can wait."

Chapter 36

Trial began on a cool, clear morning. The marine layer was burning off, and the day promised to be a beauty downtown at the court building. People were coming and going in ones and twos and threes as Thaddeus and his crew arrived inside the courtroom and began setting up. After a preliminary meeting between the lawyers and the judge in her chambers, the trial began. Jury selection was at the top of the order.

LJ Atwater drew first blood during jury selection. An older woman, Amabelle McCartney, was talking about her lack of bias. She had just told Atwater in *voir dire* that she would be able to consider the evidence without the severity of the victim's injuries coloring her deliberations.

"Do you feel like you're able to give Mr. Chesley a fair trial despite Detective Frye sitting here today in her wheelchair?"

"Yes."

"While her injuries are severe, would you be able to decide the case without regard to those injuries?"

"I know I could. People get hurt, seriously hurt, every day. Bad things can happen to good people."

Atwater couldn't resist. "Sometimes good people cause those bad things to happen."

"Objection!" shouted Thaddeus, on his feet. "Counsel is trying to get the witness to commit to his view of the facts."

"Sustained. Counsel, this is no place for closing argument. You have some leeway. I'm allowing you to ferret out bias but let's stop there without trying to get Mrs. McCartney to become a spokesperson for your client."

Undaunted, Atwater jumped right back into his strategy. He asked the prospective juror a second question. "Would you be able to set aside any bias you might have because a good person like Safari Frye was injured?"

"Yes, I could decide the case on the facts, not feelings."

Thaddeus took up the same issue a little further along. "Mrs. McCartney, there will be evidence that Safari Frye now empties her own body waste bag. Would you allow that to influence your judgment in the case?"

There, he had it in front of the jury without a word of testimony being adduced.

"I would have a hard time not thinking about her problems, I have to admit."

"But you've a strong enough will that you could decide the case on the facts, not feelings about colostomy bags?"

"Yes—yes, I think so."

Thaddeus was successful putting the facts before the jury with his questions—but only partly. Because, sitting beside him in her wheelchair was Safari Frye. Anytime the bag was mentioned, or the fact of the colostomy she would live with the rest of her life, she colored and cringed. It was an embarrassment and painful both. As it would be to anyone. But, for now, strong feelings would have to be put on the shelf while Thaddeus did what was necessary. Court isn't a place for gentle words and cuddling. Sometimes reality is portrayed in the strongest and most vile words imaginable. Colostomy was one of those vile words. Yet it would be heard again before the jury got the case to deliberate.

By the time jury selection had wrapped up, Atwater had scored his points, maybe a few more than Thaddeus even. But Thaddeus knew from long experience that trial courts bend over backward to ensure fair trials to criminal defendants. For one thing, no trial judge wanted to be overturned on appeal and a criminal turned loose. For another, defense attorneys could be flamboyant and aggressive where prosecutors never could. They had to be conservative and even mild, at times, so the jury didn't get the idea the power of the state was ganging up on a lone individual—one of them.

Flamboyant as they were, defense attorneys like Atwater pushed it further with juries than prosecutors and came away from jury selection with more pre-commitments from the jurors, a no-no with the judge but a reality in the trenches. The last thing any judge wanted was for a juror to be manipulated into one camp or the other by clever questioning or charismatic lawyers. But in the end, Atwater had scored more points with the jury. Going forward, he held a definite advantage there.

Next came opening statements. Thaddeus went first and gave a vanilla opening statement. He made no attempt to persuade during opening statement since persuasion was an absolute no-no if it came in the form of argument. That sort of thing could get a lawyer reamed out in front of the jury. So he told what the evidence would show and sat down. Now it was Atwater's chance to give his version of the facts.

"The evidence will show," he began, "that on the morning of the shooting, Kenneth Chesley was looking for paperwork in the trunk of his car before he went into the city offices on business. He was rummaging in his trunk when out of nowhere appeared a detective just to his right side. She was standing there glaring at him, her hand on her gun. It frightened Mr. Chesley to death. Then, as she went to draw her pistol, he came up with his own gun and dropped into a shooting stance so she'd know he was serious about fending her off. Out of nowhere, an over-eager Officer Rian O'Bannion shot my client and, when Kenny was shot, he was terribly confused about who'd just shot him so he returned fire at the only person he knew to have a gun. That person was Safari Frye who, in the final analysis, was shot because one of Ms. Frye's friends in a blue uniform had just shot a civilian preparing for city business. Added to that, Kenny had seen the detective start to draw her gun from its waist holder. The evidence will show she was about to shoot him, too, and Kenny probably saved his life by firing first. That's the long and short of this case."

Judge Kenyon, at the close of opening statements, admonished the jury that, "What you've just heard isn't evidence, and it shouldn't be argument. It is merely the expectations the attorneys have of what the evidence will show. You might have different opinions about the evidence, but that's why we have trials. Your job is to decide which of the opening statements you believe is true and to reject those parts you don't find confirmed by evidence. But I would also suggest you hold each attorney to his statement of the case, to look at all the facts that come out and decide if he has proven to you the case he just described."

Chapter 37

Thaddeus called Detective Vernon Maxim as his first witness. Maxim strode up to the witness stand and was sworn in by the clerk. Then he took a seat, all six-feet-four-inches of him. He was wearing a blond buzz haircut, and his blue eyes were reminiscent of the handsomest of those California surfer bands in the Sixties. He wore a wedding band and an Apple watch, just like three members of the jury, so he was familiar and looked wholesome and believable.

Maxim talked about the investigation he'd performed with Detective Staggler, all the people they had spoken with, and the evidence they'd assembled. When he was finished, it looked like a straight-ahead investigation, the kind a jury would expect and probably find reliable.

Then Atwater began his cross-examination.

"Isn't it true, Detective Maxim, that you weren't at the scene of the shooting when it happened?"

"That is true."

"So you don't know whether Detective Frye was about to shoot Kenny when he fired at her, do you?"

"No, I don't know."

"So when he says he was fearful she was about to shoot him, you don't know if his feeling was justified or not, do you?"

"No, I wasn't there."

"In fact, for all you know, she had just made a move to draw her weapon and fire, correct?"

"Correct, I wouldn't know that."

"Basically, you've been a collector of evidence, correct?"

"Yes."

"Going person to person and taking statements?"

"Correct."

"Gathering documents from the hospital, the crime lab, that sort of thing?"

"Yes."

"By the way, you call it a crime lab?"

"Yes, it's the crime lab."

"Couldn't it just as easily be called the innocence lab in a case like this?"

"Objection!" Thaddeus shouted.

The judge frowned, curling her lip. "Sustained. Argumentative, counsel. Move on, please."

"Who named it the crime lab?"

"I don't know."

"Who would we contact to get it named the innocence lab?"

"Objection." Thaddeus sighed. "Same, argumentative."

"Counsel, you are now warned. Move along."

"Mr. Maxim, did you take the statement of Safari Frye?"

"No."

"Why not?"

"We were cautioned by Mr. Murfee not to commit her comments to paper or video or recording."

"Why not? Aren't statements always taken of witnesses?"

"Yes."

"Why not her?"

"I think he didn't want us to get a statement to contradict anything."

"Mr. Murfee wanted to present her statement like he saw fit rather than how she might give it to you?"

"I guess you could say that."

"What about you? Could you say he wanted to mold her statement to fit his dog-and-pony show?"

"Yes. He wanted to mold it."

"Very well."

Then Thaddeus got him back on redirect.

"Detective Maxim, did I ever tell you not to take the statement of Safari Frye because I was worried how it might come out?"

"No."

"Why did I tell you to tread softly with her?"

"Because she was under the influence of strong drugs and probably wouldn't know what she was saying. She might tell something completely different the second or third time. You said spinal cord injuries with severe pain and narcotic drugs are never a good combination for clearheadedness."

"So, unlike what Mr. Atwater tried to make it look like, I wasn't trying to mold her testimony but attempting to let her recover first so she had her thoughts, correct?"

"That would be right."

"Yes?"

"Yes."

It went back and forth a third and fourth time, unusual for any judge to allow, but again, the rights of the defendant were being especially protected, so Judge Kenyon let the lawyers get it all out. Then Maxim was allowed to step down and take his place at counsel table, two seats from Thaddeus.

Just then, Turquoise stood, and her father called her to the witness stand.

It was time for the first on-the-record exchange between father and daughter.

"Tell us your name," said Thaddeus.

"Turquoise Murfee."

"Your business, occupation, or profession?"

"I'm an investigator with Christine Murfee Law Firm."

"You're on temporary assignment to the San Diego District Attorney's Office of Special Counsel?"

"Yes."

"Answering to me, Thaddeus Murfee?"

"Yes."

"I am your father?"

"Yes."

"Describe your duties."

"I investigate criminal cases in my usual job. In San Diego, I'm detailed to the investigation of the Safari Frye shooting case. I've talked to witnesses, reviewed evidence, and canvassed for and obtained video footage of the date and time of the Frye shooting. I've discussed these items with you."

"Are these discussions of our mental impressions of the evidence and testimony?"

"Most definitely."

"Our strategizing?"

"Most definitely."

Thaddeus shot a look at Atwater. That kind of mental impression and strategizing was off-limits to discovery. The court would likely keep it off-limits in front of the jury as well.

"What was your first assignment on this case?"

"Talk to the detectives and get their impressions then report to you."

"Did you do that?"

"I did."

"Next up?"

"Obtain all video of the incident. I did that, too."

"Tell us your sources of video."

"The City of San Diego, specifically, City Hall. Also Motor Officer Clayton Johns whose GoPro helmet cam caught most of the action and Adult Toys, Inc., a retail outlet directly across the street from City Hall. Their cameras were running and caught slices of the event between passing cars and pedestrians."

"I'm going to ask for State's Exhibit Two, the video taken by the City Hall CCTV system."

The room lights went down as the video began playing on the screens mounted above and behind Judge Kenyon. The jury had a clear view as well as the spectators, attorneys, and other court personnel. Judge Kenyon had a small screen on her desk and watched the replay there.

"Turquoise," said Thaddeus, "please narrate."

"All right, the victim, Safari Frye, has just exited City Hall. The camera is behind her and to her right, looking over her shoulder toward the street. You can see the defendant's Toyota Corolla just over and beyond her left shoulder. As she moves the next couple of steps, you can see the defendant come up out of the trunk of his car, holding a pistol and assuming a combat shooting stance. Then, from Safari's right, you can see a police officer we will learn was Rian O'Bannion suddenly draw his service weapon and fire a shot at the defendant. The defendant is going down and at the same time he is being rushed by several police officers in the vicinity. At the bottom of the picture, you see Safari Frye drop to the ground. She is immediately covered by the body of the man she was in City Hall with—you, Thaddeus Murfee."

"Very well, and now play State's Exhibit Three."

The next video jumped onto the screen. Again, Turquoise narrated.

"This video is shot from across the street looking back toward City Hall. The CCTV this comes from is meant to capture the action outside an adult toy store but it also sees across the street. Wearing the pink jacket with black piping is Safari Frye, just now exiting the building and facing the camera. Her hand touches her waistband, and the video has been enhanced to show her hand is not touching her gun. Never does her hand touch her gun."

"Yet, in his opening statement, Mr. Atwater said she was drawing her gun? Is that on there?"

"She not only doesn't draw her gun, but never touches her gun. The video is very clear about that."

"Are there other videos you've located?"

"Mr. Atwater's investigator turned up a video, but he refused to allow me to see it."

Thaddeus looked over at the jury. Some were making furious notes just then.

"What do you know about Mr. Atwater's video?"

"He was advertising in the paper for anyone with a video. He was offering ten-thousand dollars for anyone who came forward with a video he found useful. Evidently, he found one, but I called his secretary and asked for a copy, but they never returned one. I called him then, personally, and he just laughed at me."

"Objection! Attorney work product!"

The judge looked askance at Atwater. "Counsel," she said, "sidebar, please."

Both attorneys crept up to the judge's sidebar. Whispering ensued. Finally, they broke up and the judge said, on the record, that attorney work product doesn't ordinarily include videos of an alleged crime. She allowed Turquoise's last answer to stand.

Several more areas were gone into, and then Thaddeus broke off his questions. He turned the witness over to Atwater's cross-examination.

Atwater wasted no time. "Ms. Murfee, isn't it true you and I have never spoken before?"

Turquoise frowned. "Not true at all, sir. According to my notes—"

"Hold it right there! I asked isn't it true, yes or no. I didn't ask for a long-winded recitation about your efforts. So let me ask again. Isn't it true you and I have never discussed this case before?"

"True."

"Yet, you want the jury to believe that I refused to make a video available to you. Isn't that true?"

"Yes."

"And isn't it also true you could just as easily have run your own newspaper ad for video evidence?"

"True, we could have."

"But you chose not to, correct?"

"That's correct."

"Instead, you wanted to be the beneficiary of my due diligence, correct?"

"No, I only wanted to see the video."

"Calls for yes or no."

Judge Kenyon then instructed, "The witness will answer yes or no."

"No."

"But you wanted my video that I obtained for my client's defense, correct?"

"Correct."

Atwater stared with a look of contempt on his face. "Is it fair that you get my client's case workup?"

"Yes."

"But in this case, isn't it true your father also told Safari Frye not to speak to me?"

"I don't know."

"You've heard previous argument about this issue?"

"Yes."

"You were here in court when I argued to the judge I wanted to interview Detective Frye?"

"Yes."

"How is it fair your father refused to allow me to speak to a witness yet you get to see my video? How does that work?"

"Those are the rules of criminal procedure, Mr. Atwater."

She was quick with her answer. He immediately realized he'd asked her an open-ended question and got the explanation he didn't want. He wanted only yes or no. Not logic and rules.

"Defendant moves to strike Ms. Murfee's answer. She's no expert on the rules of criminal procedure."

"You opened the door, counsel. Her answer will stand."

Atwater tried grinding her down with hit-and-miss questions that jumped around in an attempt to confuse her. But

Turquoise made her father proud when she refused to be misled. Her answers were proper and swift, and Atwater got nowhere thereafter. Finally, he sat down, a look on his face like he'd just mopped the floor with her. The jury looked away.

Then, at the last possible moment, Atwater stood up again. "One last question. Isn't it true Safari Frye was there at City Hall because she was facing a sexual harassment hearing for calling a junior detective a dickless wonder?"

"True."

"I'll save the rest of these questions for her. Thank you."

All the air went out of the room. Several jurors were left staring at Safari in disbelief. Thaddeus gave out no reads with his body or face. Safari was busy, head down, writing on a yellow pad.

Several jurors finally shook their heads and looked away.

Atwater had scored his points after all.

Chapter 38

Rian O'Bannion was a four-year patrolman on the verge of being promoted the day he shot and wounded Kenneth Chesley. Thaddeus put him on the witness stand and began presenting his story.

"Tell us where you were that morning."

"I was on my way inside City Hall to testify in a driver's license hearing. I had just parked my patrol car on the right side of the street and jumped out. I came around the front of my vehicle and paused there while I scanned my notes. I looked up and there, just ahead, was a man parked on the same side as me."

"You had moved away from your squad car?"

"Correct, I paused then angled across the sidewalk to my left toward the entrance to City Hall. I was suddenly confronted with a civilian who dropped into a combat shooting position."

"What did you do?"

"I tried to see what he was pointing his gun at. I looked

to my left, the direction the man was aiming. Then I saw his target."

"How did you know it was his target?"

"It was a female detective, and no one else was near her. I saw her wearing a gun and detective's shield inside her coat. Then I looked back toward Chesley. Clearly the man was going to shoot."

"You knew this how?"

"His hand began squeezing around the gun. You can just tell when a shot's coming."

"What did you do?"

"Confirmed a field of fire behind him. When I was sure I could fire a shot at him without hitting someone behind him if I missed, I drew my gun and squeezed off a shot just a split second before he fired. He was just going down when he shot the detective."

"Were there other officers around?"

"Yes, and they all closed on him at once. Then a couple ran for the wounded detective. She was passed out, or seemed to be, then her eyes opened and she was looking at the sky. I could hear her crying. She said she couldn't move."

"Did you hit the man you shot at?"

"I did. I hit him in the left shoulder. I found out later it was superficial, but it was enough to end his shooting that day."

"What happened next?"

"EMTs and ambulances converged. They were in the area and showed up at the scene within a minute or two after the shooting. Maybe longer. I ran up to the man I'd shot and yelled something obscene at him, then I went to help the detective. She was writhing in pain and kept crying out that she couldn't move, couldn't move. The EMTs got her settled down and started an IV and hooked her up to some electrical leads then moved her onto a backboard. By now she was laying there very still, answering questions. She was worried if anyone else had been hurt and was relieved when we told her no. She was placed on a gurney and rolled up into an ambulance and off they went."

"What happened with the shooter?"

"He was also taken away by ambulance."

"Do you see that shooter in court today?"

"I do, sitting next to his attorney."

"Did you come to know his name?"

"His name is Kenneth Chesley, address unknown. Definitely the guy I shot."

"Did you ever hear him say anything at the scene?"

"No."

"That's all for now, thank you."

"Counsel," said Judge Kenyon to Atwater, "you may cross-examine."

Atwater walked up to the lectern. He slapped his yellow pad against his leg as he stood there several seconds. Then he sighed and put the yellow pad on the lectern before him. He drew a deep breath and launched into his examination.

"Mr. O'Bannion, how long have you been a police officer?"

"Four years, give or take."

"You say you heard nothing from Mr. Chesley?"

"That's correct."

"Anything wrong with your hearing?"

"No, sir."

"You didn't hear my client say the detective was about to shoot him?"

"I didn't hear anything like that, no."

"Would you remember if you had?"

"Nothing wrong with my memory, sir."

"How far were you from Kenny when you shot him?"

"Not far. Fifteen feet?"

"You couldn't miss, right?"

"We qualify on the range every month. I'm quite accurate from fifteen feet, sir."

"You could probably have shot to kill, correct?"

"Correct."

"But you didn't. Instead, you shot to wound, correct?"

"That's fair to say."

"Were you able to see the detective right before she was shot?"

"I did."

"Was she going for her gun?"

"Not that I saw."

"Would that possibly be because your eyes were glued on Kenny and what he was doing?"

"Definitely. She wasn't my target; he was. My eyes were totally on him."

"So when you say you didn't see her going for her gun, the truth is, you weren't even watching her, correct?"

"That's correct."

"For all you know, she could've been drawing her gun to shoot Kenny, correct?"

"Correct."

"And you told us you didn't hear Kenny say she was going to shoot him?"

"I didn't hear him say anything."

"Could that be because of the noise and chaos just after you fired? That you just couldn't hear anyway?"

"There was plenty of running and scuffling."

"So maybe you couldn't hear what he was saying?"

"Possibly. I wasn't taking note of how noisy it was. My

primary concern was for the safety of the people around us."

"So he could've cried out about her trying to shoot him, and it never registered with you?"

"That's possible. It was over in two seconds or less. Just bam! I saw him ready to shoot then bam! I shot him, then bam! She was down and crying she couldn't move. I think I heard her and didn't hear him because I wasn't listening for him."

"You weren't listening for him?"

"She was crying out, 'I can't move! I can't move!' You could hear her quite loud. Then she was crying in pain."

"It's not like the movies where someone gets shot and doesn't say much?"

"Definitely not like the movies. People who get shot are screaming."

"Was Kenny screaming?"

"Mr. Chesley? I'm sure he was, but I was listening to the detective. I only wanted to help her."

"Is there anything else I need to ask you about this, officer?"

"No, sir. That's all I know."

"Thank you. Oh, one last thing. I'm going to call a biker by the name of Phil Rizzoli who was on the scene. Do you know Phil Rizzoli?"

"I do not."

"If he testifies he heard Kenny cry out she was about to shoot him, would you disagree?"

"Like I said, I wasn't listening for Kenny. I only wanted to help my detective."

"And if this video shows Kenny crying out, you wouldn't disagree with the video?"

"No, I mean, how could I?"

"Thank you."

So, the video to be played by the defense had been interjected into the trial in one smooth question or two. *Nicely done*, thought Thaddeus. *Already planting Chesley's fear in the jury's mind as a fact. Already making it sound like self-defense.*

Chapter 39

"We need to have a talk," Safari said to twelve-year-old Carrie that night after court. They were sitting at the kitchen table, slurping tomato soup and dunking grilled cheese sandwiches. Safari had changed out of her courtroom clothes, done her bathroom duties with her bag and hose, then cleaned up and fixed dinner. Carrie had to finish up her homework, but she had kitchen cleanup first as soon as they finished up since Safari had cooked. Counters and cookstove tops had been lowered in the kitchen to make them more accessible to Safari. The height wasn't all that bad for Carrie either, who was somewhat small for twelve.

"The court has temporarily placed you with me, but I received news tonight the caseworker wants to review the placement now that I'm disabled. I don't mean to alarm you. I don't think anything will change, but it might. The other side of the coin is that a young girl doesn't need to be put in a position where she has to do extra duty around the house because her foster mom is suddenly disabled. That isn't fair to you."

"Wait," said the girl, "don't I get to decide what's fair to me and what's not?"

"Yes, probably. To some extent, anyway. But the caseworker really has the final say-so."

"Ellie Myers? Why would Ellie want to move me?"

"I'm not saying Ellie does want to move you. I'm just saying there's always the chance."

"What do you want, Safari? Do you want me out of your hair?"

Tears welled up in Safari's eyes. She knew this moment would come. In one way, she did, in fact, regret the placement. Now that she was married to a wheelchair and colostomy bag, she mourned the loss of her privacy. If she were going to be—what was the word, ugly?—if she were going to be ugly, she preferred doing it alone. No one would ever want her now and having a young girl around only made it more real that Carrie would be the only child she'd ever have. That was a reality she hadn't even been able to face yet, the loss of her ability to give birth. The loss of her ability to be a mother to a newborn. Besides, what man would ever want to be with her now? None, that's who. She was alone and adrift in a body that no longer worked. She wasn't feeling sorry for herself, just the opposite. She was proud she had decided to choose life over folding up and blowing away. That had only come after hours and hours of therapy and encouragement from social workers and mental health practitioners, but the decision had been made, and she wasn't going to go back to that dark place from before.

Financially, she was retired at her last pay level with COLA, Cost of Living Adjustment, in her future. Maybe there'd be more as the economy changed, but never all that much. Her future was pretty much going to be more of her present. Emotionally and fiscally. And monetary success? Any hopes of a second career? She had none now.

When Safari didn't answer, Carrie repeated, "Do you want me out of your hair?"

Safari wiped the tears from her eyes. "Honey, you're never in my hair. I look at you like—I look at you like my own little kid. I love you like a mother would. A real mother. I want nothing but the best for you, and I won't rest until I see you getting the best. The best schools, the best clothes, the best opportunities for growth, the best this world has to offer. You've already been through so much you deserve to have the good now. That's what I want for you. Out of my hair? Never!"

"Well…"

They had finished their meal and Carrie cleared the dishes from the table. As she rinsed and loaded the dishwasher, she listened to Safari.

"All I'm saying is that Ellie's got a job to do, and when there's a significant change of circumstances in a child placement, then she has to file the right papers to bring it to the judge's attention and let the judge decide all over again. This time they might decide I can't take care of you properly. Or that my attitude isn't good enough to be around you. Or that my own health is going to limit too much what I'm able to do with you. There are all kinds of factors they're going to weigh. I pray they won't take you away, but the papers I got today mean they're going to have a second look at the placement."

Carrie was now scrubbing the soup pot and grilled cheese pan. "Can I read the papers?"

"Oh, sure, your *guardian ad litem* will probably go over them with you, too, when we go back to court. You need to really be thinking about your new situation here, too, now that I'm less able than I was before. There will be no Ferris wheels with me, no runs along the beach, no walks anyplace. But I do promise to be there for you emotionally and be available for you whenever you need or just want to talk. I will help you get ready for your first prom and I will help you pick your college, if that's the way you want to go. If not, I'll help you with whatever kind of career or military service or whatever you decide to pursue. While I'm not really your mother, I can do all the mother things, and I promise you I will."

Carrie dried her hands on a kitchen towel and then hung it on the oven handle. "Can we not talk about it anymore? No one is ever taking me away from you."

"And I'll fight to the supreme court to get to keep you. So, we're even."

She placed her hands on her hips, more of a cute gesture on a twelve year old. "We're committed."

Safari turned over the paperwork, placing it facedown on the kitchen table.

The child custody hearing was set for two weeks. She had plenty to do between now and then to get ready. First up, she decided, she'd get a human factor's expert brought into her house so there could be professional testimony about all the things she was still able to do and about all the accommodations that could be made so the things she could no longer do got done, anyway.

It would cost her a few thousand, but she had the money saved.

Spending her money on testimony was the best expenditure she'd ever make. So she began making calls, looking for her expert. Then she'd need an attorney.

She wondered whether Thaddeus could help.

She picked up the phone and started punching numbers into the keypad. No time like the present to find out.

Chapter 40

Trial continued the following day.

Thaddeus's next witness was Richard Xavier Spencer, a medical doctor out of Duke with a neurosurgical specialty at UCLA. Thaddeus called him to the witness stand to prove both the mechanism of injury and the consequences, the severity.

"Doctor Spencer," Thaddeus began, "you've been Safari's primary neurosurgeon since the beginning, isn't that true?"

"Yes, I have."

"For the record, please describe her initial injuries when you first observed her."

"Severe spinal cord injury at the L4 level. Her cord was transected, meaning cut in two. A lower injury in the lumbar vertebrae, it has affected all nerve and muscle control to the bladder, bowel, legs, and sexual function. The injury is caused by a single gunshot, the bullet passing through her spinal canal and injuring tissue there, including bony processes."

"Can she walk?"

"No."

"Does she need a bag for urinary and bowel functions?"

"Yes."

"Can she get pregnant?"

"Possibly. But very unlikely. That's one we never know until enough time and attempts."

"These injuries were caused by a single shot from a gun?"

"That is correct."

"Is there any hope or expectation that her condition will improve?"

Dr. Spencer shot a look at Safari, who was smiling with her head down, appearing to write on a legal pad.

"No hope at all. Medical science is working on such things, but probably in her lifetime there will not be restoration of the functions I just mentioned."

Cross-examination wasn't attempted by LJ Atwater. There was no reason as the doctor had provided only indisputable fact.

Next up, Thaddeus called two crime scene techs who introduced video of the post-shooting scene and still photographs. Chesley's gun was then introduced into evidence, and a witness from the crime lab testified the bullet that severed Safari's spine was fired from Chesley's gun. The bullet had been located and examined under a microscope for striations and markings.

Thaddeus had proven the elements of the crime, including the defendant's identity and manner of committing the crime. Motive was never a requisite for crime to be proven in court, but Thaddeus intended to prove motive anyway. He would be doing that through the victim herself, Safari Frye.

He called her to the stand as his final witness.

He'd been over her testimony last night. Then he'd conducted the kind of cross-examination he imagined Atwater would attempt. His efforts made her angry, and he'd had to remind her they were just practicing so she wouldn't get angry tomorrow and say something to hurt her case. After that, she was able to reply to the practice questions no matter how needling.

She wheeled herself up to the witness stand, circled her wheelchair, and raised her right hand. After being sworn, she set the brake on her chair and sat beside the witness stand where you stepped up into the chair.

Thaddeus asked Safari, "Detective Frye, why would Kenneth Chesley want to shoot you?"

"I can think of two reasons. One, I was the investigating detective on the case involving Chesley's murder of Maryjane Dillon. I was the detective who said to check his Corolla for fibers that would match the window shade cords out of Maryjane's windows. When he was pulled over and stopped not three miles from her place and his car was confiscated and tested, it bore fibers that matched. I'm sure he was furious about that. Second, I was the detective in charge of investigating the cigarette burns he inflicted on Maryjane's daughter."

"Objection, move the testimony be stricken as motive isn't an issue and it's prejudicial," Atwater said slowly.

"Your Honor," said Thaddeus when they were called forward to conference out of the jury's hearing, "motive isn't a necessary element of the crime per se, but the reason he might've shot first could've been the reasons she gave, meaning he was in a rage at her and wanted her dead. The testimony is relevant and its relevance outweighs any prejudice for this reason."

"Agreed," said Judge Kenyon. "I'm going to allow it to stand, counsel," she told Atwater. Both lawyers returned to their seats.

Thaddeus continued, "You've told us he was likely in a rage at you. Let's back up to the point where you exited the City Hall building that noon. What happened after you walked out the doors?"

"Well, you immediately turned and went back inside for your briefcase. I took about two more steps, and that was when I saw Kenneth Chesley."

"What was he doing?"

"Rummaging inside the trunk of his Corolla. I couldn't tell it was him at first, but then I looked again and realized it was. My hand instinctively moved toward my gun, but just before I moved, he came up out of the trunk with his gun and didn't hesitate. A shot was fired at him at almost the exact same second he fired a shot at me. They were fired almost simultaneously."

"So you are shot. What happened next?"

"I just folded up and dropped to the ground. I lost control of my weapon. It felt like a horse had kicked me in the lower back. Just *whump!* and I was down. Next thing I know, I'm opening my eyes and trying to stand up. Except I cannot move. My legs won't work. So I inched onto my elbows and felt this unbelievable pain down there. Just a hot, searing pain burning into my back. I fell backward, and my head hit the concrete sidewalk. That time I didn't move. I turned my eyes toward Chesley, not knowing if he's coming to finish me off or not. That's when I saw a bunch of officers pinning him to the sidewalk, thank God. He would've killed me if they hadn't been there."

"Objection, speculation."

"Sustained. The jury will disregard her speculation that he would've killed her. Please continue."

"What do you remember happening next?" Thaddeus asked.

"I remember sirens. Lots of sirens. Then people running toward me. One of them was carrying a backboard. They worked on me while I had my eyes closed and answered their questions yes and no. They moved me onto the backboard and then onto a gurney, then into an ambulance. At the hospital they did scans and X-rays. They loaded me up with medicine and ran lines into my hands. They talked to me, and I had...I don't know how many doctors come in and ask me the same questions over and over. The next few days were pretty much a blur, but I was getting the big picture."

"Which was what?"

"That I was never going to walk again, thanks to Mr. Chesley. He hadn't killed me, but he had crippled me for life."

"Let me back up to the shooting. Did you ever place your hand on the gun?"

"Objection, leading."

"Sustained."

"Describe what you did with regard to going for your gun."

"As soon as I saw Mr. Chesley, he came upright with a gun and then dropped into a shooting position. At that exact moment, I went for my own gun. But I never touched it. He dropped me before I could touch it."

"So if he came in and said you grabbed or drew your gun, he would be wrong?"

"He would be dead wrong. Had I touched my gun, he wouldn't be here today."

La Jolla Law

"Tell us about the anger we just heard."

Safari rubbed a hand across her eyes. "It's difficult to manage my anger. What he did to me makes me want to reach out and do it back to him. I hope he burns in Hell for it."

The courtroom was silent while Thaddeus appeared to be perusing his notes. It was a long, uncomfortable silence, most uncomfortable for Chesley, who fidgeted and shuffled his feet several times, which grew deafening in the quiet of the courtroom. Then Thaddeus looked up. "I have no further questions right now."

LJ Atwater was immediately on his feet and headed for the lectern. He would've knocked Thaddeus down in passing, but Thaddeus was a good sized man, and Atwater wisely gave him room to pass.

Atwater began, "If we bring in a video that shows you touching your gun, would you change your testimony?"

"No."

"No? Why wouldn't you change your testimony and admit you touched your gun."

"Knowing what I know about you, Mr. Atwater, I'd first want to have video experts review the footage to see how you'd had it doctored. It would be fake."

"Would you like a few minutes to take a break and cool down before we proceed?"

"You'll find the same anger no matter how much time you take, Mr. Atwater. As long as I'm changing colostomy bags at night, my anger with you and your client will continue."

"Very well. Tell us what kind of gun Mr. Chesley brandished."

"It was silver and glinted in the sunlight when he pointed it at me. I've since heard it was a .357 magnum."

"That's a very large gun, yes?"

"Yes, it is. You can buy them snub-nosed, but only fools and people with super strength should."

"When you saw that very large gun, did you go for your gun, yes or no?"

"Yes."

"Detective, if you saw someone make a move for a gun they were wearing, might that cause you to think they were going to pull that gun out?"

"My training would cause me to think that, yes."

"Might that also cause you to draw your gun?"

"I didn't draw my gun before I was shot. I somehow yanked it out of its holster as I was going down. It was a purely defensive move at that point."

"Yes, because your gun was found on the sidewalk apart from you, correct?"

"Correct."

"The only argument between you and Mr. Chesley, then, is that he says you were pointing your gun at him when he pulled his trigger and you say not true. Isn't that about it?"

"If you say so. I'm not defending him and I haven't spoken to him, so I'm not sure what he'll say. Either way, I wouldn't believe the guy for a second."

"We'll let that go by. I'm sure you have your reasons. Or at least you imagine you have reasons."

"Well, one reason I don't believe the guy is because he murdered Maryjane Dillon then came into court and pled not guilty. So he's a liar. Were you aware of that, Mr. Atwater?"

"Objection!" cried Atwater. "Prejudicial and inflammatory! Please instruct the jury to ignore. And please allow me to move for a mistrial."

"Mr. Atwater, enough," said Judge Kenyon in a level, steady voice. "We can take up these matters on the next break. The witness is admonished against mentioning other crimes, arrests, court proceedings, and any and all other incidents other than the case we're here on. The defendant isn't on trial for any other acts. The jury is instructed to ignore Detective Frye's comments about any other case and to understand they are totally not received into evidence and shouldn't be considered by the jury in its deliberations. Please continue with your questions, Mr. Atwater."

"Detective, is it your testimony that at no time you pointed your gun at Mr. Chesley?"

"That is my testimony. Had I gotten so far as to point it at him, he wouldn't be sitting here today. That's how we know I didn't get that far."

"Your Honor, I believe that's all I have for now. Defense reserves the right to call Ms. Frye during defendant's case as an adverse witness subjected to cross-examination."

"So noted," said the judge. "Counsel Murfee, any further questions?"

"No, Your Honor. The state is prepared to rest at this point."

"The state rests its case?"

"Yes, Your Honor."

"Very well. We'll stand in recess for thirty minutes while the court attends to other business. The bailiff will take the jury to the jury room. Remember the admonition, ladies and gentlemen, not to discuss the case among yourselves at this point. Counsel, I'd like to see you in my chambers. Excused."

The attorneys followed Judge Kenyon into her office.

A half-hour later, following Atwater's motion for a mistrial, which the judge wouldn't allow, the discussion ended and the attorneys had just enough time to hit the restrooms before starting up again.

"It was close," Thaddeus told Safari, "so don't go there again if he puts you back on the stand. The earlier killings and burnings are not admissible in this case, and I've been told to advise you that you're admonished. If you do it again, you could be held in contempt of court."

"Heard and done."

"Good enough. Let's see who Atwater calls. Ready to proceed?"

"My bag isn't full. So, yeah, I'm ready to proceed, Thaddeus."

He got it. Who could blame her?

Chapter 41

David Thistle was a reformed druggie biker who now attended NA meetings and had seven years clean and sober. He used his Harley to commute to his computer programming gig downtown. He was lean and wore his hair back in a long ponytail. His shirt was black and long-sleeved the day he appeared to testify, and his knuckles were tattooed to spell out *GET SOME!* Atwater stood and shook his hand as he walked up to testify.

Thistle was sworn in then settled back and gave the jury a small, polite smile. Then he looked at LJ Atwater.

"State your name for the record, please."

"David Thistle, T-H-I-S-T-L-E."

"Mr. Thistle, I believe you work with computers?"

"I am employed in the IT department of Aetna Insurance. I program transactional software."

"How long have you done that?"

"Oh, six years now."

"And you ride a motorcycle back and forth to work?"

"Yes."

"And sometimes on your lunch hour? Like the day you were riding when you saw a shootout?"

"Objection to the characterization of this case as a shootout," Thaddeus said, taking to his feet and leaning forward. "The victim never shot anyone or anything."

"Sustained. Counsel, let's try another word. How about 'incident'?"

Atwater rephrased, "You saw a shooting incident on October Nineteenth?"

"I did. I was riding my bike up C Street when it happened."

"And, as is your daily habit, you were wearing a helmet camera?"

"Yes, I wear a GoPro on my motorcycle helmet every time I start it up. I don't go anyplace without video."

"Tell us what you saw, then we'll discuss the video."

"Like I said, I was coming up C Street, and just as I got to City Hall, I saw a uniformed police officer draw his gun, drop down on one knee, and shoot a man about twenty feet away. The man went down, and I heard him fire off a shot as he started down."

"You're saying Kenny was shot before his gun fired?"

"You can hear it on my video. First the cop shoots, then Kenny. It's very clear what happened."

"Did you bring that video today?"

"Yes. You told me to."

"And I'm going to ask my paralegal to play the video for the jury at this point. Mr. Clark?"

The room lights went down, and the TV screens leapt to life as a moving camera began capturing pedestrians and automobile traffic along C Street in downtown San Diego.

"Please narrate for us, David."

"Well, I'm coming up C Street, and I see the people

coming out of City Hall. I think it was about lunchtime so there's plenty of pedestrians. Okay, I'm almost across from the woman who gets shot. The man turns around from his trunk and raises his gun and you can hear the two gunshots. The man falls back; he's shot. Then the woman collapses in a heap. She's shot. Then it's pandemonium. I pull over to see if I can help. I was a combat medic in Iraq, and I've seen plenty of gunshots. Here we go, closing in on the woman. I'm one of the first ones. You can see all the hands. I order everyone to stand back and don't touch her. Now you can see my hands pulling her shirt aside and checking the wound for bleeding. It wasn't that bad so I tear the Harley handkerchief off my neck and compress the wound. It wasn't sterile, but it was the best I could do. Better a little grime in the wound than bleeding out.

"Now the EMTs are arriving and I'm backing away. I turn and look at the man who got shot, but he's been swarmed by the cops, so I stand down on that one. I'm not getting any closer."

Atwater asked, "We heard two gunshots on your video. How do we know which one came first?"

The biker shrugged. "Does it matter?"

Atwater stared at him. "Maybe not since you put it that way."

"I mean, if the guy shot first, then the cops shot him, you still have the question whether she was going for her gun. If you check out the video again, you'll see her hand reach inside her jacket. Did she actually touch it? How would anyone know since it was under her coat? But I can say it would be enough to spook me into thinking someone was going to shoot at me."

"Objection, speculation," Thaddeus said without looking up from his notes.

"Sustained. The jury will ignore the part about being spooked into thinking he was being shot. Please continue."

Atwater checked his notes. He appeared to be carefully going over his questions one-by-one as the biker, David Thistle, began fidgeting on the witness stand. Finally, Atwater looked up. "I believe that's all I have, Your Honor."

"Mr. Murfee?"

Thaddeus stood and went back to the lectern. He gave Thistle a curt nod. "Now, you asked what difference it made who shot first?"

"Yes. I just don't get it."

"You were a combat medic?"

"Yes."

"What's the first thing you do when you hear gunfire?"

"Try to suppress it with returning fire."

"Wouldn't it make sense that if the woman sees the man with a gun and hears his gunfire that she would be going for her gun at the same instant?"

"I—I guess so."

"I mean, if the police fired first, then Mr. Atwater can argue his client was frightened into shooting, correct? That he was returning suppressing fire?

"Yes. I guess that's true. But you can also argue he was firing at her and then got shot. I don't see how you can tell from the video who went first."

"But your testimony is the police fired first?"

"I thought I saw the cop firing first."

"Let me ask Mr. Clark to replay the video."

The video began playing again.

"Mr. Clark," said Thaddeus, "half-speed, please. Now, at the moment we hear the first gunshot, freeze it. There!"

All eyes were fastened on the screen, frozen just a frame or two after the first gunshot.

"At this point, Mr. Thistle, the Toyota Corolla is blocking your view of the defendant, is it not?"

"Yes. My helmet cam has the Corolla but not the man at the trunk."

"Can you see the police officer with his gun out right there?" Thaddeus walked to the screen and pointed out the man he meant. "This officer here?"

"I can see him."

"What does he appear to be doing?"

"Drawing his gun."

"Yet, we've already heard the gunshot?"

"Yes, but I'm thinking it was another cop who shot. There were half a dozen of them going in and out. It could've been any of them."

"Why do you suppose you're so certain the cops shot first?"

"I just remember it happening that way."

"But your video isn't certain of that. In fact, wouldn't you agree your video doesn't answer the question at all?"

"I just remember it that way."

"Mr. Thistle, I want to show you an advertisement we clipped from the newspaper. Please look at it."

He handed the witness a newspaper clipping, which the witness studied.

"Have you seen that before?"

"I have."

"What is it?"

"It's a newspaper ad I answered."

"Whose number is on the ad to call?"

"Mr. Atwater's."

"And what does the clipping want?"

"It's looking for a witness with video of the shooting. It

offers ten-thousand dollars for anyone with video who answers the ad."

"Did you receive the ten-thousand dollars?"

"I did. Mr. Atwater paid me, and I paid off my ride."

"You paid off your motorcycle."

"That's right."

"Did the ten thousand include you coming here to testify?"

"No, that was extra."

"So, tell the jury how much you were paid to come here and testify."

"Another ten-thousand dollars."

"Who paid you another ten thousand?"

"Mr. Atwater."

"So, Mr. Atwater paid you ten-thousand dollars to come here with your video and testify. Is there anything else?"

"I get another ten-thousand if Kenny Chesley walks."

"If there's a not-guilty, you get another ten-thousand dollars from Mr. Atwater?"

"Yes."

"Mr. Thistle, I believe that's all I have."

The newspaper clipping was admitted into evidence and passed around to the jury.

Atwater said he had no further questions, and Thistle stepped down.

Chapter 42

A heated argument broke out at defense table. Thaddeus knew exactly what was going on since he could overhear bits and pieces. Chesley wanted to testify; Atwater was telling him no way. Atwater warned Chesley he would be impeached with evidence of prior bad acts based on strangling Maryjane Dillon and burning Carrie Dillon with a cigarette. Chesley argued that was all nothing, and he could convince the jury he was shot by the cops and fired back in self-defense.

"Except you didn't fire back at the cop who shot you," hissed Atwater, who was losing it altogether. "You shot someone who didn't even have her gun out!"

That, thought Thaddeus, *is my closing argument*.

Then Chesley threatened his lawyer. He would sue him if he didn't call him to testify. He handed his lawyer a letter written on jailhouse stationery demanding that he be allowed to testify. He said the jail had taken a copy of the letter and kept it on file as an official letter from an inmate to his lawyer. Undaunted, Atwater called for a ten-minute recess in the trial, which the judge granted. The defense lawyer immediately went to the clerk's official file and checked for letters. He was stunned. Chesley had, indeed, written him the exact letter, and it had made its way into the court's official case file. Now Atwater had no choice. Chesley would testify.

Thaddeus was elated. His questions for Chesley, he told Turquoise, "Are etched in stone. Every law student to eighty-year-old lawyer knows what I'll be asking about prior bad acts.'"

Before the recess was up, Atwater had requested and gotten a conference with the judge in chambers. He wanted to present an oral motion, he warned Thaddeus, to bar any questions being put to the defendant about prior bad acts when he testified.

Thaddeus and Atwater disappeared into the judge's chambers. There, they found Judge Kenyon wearing her black robe, her court reporter waiting with her machine and tripod at the ready. Chesley was taken there, as required by law. Now, two burly deputies watched over him.

"Your Honor," Atwater began in a voice pegged with neediness, "Kenny Chesley wants to testify. It's against all my advice, but he's written a demand letter to me and I cannot stop him from taking the stand. But, as his lawyer, it is incumbent on me to request the court bar any and all questions the state might wish to ask my client against any bad acts. The reason I believe this motion should be allowed is two-fold.

"First, Kenny has been charged with the murder of Maryjane Dillon. But that case is a strangulation case. Those allegations against him have no congruity with the allegations of shooting a gun in this case. So counsel should not be allowed to go into those very disconnected events.

"Second, and more important, is that this case deserves to be decided on the facts. And the facts at this late time in the case demand we decide whether Kenny rightly or wrongly believed he was about to be executed and fired a bullet at Safari Frye because he believed she was gunning for him. That's the whole case, right there. The case shouldn't, then, be colored with an immaterial and irrelevant strangulation allegation that isn't remotely connected to the kind of bad act the state alleges in our case.

"For these reasons, we move the court silence Mr. Murfee on any and all questions concerning prior bad acts. Thank you."

Judge Kenyon nodded at Thaddeus. "Counsel?"

"You know, Judge, hearing Mr. Atwater's argument reminds me that some defense lawyers think the worst thing that can happen to their client in a courtroom is for the jury to get to know them. If that was such a terrible thing, what are they hiding? In our case, what they're hiding is evidence of Mr. Chesley's degree of depravity. He not only strangled Maryjane Dillon, he also burned her daughter, aged twelve, with a cigarette on three places along her arm. It's that kind of depravity the jury needs to hear about in order to judge correctly just why, exactly, he happened to be parked along the street directly outside where he knew Safari would be exiting a hearing. Was it just coincidence? Maybe, just maybe, some unsophisticated juror might believe it was coincidence...until they hear about the strangulation and the incineration of a child's arm just because.

"The jury is entitled to know this man. To ask that they deliberate inside a vacuum isn't fair to the jury, and it sure as hell isn't fair to the victim, Safari Frye. This woman was sought out, followed, and attacked by a predator of the worst kind—the coward who shoots first when he thinks no one is watching."

Chesley, who was sitting in the room taking it all in—a burly deputy on all four sides of him—stared daggers at Thaddeus as he said this. If looks could have killed, Thaddeus would have been the first to go. But looks couldn't kill and, besides, Thaddeus wasn't running, and he wasn't turning his back on the guy. As he spat out the words about "the coward," he had looked Chesley dead in the eye and spoke slowly and steadily so the defendant didn't miss a syllable.

Then it was over, and the judge indicated she was ready to make a ruling.

"The Court has heard arguments of counsel, and the court is well-versed on the law of evidence both in California courts and the Ninth Circuit to such a degree that what I'm about to say falls on all four corners of the rule. The state, the District Attorney, is barred from asking or referring in any way to any other acts of the defendant other than those we've heard about in the evidence in this case thus far. Mr. Murfee, you are specifically barred from asking questions about Mr. Chesley's allegations of wrongdoing regarding both Maryjane Dillon and her daughter, Carrie Dillon. All other bad acts are likewise barred. There will be no questions, no commentary, and no inferences regarding the same. Specifically, Mr. Murfee, you shall instruct the victim that if she is recalled to the witness stand, she shall not make any such references either. Let us rejoin the jury in the courtroom. That is all."

There comes a time in every trial where the jury sits up straight, the steno pads are set aside, and the ink pens are capped. That time came the moment LJ Atwater announced he was calling Kenneth Chesley to the witness stand. The jury didn't want to miss a word.

Chesley, dressed yet another day in his ill-fitting gray suit and black tie, stood forlornly before the clerk and swore to tell the truth. While the suit was ill-fitting, it also resembled the kind of suit a meek back-room accountant might wear to work, lending Chesley that same air of meek and retiring. Thaddeus considered that such an air might be exactly what Atwater was trying for. The man left nothing to chance, of course, including the very suit of clothes his client would wear to court.

Chesley sat down in the witness chair and avoided even a glance at the jury. His eyes were fastened on the floor just in front of counsel table, and there they remained until Atwater launched into his first question.

"Tell us your full and complete name."

"Kenneth Myram Chesley."

"Mr. Chesley, where do you live?"

"Right now? In jail."

A murmur among the jury. Then the attorney continued.

"On or about October nineteenth, were you parked along C Street in San Diego about noon?"

"Yes."

"In your Toyota Corolla?"

"Yes."

"What year is that car?"

"2004."

"Why were you parked there?"

"My wheels were wobbling. I was getting ready to tighten lug nuts with my tire iron."

"Had you tightened any lug nuts before the shooting?"

"No."

"Tell us what happened."

"I was looking in my trunk for a tire iron when I spied Detective Frye out of the corner of my eye. I could see her spot me and go for her gun, so I pulled my own gun out of the trunk to defend myself. At the very second I heard a gunshot, I reacted and fired a bullet myself. I wasn't looking at anyone special. Just pulled the trigger. It was a stupid thing to do, but the gunshot I heard just scared me to death and I overreacted."

"Were you aiming your gun at Safari Frye?"

"No, sir. I wasn't aiming at anyone."

"So the gun just went off?"

"Best I can tell, the gun—I mean the bullet—hit exactly where I was looking. That's all that makes sense to me. I was looking at her, watching her go for her gun, when the police shot me. The shot in my shoulder made me shoot. That's the honest-to-God truth of the whole thing right there. I didn't want to, but they shot me, and I just reacted."

"All right, I think that's all the questions I have right now."

Good, thought Thaddeus, *smart fellow, keeping it short and sweet.*

Thaddeus immediately began, "You say she looked at you when she came out of the building?"

"Right at me, yes, sir."

"Why would she look at you?"

"I—I don't know."

"Did you know her from before?"

"Did I know her? No."

"Did she know you?"

"Objection! The witness can't possibly know who she knew."

Over her glasses, Judge said, "Sustained. Move along, counsel, remembering my admonition."

"There was a look of recognition?"

"She recognized me, yes."

"Where would she have known you from?"

"We saw each other around. I mean, I know lots of the police in La Jolla where I live."

"Why would you know the police there?"

"I—I—"

"Objection. Admonition!" shouted Atwater.

"Counsel, please move along." Judge Kenyon gave Thaddeus "the eye," like *don't push it.*

Chesley then added, "She arrested me before."

There. It was done. Chesley had just strangled himself with his own words. Thaddeus took his time.

"She arrested you where, in La Jolla?"

"Yes."

"Did she take you to jail?"

"She took me to jail and booked me."

"How did you feel about that?"

By now, Atwater had thrown his hands up. His own client had blurted out the one thing Atwater had fought so hard to keep out of the jury's hearing when Chesley said, "She arrested me before." Because that opened all doors, and Thaddeus walked right through them. Now he bore in even harder.

Chesley's face had turned a blotchy red. "How did I feel about her arresting me? I hated it."

"Did you hate her?"

"I wasn't happy."

"That wasn't my question. Did you hate her?"

"I tried not to, but it sure as hell pissed me off."

"So you followed her to City Hall and waited there to shoot her?"

"Whoa, mister, no one was waiting to shoot anyone."

"You say. How about the fact you had a gun in the trunk you just happened to have wide open?"

"Like I said, I was working on my car. I normally carry a gun in my trunk in case I break down out in the boonies."

"Was the gun in a holster?"

Thaddeus knew it wasn't. No holster had been found.

"No."

"Just a gun free and loose in your trunk, no holster? Was that so you could grab it up and shoot Detective Frye as soon as you saw her march forth?"

"No. I mean, I just carry it there. No meaning."

Then he asked the question every juror wanted to hear. "What did she arrest you for?"

Atwater tried, but his heart wasn't in it. "Objection. Admonition."

"Overruled, the defendant himself opened the door. Please answer, Mr. Chesley."

Chesley cleared his throat before, "What was the question?"

"What did she arrest you for?"

"For killing my girlfriend."

"Did you kill your girlfriend?"

"Do I have—? Judge, do I have to talk about that case? Didn't you just tell us in your office he couldn't ask me about that?"

"Just answer the question, Mr. Chesley," said the judge very low-key and matter-of-fact. Everyone's favorite horse was out of the barn now.

"What was the question?"

"Did you kill your girlfriend?"

"I did not."

"Did you burn the arm of her little girl with your cigarette?"

"I did not."

"If the twelve-year-old daughter of Maryjane Dillon says you held her down and burned her arm in three places with your cigarette, would she be lying? Is that what you're telling this jury?"

"I don't know if she'd be lying. Hell, I don't even know her."

"You don't know Carrie, age twelve?"

"No."

"You don't deny living with Maryjane for a time, do you?"

"Do I deny it? No, I don't deny it."

"You don't deny that she had a twelve-year-old daughter named Carrie living with her, do you?"

"No, I don't deny it."

"But you do deny burning her with a cigarette?"

"I deny that. It's a damn lie."

"Mr. Chesley, do you smoke cigarettes?"

"Yes."

"Did you smoke in Maryjane's house?"

"No—yes."

"But you didn't burn Carrie with one of your cigarettes?"

"No."

"If I bring her to court and show you the burns where she's going to need plastic surgery, would you still say you didn't do it?"

"It's a damn lie."

"And you didn't murder Carrie's mother by strangling her with a curtain cord. That's a lie, too?"

"They're all lies."

"And you didn't lie in wait to kill Safari Frye because you were in a rage at her?"

"No, sir."

"You just happened to be stopped and parked in the one spot in the city where she would be walking that day?"

"It just happened. Stuff happens."

The jury got it. There was no need to continue.

"That's it," Thaddeus told the judge. "I have no further questions for this—this person."

Chesley then stood.

"Defense rests." Atwater was already shuffling papers together on his desk.

Thaddeus took a minute to confer with Turquoise.

She insisted, "We have a chance to hit Chesley with testimony about his role in Vicki Pelham's case."

"I'm sure he won't let us go into Maryjane's case again. But I need one more against him. If I could get to Vicki Pelham's case, I'd have him in prison for thirty years."

"Put me on the stand. Ask me about other cases. Let me see where I can go with that."

"Hair and fibers?"

"Exactly. I have reports. You've seen them."

"Will do."

Thaddeus stood and addressed Judge Kenyon. "The state has one rebuttal witness. The state calls Turquoise Murfee to the witness stand."

A rebuttal witness was one who was called to refute what a witness had said during the other side's case.

Here, the rebuttal witness, Turquoise, would be called by the prosecution to provide contradictory evidence of the accused's character and would testify that the person was violent, bad tempered, and abusive.

Fifteen minutes later, they were back in session with Judge Kenyon presiding. Thaddeus announced, for the jury's sake, he was calling Turquoise Murfee to the stand. She went forward, raised her hand and was sworn, then he asked the preliminaries—name, address, employment, duration, and so on. Then he went after what he'd called her for.

"Now, you have monitored the San Diego Police Department's investigation of Kenneth Chesley and Maryjane Dillon?"

"I have."

"Describe the case."

"Objection," cried Atwater. "Seeks to impeach with evidence the court has barred. Repetitive."

"Sustained. We've been there, Mr. Murfee. Move along."

Thaddeus asked, "Anything else?"

"Yes, there is the Vicki Pelham murder case. A link between that crime and Kenneth Chesley has also been found."

"Same objection!"

"Overruled. Please continue."

"Please tell us about that."

"Vicki Pelham was murdered in her upstairs den. It is connected to her bathroom. She had evidently just finished her bath when she was attacked in her bathroom. She managed to make it into her den and almost out the door to the hall before she was stabbed to death and died. The den was carpeted. The Police Department took fiber samples out of her carpet. Just as a matter of doing due diligence, the carpet inside Mr. Chesley's Corolla automobile was examined in the crime lab. That carpet was found to contain fibers from Vicki Pelham's den carpet. But that's not all. The police crime lab then tested Vicki's carpet and found fibers from the carpet in Mr. Chesley's Corolla. He's been tied to that murder in two ways then. A workup on his knife is underway at this time for blood, DNA, and fluids, but we don't have those test results yet."

"So Kenneth Chesley is implicated in two murders that occurred in La Jolla, California?"

"That is correct. He has been indicted for the Dillon murder. The Pelham case is still under investigation, but I understand from my sources that another indictment is coming Mr. Chesley's way."

"This is the same Kenneth Chesley who gunned down Safari Frye?"

"The same man, yes."

"The same man who is now claiming the detective was planning on shooting him so he shot her first?"

"That's the same man, yes."

"Thank you, Ms. Murfee. Your Honor, that's all I have and that's all the rebuttal the state has to offer."

"Your witness, Mr. Atwater."

There was a moment of silence before Atwater answered, "No questions."

The judge took over. "Very well. Ladies and gentlemen, this concludes the testimony in this case. We'll now stand in recess the rest of today while the court settles jury instructions with the lawyers. Court will resume in the morning at nine a.m. with the closing arguments of counsel for both sides. We're adjourned."

Chapter 43

The Sunday before the Chesley case ended, Reginald Pelham paid a visit to Thaddeus Murfee. They were sitting in Thaddeus's temporary office off his hotel room and had just been served a carafe of coffee. The server finished pouring and left the two men alone.

"So," said Thaddeus, "how are things going for you since poor Vicki's death?"

"That's one thing I want to update you on," said Pelham. "It turns out her heirs are her siblings, a younger sister and her older brother, Everett Penstone."

"Butchy's dad?"

Pelham nodded. "Yup. He and Butchy and the rest of Boyz 'N Luv have been living at our place for the best of six months."

"What is everyone trying to grab?"

Pelham answered Thaddeus's question with him asking, "They want her estate, which is one-half of my assets."

"That should make them happy, certainly," said Thaddeus. "I expect you're not at all happy about that."

"Not at all, especially after all I did for Everett and the boys. But, hell, he's a good guy. I just would've never expected it." Reggie stopped to take a sip of coffee and then, "I'd like you to review their offer to settle. My divorce lawyer is at a loss about how to proceed. They're after SkoolDaze, Thaddeus. One-half of SkoolDaze."

"Which you obviously don't want to give up. Is there any chance of a like-kind exchange? I'm talking money and assets in an amount equal to one-half the value of SkoolDaze?"

"That's out. I've talked to them. They say they're convinced SkoolDaze is only going to increase in value, and they want in on that. No, they want SkoolDaze stock, not other assets or money, not an equivalency."

"Incidentally, I sent you Turquoise's testimony from the Chesley trial. Did you look that over?"

"I did. I was shocked to learn about the fibers between Chesley's car and Vicki's carpet. And vice-versa. The detectives hadn't told me yet. Wow."

"I know. They're doing a fine workup there. Hats off to SDPD."

"They sure are." Reggie stared out the window at the ocean beyond. "Ya know, Chesley has been around the house before. He's met the boys there a couple of times to go over tour stuff. I never took much of a liking to him then. A bit of a greasy fellow, if you know what I mean."

Thaddeus nodded. "That I do. He's not a good man."

"Well, I hope they get the bastard, and you can put him away for life. Hell, if California had the death penalty, I'd be all for that for him taking Vicky's life."

When Reggie started to tear up, Thaddeus tried to divert him. "So what are you thinking?"

Reggie inhaled a long breath and then exhaled in a quick snort. "Thaddeus, would you consider making up a plan to settle with these folks? I just cannot have them in my business, mucking things up. I don't mind paying them what Vicki owned, but I don't want them coming into my business with their stock ownership and trying to serve on the board of directors or elect one of their own as an officer. They might even oust me if they get a few other stockholders on their side of the ledger. I can't think of any who would do that, not so far, but what if we have a rocky year? Then what happens to me?"

"I'd agree to take a look. Hell, I'll even do it for you, but there's a price."

"How much?"

"I want two-hundred-and-fifty-thousand dollars put into an irrevocable trust for Carrie Dillon. She's the little girl whose arm was burned by Chesley. She's going to need plastic surgery, and she needs a college fund. Or a fund to start her own business, whatever."

"Done. When can you start?"

"You didn't let me finish."

Reggie raised his eyebrows. "Okay."

"I also want you to hire Safari Frye as SkoolDaze's Chief of Cybersecurity. She's a fast study, and she needs work since she was paralyzed. Otherwise she's looking at a lifetime of lesser jobs. I'd like to see her get a chance with you. Your job pays her two-fifty a year and a master's program in cybersecurity."

"Now you're driving a hard bargain."

"Not really. These are things a guy like you will do with

his mad money during the year anyway. Might as well keep it local. Two ladies who deserve it."

"All right, Thaddeus. Tell Safari to call me. She can begin whenever she's ready."

"She's ready now. I'll have your plan back to you in forty-eight hours. Stay by your phone."

"Roger that. I'll be waiting for your call."

After Pelham's departure, Thaddeus began making his notes to settle the case. He was certain he could draft a plan that would have Vicki's heirs surrender their common stock in return for equal benefits plus. He was lost in thought and study for the next several hours, using the SkoolDaze balance sheet and income statements to make his case for settlement. When he finished up, he was sure he had a plan the heirs would jump at. Then he began reducing it to writing, a settlement agreement, and release of liability that would restore Reggie's business to him and make the heirs happy they were alive.

Chapter 44

At the end of the last day of trial, Thaddeus argued to the jury that Chesley shot someone who was no threat to him. He argued that Chesley was lying in wait for Safari.

Atwater argued self-defense. He argued his client was startled by the detective going for her gun and then heard the gunshot and fired back at the detective, who he thought had shot him.

Thaddeus argued she had no plans to shoot him at all, only returning to her car after a hearing. Atwater argued the hearing was about her right to continue as a police officer. Thaddeus argued the sexual harassment hearing was a red herring and had no bearing whatsoever on what happened when she went outside.

The jury was out almost three hours. But in the end, they returned a guilty verdict. Chesley was taken away in handcuffs.

Atwater held no after-court press conference. He slunk

away in a black Escalade and wasn't seen on TV again that day or the next.

Chapter 45

Juvenile court began early, seven-thirty a.m. This was so the working mothers and fathers would miss only the first hour or two of work. Juvie cases rarely lasted more than sixty minutes because the psychiatric and psychological reports, case manager reports, and guardian ad litem recommendations were all in the judge's hands at least a day before the hearing, and the hearing would consist only of argument, no evidence taken. Most judges had their minds fairly well made up before entering the courtroom. In Carrie Dillon's case, however, it was more complicated: the foster mom, a former police detective, had been severely injured at work and was now disabled. Would that impact—and how hard—her ability to serve as a twelve-year-old's foster mother? Or should the judge even give it any notice?

Denise Gordon, Judge of the Juvenile Court, was mindful of these things as she took the bench and called the hearing to order. It was two weeks after the Chesley conviction. Safari and Thaddeus were in court that early morning, preparing to make their case.

There was one troubling facet of the case, a twist that had Judge Gordon on edge. The case worker's report included reference to the fact the foster mother was still medicating with strong pain relievers for the ongoing pain from the shooting. The caseworker claimed the drugs left the mother confused and sometimes "bewildered" by even the most minor of tasks, such as making a call on her iPhone. Or allowing the Keurig to quit its brew cycle before removing the receptacle so new coffee didn't run out on the overflow. Things like that, which the caseworker had actually witnessed herself. She'd had to posit that the foster mother might be unable to function at some moment when the child's needs demanded a quick and proper response—say a fall from her bicycle, a kitchen accident, a sudden illness. A mother had to always be available, the report went on to remind Judge Gordon. There could ill afford to be momentary lapses of the ability to provide care as needed.

Judge Gordon couldn't argue with that. But was the possibility of diminished judgment from the pain pills such that the foster placement should be re-done, the child moved out of what was clearly a nurturing environment? If so, what of the emotional damage to the child? What of her needs? What about her bond with her foster mother?

"Ladies and gentlemen," said Judge Gordon, "we're now in session on the case of Carrie Dillon. As we know, she was previously placed with Safari Frye, a certified foster mother with an excellent history of providing foster care and complying with placement requirements and child needs. We also know Ms. Frye has, since the placement, suffered a terrible work injury as a detective in this city.

That injury has left her partially disabled, incapable of moving about except with a wheelchair.

"But there's another aspect to this case since the injury. The report has it that the foster mother now requires regular medication with pain relievers that render her, at times, susceptible to lapses in judgment and even motor ability so that the simplest of tasks can turn on a dime into insurmountable problems for her.

"No party, no official, regrets this development so much as the court. Yet, my sworn duty as a judge, and especially as a juvenile judge, is to look first and always at the welfare of the minor. There is no other duty the court owes, actually, other than the minor's best interests. And so, with this duty balanced against the foster mother's new challenges, I would like to open this hearing to statements from all interested parties. We will begin with Ellie Myers, MA, the caseworker. Ms. Myers, may we hear from you now?"

A middle-aged woman with fleshy arms and a red face took to her feet and leaned against her hands placed firmly on the table before her. She shook her head then reached and rubbed her neck with one hand. Then she removed her eyeglasses and closed her eyes. "It is the most burdensome moment of all, in my work, when a solid, happy placement is suddenly threatened. Yet, when it happens, each time I have to set aside my personal feelings and consider what changed circumstances have come to my attention that need to be addressed. In this case, Safari Frye is one of the finest placements I have for a resource. She has always been gracious, loving, helpful, and fully attentive to the special needs of the children I have placed with her, particularly those requiring lots of foster mother time spent waiting in doctors' offices, child psychologists' offices, parent-teacher meetings, and the jillion-and-one other time sucks that foster parenting means. Safari comes in number one here. But now, with this injury, as I said in my report, there is this overlay of medications. Medications that have side effects that are never in a child's best interests. Here is where the needs of the child bump up against the realities of the foster parent. The two don't mix. There is now presented the daily possibility of some unseen incident or moment of serious need that the foster mother won't be able to meet. She won't be able to handle something because of her medications. Ordinarily, I would take the long view of this. But here, the long view is very long indeed. Safari's own doctors cannot predict how long she'll need these medications. I know because I've visited with each and every one of them.

"So I am sad to report to the court that the state's position must be a request for a change in placement. At least until the foster mother's twenty-four/seven freedom from drugs is guaranteed once again. How long might that take? We just don't know, so I must suggest we look for a new, permanent placement for Carrie Dillon."

Thaddeus looked down at Safari, who was one with her wheelchair and her pain. There was nothing he could say to console her. As he watched, her eyes washed over with tears until they were brimming and then running down her face. She raised her hand, as if asking a schoolteacher for permission to speak.

Said Judge Gordon, "Ms. Frye? I was going to call on you last, but you can go now if you wish."

"Just let me say how sorry I am. I've let the court down. Even worse, I've let Carrie down. The little girl I love like my own. Or maybe more. I would give everything I'll ever have just to get to spend my life with her. We're one, Judge. you know what I mean?"

"I do."

"Well, then I get shot. Out of the clear blue sky, I'm lying on the sidewalk, looking high overhead, and all I can think about is my little girl. I knew, lying there, that I was going to lose her. I just knew my life had gone terribly wrong.

"In law enforcement, we don't know from one shift to the next if our lives are going to suddenly change. We can be happy in our jobs, in our homes, playing league basketball two nights a week and surfing on the good days, then all of a sudden be married to a wheelchair. Then everything and everyone just gets up from the table and leaves. It's just over. That's what happened to me. I had my daughter, had my basketball league, had my surfboard, had my Harley, and a job I loved. Now, phhht! just gone."

"Do you have any answers for your dilemma with the drugs, Ms. Frye?" asked the judge in a soft, dear voice.

"Only one. I no longer take those drugs. From this minute forward, I do not take pain relievers or any other mind-altering medications. I cannot lose this child."

The judge leaned back. "How wise is that, really? Your pain level must be excruciating to be on such strong medications."

"Wise? It's not wise at all. But it's necessary, and it's something I can do. I have no choice. I would ask that the court leave the placement as it is and that the caseworker, Charlotte, come to my house every day to check on me. I will be clean as a whistle, no drugs, no funny thinking."

"Yes, but what will you do for the pain?"

"I will do para-yoga. I will do mind control. I will cry until it passes. But I will not allow it to affect my thinking, my ability to take care of Carrie. That it will not do."

"Ms. McNamara?"

Charlotte McNamara stood and spread her hands. "I

would like nothing better than to leave the placement unchanged. I would be willing to do a series of daily check-ins with the foster mother over the next several weeks to see where this goes. But I reserve the right to remove the child without notice if I see even the slightest indication the foster mother is impaired by drugs. And there won't be a second chance. I'm sorry, Safari, but that's how it has to be."

"I understand," said Safari. "You won't regret this."

"Very well," said Judge Gordon. "We're going to put the Notice of Changed Circumstances on the back burner for twenty-one days. At that time, we will meet again and see where we are. We stand in recess."

Safari reached and touched Thaddeus's cuff. "Let the others leave. Give me a minute, please."

He stood back, crossed his arms, and waited. The room cleared, including the bailiff, who was the last to leave. She didn't turn out the lights on her way out. She understood.

At long last, Safari raised her head and sat back in her chair, squaring her shoulders. "Okay, it passed."

"That bad, huh?"

"That bad."

"What did you do?"

"Talked to a God I no longer believe in and said I'd do anything."

"Well?"

She shrugged. "It's passed, so let's leave it up to Him when He'll call in the debt. We can leave now."

Chapter 46

Of course he would have to take the California State Bar Exam as there was no reciprocity. Which meant he would have to hit the books and re-learn the law, this time in another state than Illinois or Arizona or Colorado, the states where he'd once been licensed. But it didn't matter how long it took to earn the California law license because Thaddeus was in no hurry, anyway. Sure of the commitment he was making, and sure he was ready for the Southern California experience, Thaddeus rented a suite of offices in downtown La Jolla overlooking the pristine blue Pacific Ocean. His offices were above a bank and consisted of the entire floor, "Talk about optimistic," he told his wife. "I've taken over an entire floor." Room to grow, she told him. Christine—the wife— was all in with the idea of moving to California. She was burned out with the cowboy west of Arizona and Colorado and ready for the golden sunsets of SoCal.

And so he had his office ready for the meeting between Reggie Pelham and the heirs of Victoria Pelham. Thaddeus had promised he would create a settlement plan the heirs would jump at, and he felt like he had.

They arrived on a Friday morning, looking anxious and somewhat greedy to Thaddeus' practiced eye. Which was a good thing for it meant they were ready to settle and get their hands on the loot they stood to inherit from Vicki. *Bring it on*, said their eyes.

They were all represented by one attorney, a woman named Madison Reyes. She hailed from Bel Air in Los Angeles and was reputed to be the LA area's top estate lawyer. While her specialty was estates, Thaddeus' opinion was they needed more of a transactional lawyer rather than an estate lawyer but, hey, it wasn't his call. They shook hands, gathered around a football-field-size table in Thaddeus' conference room, and tried to remain collected and cool while coffee and juice was served.

Then Thaddeus smiled and raised his hand to speak. He was seated with Reggie Pelham across the table from the heirs, two of them versus a half dozen of the others, counting the heirs, the lawyer, and her staff.

"One-point-two-billion in common stock remains to be distributed," said Thaddeus, "after costs and legal fees and the rest of it as detailed on the settlement sheet you've all received. One half of that one-point-two remains with Reggie, being the sum of six-hundred-and-twenty-million and the same amount goes to you folks, the heirs of Vicki Pelham.

"The hangup has been the valuation and distribution of the company known as SkoolDaze. SkoolDaze is, of course, the brainchild of Reggie. It is a viable company, growing by leaps and bounds, and Vicki owned one-half. Now you, the heirs, stand to inherit that one-half through Vicki's last will and testament. So, congratulations, you're all instant multimillionaires. Good for you. Vicki's ownership, incidentally, is the common stock of the company, one million shares in all. It is to be divided in equal parts between Vicki's two sisters and one brother.

"The stock is the key issue," said Thaddeus. He took a drink of his coffee and continued. "The heirs, and Ms. Reyes on their behalf, don't want to give up the stock because the company it owns is growing by leaps and bounds. On the other hand, Reggie wants his stock back because he wants control of the company he created and babied along to what it is today. He wants and needs to be able to turn on a dime without the need for shareholders' meetings and shareholders' consents for whatever twists and turns he might like to make. Completely understandable, as Reggie is an entrepreneur and these are people you want to give free rein to and turn them loose to make their millions and sometimes, like here, billions. So what to do? How give Reggie his freedom to operate and still protect the heirs in their desire to remain hitched to a shooting star. That's the question. That's what I've been brought in on the case to solve, and I think I have.

"My solution is simple and elegant. The heirs will receive non-voting preferred stock that owns the right to share fifty percent in the net earnings of SkoolDaze according to its annual report filed yearly. SkoolDaze is not a publicly traded company, so the report is filed and available only inside the corporation itself. But it will carry the same weight and have the same accuracy and considerations as one filed under SEC rules. In other words, you will be able to rely on its accuracy and its numbers will be easily available to your accountant for confirmation. So there you are, you will be owners with the right to receive fifty percent of the earnings of SkoolDaze. In this manner, you remain hitched to a rising star as you would as owners of the company's common stock, but you give up voting rights. You give Reggie Pelham the right to make money for you. You retain your one-half ownership in his genius and ingenuity and creativity. It's a win-win. Any questions?"

Madison Reyes, the attorney for the heirs, had received a copy of the proposed settlement several days before. Reportedly, she was onboard with the idea. Now all that remained were the details but that would be done easy enough. She said, "I'm recommending my clients accept your solution, Mr. Murfee. There are tax consequences to receiving continuing income, but that's better than no tax consequences because no income. And, most important of all, there are no tax consequences on the exchange of common stock for preferred. And as I understand it, the heir can sell out their rights at any time for the face value of their shares and take their money elsewhere for investment. So if they don't like your deal, they will be cashed out and paid off and can go elsewhere and everyone is happy. Is that correct?"

"Absolutely correct," Thaddeus said. "Reggie will buy you out at any time."

"And there are other details to be hammered out."

"We're happy all around. I'm going to recommend my clients accept the deal. I've discussed with them all and there is one-hundred percent acceptance. They're onboard."

"Excellent," said Thaddeus. "We'll hammer out the details over the next couple of weeks and then make distributions to the heirs in equal shares of the YTD earnings of the company. This is to show good faith, as I set out in my plan."

"Everyone can buy a new house or two," Madison Reyes laughed.

"Whatever they choose," Thaddeus agreed. "Now, I've drawn up settlement letters that indicate agreement in principle to my plan. Let's all sign and we'll be done here today."

The letters were passed around and signatures attached. Then it was done.

Everyone shook hands and the heirs with their lawyer left the building.

Thaddeus, alone with Reggie Pelham, breathed a long sigh of relief.

"And all you have to do is hire Safari and set up Carrie's irrevocable trust."

"Done on both counts. She starts Monday next. Carrie is funded and in the hands of my bank."

"Excellent. So our business is done."

"Except for one thing. I'd like you to come onboard as general counsel to SkoolDaze."

Thaddeus smiled. "No can do. I don't want to work that hard."

"No need to work that hard. There will be a full staff and all the trimmings."

"It's certainly inviting."

"Think about it."

"I will. I will think about it."

The men shook hands, their business finished. Then Pelham left the office, left the building.

Now Thaddeus was alone in his new office. He began turning off lights and took one last look around before he climbed inside the elevator. He shook his head.

"What have I done?" he said to no one.

Chapter 47

Turquoise was waiting for him downstairs in their new car rental. It was a Mustang convertible. Now that the Murfee family had decided to take a break from cowboys and the West, they decided they would go all-in SoCal. So the Mustang it was.

She was waiting with the top down, and when Thaddeus hopped into the passenger seat, he gently reminded her about sunscreen. Turquoise smiled at her dad and, without a word, merged into La Jolla traffic. They didn't have far to go, only over to Safari's apartment, but to Thaddeus, it seemed to take forever. He couldn't wait to see her face.

They pulled up on the street in front of her complex and got out. On the sidewalk already waited Safari's sister, Elaine, Safari's friend Janet and her young son, Jamison, and Safari's ex-boyfriend, Max. It was Safari's twenty-seventh birthday. When asked previously, she had turned down all offers to celebrate, even to go out to dinner. So Thaddeus had arranged for the party to go to her.

Max had his guitar case to supply the music, Janet held a homemade cake, and Turquoise held a bag with presents.

After hellos and how-are-you's, Thaddeus led them to Safari's ground-floor apartment and rang the bell. As usual, Carrie answered the door, but this time with a big grin on her face. She was in on the surprise, too. She'd had to make sure Safari would be home, and Thaddeus had asked her to clean the house and get it ready. He didn't want Safari to be embarrassed in any way. He knew how hard it was for her to even do the simplest housework like dusting and vacuuming.

Carrie opened the door wide and yelled out, "Mom, someone is here to see you."

From a room down the hall, they could hear, "Be right there."

A moment later, Safari wheeled into the living room, and at the sight of everyone standing there, brought her chair to a fast halt. Her mouth hung open as she traded looks with each of them in turn. "What's going on?" she asked to no one in particular.

"On the count of three," said Thaddeus. "One, two...three!"

"Happy birthday!" they shouted as one.

Turquoise threw a bit of confetti into the air, and Carrie and Jamison blew on cheap cardboard party horns that made an obnoxious squawking sound, which made everyone laugh.

Except Safari, who still didn't move or say anything.

Thaddeus stepped forward and gave her a hug. "Happy birthday, Safari."

Then Turquoise stepped up and gave her a hug, followed by Elaine, Carrie, Janet, Jamison, and Max last. He knelt down beside her and lingered in his hug until she finally hugged back.

When at last he released her, she asked him, "What are you doing here?"

He smiled. "I'm here for your birthday, ya dickless wonder."

She finally laughed at that. "So you heard, huh?"

He glanced at Elaine, who grimaced. "Oops."

But Safari just laughed again. And that made Thaddeus happy. She was slowly coming around to her visitors after the initial shock.

Safari snagged Max's hand and asked again, "No, really, why are you here?"

He kissed her knuckles. "Because I want to be with you. I'm still in love with you."

Thaddeus could see the tears welling in her eyes and how Safari tried to harden herself so they wouldn't fall. "Why would you want to be with me now?"

"What? You think I'm the kind of guy who cares if you are in a wheelchair? That's not my style."

Safari chewed on her lip as if she still couldn't believe it. But when Max leaned in and gave her a hard kiss on the mouth, a heartfelt smile broke through and, yes, a couple of tears finally fell.

"Okay, enough of the tears," said Janet, "Let's eat cake!"

With that, everyone cheered, especially young Jamison. What kid didn't think cake was the best thing about a party? They all gathered around the kitchen table and sang "Happy Birthday" once the candles were lit. Then Turquoise and Elaine sliced and dished out the cake for everyone.

"Open your presents!" Carrie yelled. "I can't wait to see what you got."

Safari still had most of her cake left but gave in to Carrie's pleading. Thaddeus could see the love she had for the child all over her face.

Safari waved her hand at the bag that sat at the end of the table. "All right, hand 'em over."

"Mine first," said Elaine. So Safari started with her sister's, who had gotten Safari a new outfit, a blue shirt with lace at the neckline and a matching skirt. Safari smirked at Elaine. "I never wear skirts."

Elaine only smiled back at her. "Well, there's a first time for everything."

"You're right." Safari held up the skirt to her waist. "There sure is."

Then she went on to open the gift from all the Murfee family. Thaddeus had picked out a high-tech Smartwatch that he knew would help her in her new job. Janet and Jamison got Safari a quilted wheel pouch for her chair so she could load it up with everything she might need for work, her phone, paperwork, books, or water bottle.

And Max... Well, Max—in love as he was—Max got her a ring.

Chapter 48

The door to room 9 opened and out walked Dusty Zamboa. The Boys 'N Luv crew had shifted from Uncle Reggie's house to the Pantai Inn, a smaller, more intimate setting, one that didn't associate the young men with violent crimes—the shooting of Joan and then the slice and dice of Victoria Pelham. Their new PR company had suggested as much while they finished recording, hoping the distance would remove the boys from the negative spotlight.

Dusty went next door to number 10 and knocked. A small blond woman in a bikini and a necklace of seashells answered. She was Jonny's latest and was clinging to him stronger than a starfish to coral. Dusty didn't understand why Jonny kept her around. She was just a slut like the rest of them. He couldn't even remember her name. Diana or Denise or something.

But he'd play nice. "Can I get Kenny's car keys from you?"

She shrugged. "I guess so, but ya know the cops had it in custody. They might be watching it."

"I doubt that," said Dusty. "Not with Kenny in jail. They got who they wanted."

"Why do you use Kenny's car, anyway? It's not like you can't afford something a lot better. I don't get it."

"It's not for you to get." *Bitch*, Dusty thought. "Anyway, we're going on tour again so I don't need to pay to store a car. And it's not like Kenny is going to need it now."

"Too bad Kenny can't go. He loves Butchy and you guys. He loves being your roadie."

Dusty snorted. "Yeah, too bad."

She held out the keys, but just as he reached out to grab them, she yanked them back. "I might need to use it later."

Dusty's inner demon was about ready to explode. "Fine."

She smirked at him and tossed the keys before shutting the door in his face. He missed catching them so had to scoop them off the ground. If Blondie wasn't always glued to Jonny's side, she'd be next.

He walked into the parking area and unlocked the Corolla. He slid inside, his butt settling easily into the driver's seat. The car was like an old friend, musty and ancient, one he'd driven many times. Even the amber carpet was like an old friend. He reached down beneath the driver's seat and peeled back the carpet.

Pruning shears.

Still there. He picked them up and slipped them into his pants pocket. He looked at his own stub of a ring finger. "Ow," he said to the remembered pain.

Off he drove down the Pacific Coast Highway.

Where would he find her? In the parking lot of a 7-

Eleven? Perhaps walking along the beach? Or alone, in her bath, smelling the newest soaps? *Snip-snip.* The world was a delicious place.

He had only to dine.

Chapter 49

Their swimsuits were still damp as they lay in the sun beside the pool. Sunscreen was applied copiously and dark glasses blocked the UVs. Turquoise, from her lounger closest to the pool, reached and touched her father's arm.

"We've gotta talk," she said.

Without opening his eyes Thaddeus muttered, "Uh-huh?"

"It's about Vicki Pelham."

"I thought it might be sooner or later."

"Do you know?"

"I was never certain. There's just no motive for Chesley to kill her. What do you have?"

"It was Dusty."

"And how do we know this?"

"I followed him there that day."

"You have got to be kidding."

"No. He parked in the alley and went over the fence. I

waited down at the end. He wasn't gone ten minutes. Maybe only five."

"You're sure it was the day she died?"

"Sure? Of course I'm sure. I heard about it that night on the news."

"Why else would Dusty go over Pelham's fence. Of course you're sure. But why would Dusty murder Vicki?"

"You know why? She told him she'd seen better mascara on Macy's dummies than what he was wearing. She said it in front of his friends and it mortified him. It pissed him off. Butchy happened to mention it during my investigation."

"OMG. That was it? Mascara?"

She shrugged. "Anyway, I just thought you should know. But the bad part is that the cops can't make a case against him. He was driving the Corolla but it's registered to Chesley. They naturally thought it was Chesley who killed her."

"Why didn't you come forward?"

It was quiet at poolside for a minute. Only the shrieks of the kids in the pool were heard. Then, she spoke again. "I didn't come forward because you needed for it to be Chesley. You needed it to put him away on Safari's case. That's why I asked to be your rebuttal witness."

"Kid, we must be related."

Chapter 50

The highway south of La Jolla rose a hundred feet above the rocky coastline. Thaddeus was unfamiliar with the road. He only knew he wanted to be headed northbound and cross the centerline in the oncoming lane when the Corolla approached. Thanks to the workup done by Turquoise, Thaddeus had known for some time about the link between drummer Dusty Zamboa and Kenneth Chesley, the boy band's roadie. Now Thaddeus approached the first set of switchbacks and turned his headlights on high, though it was only noon.

Turquoise had called Dusty's cell. She had told him she was a fan dying to meet him and, funnily enough, he'd agreed to meet her, especially since it was an out-of-way place, somewhere a psychotic like Dusty could easily kill her. The address she'd given led Dusty to these switchbacks on this craggy hillside. Now, Turquoise's voice crackled in Thaddeus's earphone. "He just entered the switchbacks. He's alone."

Thaddeus was chugging around the second curve when

he spotted it, an old but very serviceable Corolla being driven by the drummer. "C'mon," Thaddeus breathed to himself, "swing out toward the edge. That's it—that's it—"

Thaddeus shied away from the centerline. The two vehicles passed in a blast of air, each continuing on his way.

Thaddeus pointed into the rearview mirror at Dusty's taillights. "I'm here now," he said. "And I'm after you."

Her voice crackled over the earphone. "Where do you want to eat tonight?"

"Safari's invited us over. She and Carrie are making fish tacos."

"I love fish tacos. Should we call mom and get her over?"

"I already called and told her our work was wrapped up. She's on her way."

"Are you seriously going to keep the La Jolla office?"

"Serious? As in, am I going to practice law here?"

"Yes."

"Yes, I'm serious. Mama Chris is bringing all the kids. Tomorrow we're house hunting while you watch the kids in the hotel pool."

"How many bedrooms?"

"There'll be room for you. If you want."

"I wasn't saying."

"Yes, Turquoise, you were saying. You're my kid, and I always want you nearby."

"I want to work for you."

"It might be boring."

Long pause.

"Right."

THE END

Next in the Thaddeus Murfee series

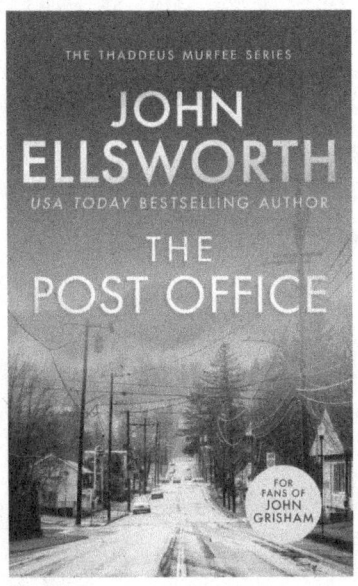

vinci-books.com/postoffice

This is the story of Rachel.

A young girl who needs to die.

Thaddeus takes on the case of Rachel, a young girl seeking the right to die with dignity. As medical options dwindle, Rachel and her family journey from California to Oregon, where they encounter Johann, a nurse with a dark past.

Turn the page for a free preview.

The Post Office - Preview

PROLOGUE

Herat Province, Afghanistan

The smoke was thick in the air, and the sounds of sirens bleating overwhelmed his senses. Johann Van Giersbergen covered his ears but realized he couldn't keep his balance like that as he waded through the rubble—cement, metal, and glass everywhere—looking for survivors. After uncovering his ears, the sirens penetrated his body, the sound thrumming through his veins. He coughed into his elbow, his eyes and nose watering.

Johann had been drinking tea with the other nurses at the hospital when the drone attack came out of nowhere. There'd been no warning, no rumors beforehand like there usually were before something big like this happened.

All the nurses had scattered to the village, doctors, too, to locate the victims, help anywhere they could.

"Save my baby!" a woman wailed in Arabic. The

woman in a full burqa knelt next to a tiny figure, gray with dust and half covered in debris.

Johann almost didn't hear the woman over the sounds of war. The sirens and people shouting, the deafening thunder of buildings in collapse. The wails and moans of those dying.

He quickly moved next to the woman who was rocking back and forth, her hands fluttering about as if she didn't know where to place them. Johann cleared a large slab of cement from the child's legs and then dusted away smaller pieces of wreckage. It was a young boy, no older than four, Johann guessed. He lifted the body gently and shouted for the woman to follow. His Arabic was excellent and the reason he'd been posted in Afghanistan with Doctors Without Borders.

The older woman struggled behind Johann, who was only 21, strong, healthy, and at the prime of his life. The posting to Afghanistan was the first job he took upon graduation from nursing school. He had meant to somehow payback for the education he had received. He led the woman back to the hospital, which luckily had gone unscathed in the attack. Men and women ran in and out of the building, some carrying an adult body between two or three of them.

Out of the worst smoke, Johann was able to get a better visual of the small child in his arms. He wasn't moving, no breath, and without having to take his pulse, Johann knew he was dead. The boy's dark lashes sat like dark half-moons on the cheeks, his small mouth in a slight frown. Johann couldn't tell the mother, couldn't be the one to bear such news, so he led her to the emergency room.

Inside, it was chaos. All the examination rooms were already full, so people sat and lay everywhere in the hallways and waiting room. Johann looked for his boss, an English doctor from Manchester, Dr. William Blake, and finally spotted him across the room.

Johann took the boy to him. With a barely discernible shake of his head, Johann handed the boy over to Blake. It was enough. Blake would understand. With the boy still in his arms, Blake told Johann, "Go. Find as many as you can and bring them back here. Quickly!"

Johann didn't hesitate but turned on his heel and weaved his way around bodies until he was at the emergency room doors. On their way in were two of Nangyalay's men with a young man, maybe twelve or thirteen years old, strung between them. One of the teenager's arms was missing, and he was bleeding profusely from the hole. Johann knew the boy would not make it. Johann bit his lip. By thirteen, Johann had already surfed most of the beaches along the California coast, had traveled to Europe on a family vacation, skied in the Rocky Mountains. This boy would have never known a life like that. But now, this Afghani boy would know no life at all.

Johann let them pass, but two other men from the Taliban followed right behind, another two Johann recognized as part of Nangyalay's command. They each carried young girls on their backs, holding the girls' arms around their own necks.

"Who made the strike?" Johann couldn't help but ask. All this pain, blood, and death! Who had created this?

The last man through the door smirked at Johann. "Who do you think?"

Johann pushed through the door and stopped to take in a few deep breaths. The air was just as bad outside as in. He stepped aside as two men with a makeshift stretcher carried an old man with a long gray beard. His leg was twisted unnaturally, but the man was still conscious, murmuring prayers with his hands clasped to his stomach.

Johann took a long look around at the horror of the drone strike. Then he bent to his work, the nurse doing what he could to save lives.

But he would remember it forever. He would never forget what he saw and heard that day. He would never forget the death that screamed down from the pale blue sky and the cries of the innocent.

He would never forget.

CHAPTER 1

Celena Murfee's birthday was Valentine's Day, and the party for the fifteen-year-old started at four o'clock. This allowed time for the partygoers to get home after school, change clothes, and pick up their presents for their friend.

Celena was Thaddeus and Christine Murfee's second eldest daughter after Turquoise who, like Celena, was adopted and held a special place in her parents' eyes. She was five-six and tall for her age, blue-eyed with flouncy blond hair that insisted on coming down across her forehead in a sweep no matter how hard she tried to keep it up. On the day of her birthday, her hair was pulled back in a ponytail to allow for the showing of her newly-pierced ears, four holes on the left, one on the right. Celena, a student of the clarinet, wore a turquoise and coral Southwestern Indian flute player figurine, the Kokopelli, in her right ear.

Thaddeus gave his daughter a Westphalian dressage horse for her birthday; his wife Christine gave her the gift of horse boarding and care at La Jolla Equestrian Center in the Tassajara Valley of the East Bay. Celena had already all but moved into her gelding's stable, spending hours with a curry brush and happy voice, getting to know her mount.

It was just after four when Celena's friends—mostly classmates—began arriving in carpools. It was an all-girls shindig, a sleepover since it was Friday night and no school the next day. Thaddeus was certain he'd be awake most of the night, lending a male referee's voice to Christine's pleas for less Jonas Brothers and more quiet time when some of the crowd wanted to actually sleep. Even if it was only just Christine and Thaddeus who did!

The west-facing family room opened onto the beach so there was a round of surfing to be followed by Thaddeus's charbroiled burgers on the grill and Christine's angel food chocolate cake, Celena's favorite. Thaddeus was one cut above a "poor" surfer, said Celena, who had picked up the sport very quickly, as had her brothers and sisters: Sarai 13, Parkus 12, Chad 12, and Missy 10. The surfing would be followed by a quick burger, then off to the stables for a twilight ride along the main trail. Then would come videos and music and late-night pizza.

Turquoise arrived home at five to help keep the peace. She shared a two-bedroom apartment with a young investigator from the San Diego District Attorney's Office, a woman about her own age. Turquoise and Dana had been spending a lot of time together outside of work, socializing with other colleagues and going to the pub or movies. Thaddeus was happy that she had friends outside of the family and had finally started living a little outside of work.

But Turquoise had given up one of her night's off to lend a youthful voice of authority to the melee and let Mom and Dad catch a few hours' sleep if possible.

Following the trail ride and snack, everyone gathered around the fire pit while Sarai led a sing-along with her guitar. Parkus and Chad pulled out drums and a bass guitar, and soon the place was rocking.

Just after ten, when the local custom was for the outdoor music to shut down, Thaddeus was emptying his coffee cup and preparing to go inside when he was approached by Rebecca Sundstrom, or Becca as she liked to be called, Celena's best friend. There had been a sorrow wrapped around her family ever since her older sister's leukemia had come roaring back from a period of remission. Becca's sister was now wasting away.

"Mr. Murfee," said Becca, "can I ask you a question?"

"Sure, Becca," he said, settling back into his patio chair, "what's up?"

"Rachel doesn't want to go on living."

"I'm so, so sorry to hear that. Bless her heart."

The girl shook her head. "Her pain is so bad—" Tears streamed down her cheeks, and she could barely speak. She drew a deep breath and continued, "The medicine quit working. It used to make her sleep and took away the pain. Now she says it doesn't help at all."

"How sad. If there's anything Chris and I can do…"

Becca stared at the floor, worrying her fingers together. "Maybe there is."

"What's that?"

"Rachel wants a doctor to help her end her life."

"Well, how old is Rachel?"

Becca looked up at him. "She's seventeen."

"What do your mom and dad say?"

"They say absolutely not. They say they'll find a doctor with stronger medicine. So, Rachel cries herself to sleep every night and wakes up and cries some more. In the daytime, it's even worse." Now Becca's body was shaking with sorrow and sobs.

Tears came to Thaddeus's own eyes as he fought to remain a good listener. "How can I help?"

"Maybe if you talked to my parents. They talk about you and Christine with admiration. They love that Celena and I are best friends. They were so glad when you moved to La Jolla and when Christine helped my dad's medical practice with its new forms. They might listen to you if it's both of you. Please help my sister leave this world and stop the pain."

The girl was drying her face now on her beach towel. She was wearing cutoffs and tennies and a Fender T-shirt. She looked cold. Thaddeus offered her a dry towel, but she waved it off. "Could you call them and talk? Celena says you can talk the birds out of the trees. Well, maybe you could talk my mom and dad into listening to Rachel. She's seventeen, but pain is killing her. That's what her doctor says."

"Are your parents religious?"

"Yes. Our religion doesn't believe in assisted life termination. That's the big problem for Rachel."

"Well, Becca, let me talk to Chris and see if we can get together with your folks. Do I have your permission to tell them you approached me and asked me to talk to them?"

"Yes, sir."

Thaddeus pulled out a chair and gestured for Becca to sit. "Can you tell me a little more about Rachel?"

Becca sat, but on the edge of the chair, and dropped her hands between her knees, squeezing her wrists together. "She's almost three years older than me. She'll be eighteen in a few months. She's taller than me and gotten real thin, but before she got sick, she played on the line in volleyball. She was a spiker big time."

"What kind of music does she like?"

"She plays the violin. All kinds of classical and some bluegrass, believe it or not. She was just getting into Nickel Creek when she got sick. She loves Sara Watkins of Nickel and she'd marry Chris Thile. Big fan."

"What classes does she like in school?"

"Did like. She's not going this year. Loved history and English. Hated chemistry but she was straight *As* in chemistry and trig. She loves to read romance and spy novels. Her big hero is Joseph somebody, *Heart of Darkness*."

"Joseph Conrad?"

Becca pointed at Thaddeus. "That's the one. She loves him. Also belongs to Oprah's Book Club. About the only thing that helps her anymore is reading and listening to music. It gets her mind off her pain for a minute or two so it's really good for her."

"What about her own religious beliefs?"

Becca twisted her mouth in thought before she said, "I would say Rachel is probably someone who doesn't believe in anything. I know she doesn't pray, and when I try to talk about God and stuff, she just rolls her eyes and plays like she's about to vomit. So, we don't go there anymore. Mom and Dad still have their church, and their pastor comes once a week and gives her communion, which she takes because Mom and Dad are watching. She doesn't want to hurt their feelings. Rachel is a very sensitive girl and hates seeing anything in pain. She belongs to the Sea Shepherd and PETA, and when we were little, we always had a stray dog or cat or two hanging around. In fact, she wants to be a marine biologist when she grows up. *If* she grows up."

Thaddeus didn't know what to say about a girl with very little hope in life so shifted to Celena's best friend. "What about you, Becca? How are you holding up under all this?"

Becca began crying again. The tears rolled heavy and

fast down her cheeks, faster than she could swipe them away with the towel. "I just want my sister to stop hurting. I would do anything to help her, Mr. Murfee. Just sit with her once and watch her pass out from the morphine, listen to her cry. It's horrible, and I hate her cancer. I hate all cancer. I wish they'd find a cure instead of making more bombers and bullshit tax breaks for the top one percent."

"You sound like someone who keeps up."

"Nowadays, we get so much information from the internet, whether we want it or not. Like Tik Tok, Instagram, Snapchat, Twitter, news alerts constantly pinging our phones. It's always there, the world and everything that is going on."

Thaddeus didn't envy their generation. "What else should I know?"

Her head tilted to the side in confusion. "What do you mean?"

"Like is there anything else about this situation I should know about before I meet with your parents?"

Becca stood from the chair, her fists clenched at her sides. "I'm about to buy my sister some heroin and let her OD, that's what. If somebody else doesn't do something, then I will. She shouldn't have to keep hurting like this. I say let's cure her or let her go. It's not fair, and I hate my parents for not helping her."

Thaddeus understood the emotion radiating off the young woman but needed to keep things calm, keep her calm. "Please sit back down with me, Becca." Thaddeus patted her vacant seat, and when she sat again, he continued, "What would you like to see your parents do?"

"Give her enough drugs to allow her to go asleep peacefully and not wake up. She doesn't want to be alive anymore. Why does she have to be?"

He shook his head. "I'm sure I don't have that answer for you," said Thaddeus. "Tell you what, though, how about I call your parents and try to talk to them about what's on your mind? I'm sure it would be extremely difficult for them to let go."

"Wow, I can't believe you said it that way."

"What, let go? It sounds to me like you've made your case for letting go. Why complicate a terrible situation?"

"You could sort of be my lawyer with them?"

"Something like that. But you have to promise me one thing. You have to promise me you won't buy heroin and give it to Rachel. That's definitely not the way to handle this. Okay?"

Becca squirmed in her patio chair. "I don't know. How can I promise something when I don't know what might happen? If it just turns into a bunch of adults talking but doing nothing to help my sister, I want my options open. I don't think I can make that promise, Mr. Murfee. Does that mean you won't talk to them for me? For Rachel?"

Thaddeus smiled. He appreciated her honesty. "No, it doesn't mean that. I'm still going to talk to them. At least give me a chance to do what I can do first, okay?"

"Okay. But I reserve the right to help if I have to."

"All right. I know you have to do that, and I respect that. I respect your judgment and your right as Rachel's sister to step up and help if nothing else works. I understand."

"All right, then." She clapped her knees and stood. "I'm going inside for pizza. I heard the doorbell and those guys won't leave me any. Thanks, Mr. Murfee!"

"You're welcome. I'll call them right away."

"Bye!" She waved as she left. "And thank you!"

CHAPTER 2

Thaddeus and Christine took Jim and Louisa Sundstrom to dinner the next night. They knew each other well since their daughters were best friends and they could always be located at one house or the other. After drink orders were taken and the waiter returned with two wines and two coffees, Thaddeus took up the question.

"Let me begin by saying we were crushed to hear Rachel's problems had returned."

"Yes," said Jim Sundstrom. "It's really got a foothold this time." Jim Sundstrom was a family doctor in downtown La Jolla with a sub-specialty in gerontology. The Sundstroms and the Murfees had spoken before; Jim didn't pretend to be a cancer specialist or have any oncological insights into his daughter's case. She was being managed by a team of oncologists out of La Jolla and her treating physician was one of Jim's classmates from UCSD med school.

"So sorry to hear that," said Christine. Like Thaddeus, she was a lawyer but practiced separate and apart from him. Their theory was the too-many-cooks one. So far, it seemed to be working to keep their respective distances.

"I know," said Jim. "We've been everywhere, talked to everyone, tried every medication and treatment modality. If it's approved or even experimental, we've done it all."

"Now all we can do is pray," said Louisa. "We're strong believers."

"What about Rachel?" asked Thaddeus. "Is she a strong believer, too?"

"She blows hot and cold," said Jim. "Near as her mother and I can tell. She's young, that's all."

"Well, if there's ever anything we can do to help, please let us know," Christine said.

"I really wanted to talk to you tonight," Thaddeus said, "partly because we've missed you guys and partly because Becca spent the night at our house last night. She posed a particular question to me, and I wound up promising her I would come to you and ask you myself. She's very persuasive, that one."

"Bless her heart, seeing her sister like this is killing her," Louisa said. "I don't even know where to begin with her anymore."

"Well, your Becca is very mature for fifteen," Thaddeus said. "Frankly, I was impressed. So, here it is, without beating around the bush. Becca tells me that Rachel is suffering terribly and there's no hope for her—"

"Prayer, Thaddeus," Louisa broke in. "The Divine Healer."

"I understand that. But in the meantime, Becca sounded pretty despairing of her sister's condition. She says the pain is unbearable and she cries the entire time she's conscious. She says the drugs have stopped working. Please forgive me for barging in like this, but the lawyer inside me promised your daughter I would come before you on her behalf and ask whether there'd been any thought given to allowing Rachel to terminate her own life? To ask for physician-assisted ending of her life? Is that something that's discussed or being considered?"

"Thaddeus," Louisa said, a deep frown on her face, "you've really crossed the line this time. This is a very private family matter, and I'm not comfortable discussing it with you. Can we change the subject, please? I hear there's a new horse in Celena's barn."

"Forgive me," Thaddeus said, "but I promised Becca I would act as her attorney and try to help her understand if there was any discussion of just letting Rachel go?"

"Thaddeus," said Jim, "our religion doesn't believe in physician-assisted suicide. We consider it a sin. A dreadful sin. And that's our answer and that's Becca's answer. We've been over it and over it with Becca. We've discussed it with Rachel, too. She asked, and it was the hardest thing I've had to do in my life to tell her we don't do that in our family, that our beliefs don't allow it."

Thaddeus cleared his throat. He shot a look at Christine.

Christine said, "What if your beliefs aren't Rachel's beliefs? Should she be consulted and listened to?"

"She's only seventeen. That isn't old enough to decide," said Jim. "You're both lawyers. I don't have to remind you she's still a minor."

"I know that," said Christine, "but it seems it isn't a legal question requiring someone to be an adult as much as it's an ethical question, a question that people of any age should be allowed to answer."

"We disagree," said Louisa. "She's too young to decide. Now, please, let's talk about something else. I'm getting very uncomfortable sitting here and discussing such private business."

"I appreciate that," said Thaddeus, "but I also know I feel an obligation to my client, Becca, to come back to her with an answer. Will it ever reach a point where you can let Rachel go, so she doesn't have to suffer anymore? Is that even a possibility?"

"Not a possibility, Thaddeus," said Jim. "That's a position that our God takes, and we cannot disagree. Her life cannot be taken from her by men."

"All right then, thank you," Thaddeus said. "With your kind permission, I'll report back to Becca that the matter is closed."

"Report away," said Jim. He dropped his empty coffee mug heavily onto the table.

"I hate the sound of that," said Louisa. "I cannot imagine in my wildest dreams one of our best friends stepping up to act as our daughter's lawyer against us."

Thaddeus shook his head. "I would say I'm acting more in the support of the family than I'm acting against you. I'm your friend and supporter. Always will be. I also know where I'm not wanted insofar as discussing a matter, and I respect that. I won't ask again. Please forgive me for crossing any lines."

"And me, too," Christine added. "We aren't those people."

Louisa reached and took Christine's hand. "We know you're not, sweetheart. We just know our little girl got to talking and lured you in. Becca's quite good at that."

"I wouldn't say lured us in, not at all," said Thaddeus. "I'd say she acted as a mature and responsible member of your family, and you should be proud of her for reaching out for help."

"Agree," said Jim, "but let's move on. Tell us about the Lakers game at the Staples Center you went to. Was it amazing?"

"It *was* amazing," said Thaddeus.

"Excellent. Next time, we're going. Sorry we had to miss out this time."

"No worries. We'll go again."

CHAPTER 3

Johann Van Giersbergen arrived at the post office on Grayling Drive at 8:13 a.m. He pushed through the glass doors and made his way inside. The clerks were ahead and to the left through double doors, while directly in front of him was a long, wide table with pigeon slots holding mailing labels and envelopes of all sizes, as well as a dozen ballpoints secured by chains at the corners. When he pushed through the interior doors, his heart fell. There were already ten in line for the clerks. The line of patrons started at the far end of the table, wound back around the near end, and bodied up to Johann. He took a service ticket. It said he was number eleven. He inhaled a deep breath, holding the manila mailing envelope against his chest. He was in a hurry, yes, but he might as well not have been. It was time to dawdle.

Dawdle. It sounded like something a duck might do. Or maybe something a high school student would do in his trig class, behind a curled hand, with a ballpoint pen. "Let's play hooky and go dawdle in the pond," he whispered to himself, last in line where no one would see his mouth move soundlessly. Except for maybe the postal employees facing his direction. But they were all underwater with so many impatient patrons stamping and steaming at the molasses bureaucracy they had voted into office yet again. *Now how did that happen?* wondered Johann. He was twenty-two but had never voted in a presidential election. Next time he would vote non-molasses, he told himself. Which was the moment when —just then—the line moved ahead three people, placing him perpendicular to a corkboard and its 9 x 12 notices.

His gaze roamed to the row of faces on the FBI'S TEN MOST WANTED. The wanted poster was behind glass and under lock and key. Number One looked insane. No problem with him getting put behind bars. Number Two looked like a prostitute with a swastika tattoo on her forehead. Number Three was a bank robber who looked like he might have played piano in a church at one time. Number

Four was... Johann looked closer. Number Four was—was—him!

He strained to see clearly. The picture wasn't fuzzy or faded. The photograph could've been made as recently as that morning, in fact, and it looked like no one but him, complete with the mole at the corner of his mouth. He sucked in his breath and shrugged his head down between his shoulders as far as it would go, a reflexive effort to hide himself away from the three people behind him who, thank God, hadn't yet drawn abreast of the bulletin board and caught a glimpse of him, too.

Thoughts tumbled through his mind. He couldn't breathe. He gasped hard, but his lungs wouldn't fill, and he felt paralyzed from the waist up. His mouth was fixed in a crazy smile expressed out of trauma and horror. Worse, his brain was racing and his thoughts receding, carrying away information that he desperately needed.

Needed or not, he was unable to access his mind. He felt the artery threatening to explode in his neck while his pulse galloped and called all blood home to his core. His hand left a sweaty palm print against his manila envelope when he turned, dropped his eyes to the floor, and passed back along the line of people waiting behind him, fleeing the post office and its rogues' gallery.

He stepped into the cool morning air of San Diego and came to a complete stop. One thought had come full-circle: he had no idea what crime the wanted poster said he had committed. His first impulse was to dive back inside, reclaim his place in line, and study the poster close-up. But he came back to his senses. Going back inside was an arrest waiting to happen should any of the citizens in line match the poster and his face. So, a trip back inside was definitely out.

Down the sidewalk he went, stepping off the curb at Gerry's new Yukon XL. He had tossed him the keys that morning and told him to make a special trip to the USPS to mail the manila envelope Johann still carried. Turning, he ducked his face and retraced back to the curbside slots and dropped his envelope into the red-white-and-blue receptacle. Then he turned and hurried back to the SUV. He climbed up and inside and punched the starter button. The V8 jumped to life, and the rear camera flashed on the second he dropped it into reverse. Two cars coming, slowing and searching for parking—nothing to do but wait.

Sweat had formed on his upper lip and brow. He ran his tongue along his lip and removed his right hand from the wheel momentarily to wipe his brow. Good God, this can't be happening. The man on the poster even had the same exact mole at the side of his mouth. It was him. It had to be him. He had to get to a computer and hit the FBI homepage.

Traffic cleared, and he was able to take his foot off the brake and let the SUV back up. He was inching away from the tight confines of his parking spot when a car suddenly came roaring out of nowhere—off to the right side—and clipped him in the right rear quarter panel. His Apple watch immediately asked if he had taken a fall. His first impulse was to leap from the car and tear some dumb driver a new asshole. Johann had a mouth and quick temper, and this was one of those moments made for his anger.

As he was about to leap out—opening the door to let himself slide to the ground—he realized there would be a cop here before it was all over. Someone with a badge was going to get a good look at him and probably match him up with the face plastered on the wall inside the post office. Hadn't he heard somewhere that all cops study the pictures of the Ten Most Wanted every day before they go out into the world? Hadn't he heard that on TV?

But Johann was sharper than your average criminal. He stepped around the Yukon, back around to the hapless woman driving the Ford that had just hit him. "Hey," he cried at the woman, "are you okay?"

The startled woman's mouth fell open. Then, "I should be asking you that. I hit you! I don't know what to say."

"Wait here," commanded Johann. "I saw a cop inside. Let me go grab him so we can answer some questions and be on our way. Is that okay?"

"I'll pull up and park at the end," said the Ford driver. "You can't miss me. I'm the one with the crumpled front end her husband is going to leave her over. It's my third accident this month."

"Don't move then. I'll be right back with a cop."

As the woman nodded then pulled ahead, moving down toward the end of the parking zone, Johann, instead of returning back inside, climbed up into the Yukon's driver's seat and restarted the engine. He continued backing into the slot behind and then immediately shot forward, making a right turn in the parking lot and heading for the entrance where the Ford driver had come from. He made it to the entrance despite being waved at and shouted at for going against traffic. He waited there while a car in the street was trying to turn in. He surrendered to the inevitable, backing away, but flipped the driver off before he made his escape and made a left turn onto the road.

He headed for Rady Children's Hospital. For the last two weeks, Johann had been working for Gerald M. Isherwood, M.D.—the city's top diagnostician and treating pediatric psychiatrist. Johann was one of many nurses who provided nursing care at the Chadwick Center of the hospital. He had, at Dr. Isherwood's suggestion, even undergone psychoanalysis as part of his training and had come away with a gold star for mental health.

His shifts now were dedicated to children of abuse, the kids who had been thrown against walls, burnt with cigarettes, and sexually used, photographed, and discarded. The toughest of all were the head-bangers, the three, four, and five-year-olds who threw themselves against the walls of the unit and slammed their heads against hard surfaces until they acquired their sweet comatose. In the short time he'd been at the hospital, they'd become his kids, each of them, and he knew they would be his life's work. The kids had his heart, his mind, and his soul. While he gave them their medicine, helped them bathe, held their hand while they cried, Johann vowed to protect them.

Johann studied his rearview. Good, it was clear. No one following. He felt himself gasping for air and realized he was all but anoxic with panic and fear. He shut his mouth, forcing himself to breathe only through his nose and slow down his oxygen exchange.

He made a left and headed up three blocks to the stoplight on Sandrock and Aero Drive. At the light, he covered the side of his face with his hand, pretending to be adjusting his sunglasses but actually shielding his face from the older man in the passenger's seat of the car beside him. So far, he hadn't looked his way even once, but that didn't matter.

He realized, with a drop of his stomach, that he couldn't be too careful now. Then another thought formed—he needed to get home to his laptop to try to figure this out. When the light changed, he gunned it, raced ahead of the car on his left, moved into the left-turn lane and spun a U-turn at the next intersection. Then he was heading eastbound, back toward his apartment complex. It came up on his right a mile later, and he was soothed to see the familiar sign Sunnyside Meadows, where he turned in and raced ahead for his parking spot beneath the carport.

He leaped from the Yukon and jogged toward his apartment. As he went along the walk, thoughts sailed through his head at lightspeed.

At the top of the first flight of stairs, he had just turned to his right to work his way three doors down to the safety of his own apartment when he came face-to-face with two clean-shaven, short-haired Caucasian men wearing dark suits, sunglasses, and carrying a walkie-talkie. He dropped his head and hurried past them, down to the end, where he made another right turn, this time out of their line of sight.

He was scared to death when he climbed back inside Gerry's Yukon and slammed the door shut. The motor caught instantly. He pulled the shift into reverse. He was stunned and panting for air, and he was gone before the men in the suits came looking. The suits had been about to knock.

On his door.

CHAPTER 4

Johann had never been treated for mental illness. Never had a bout of forgetfulness, hadn't been in some kind of accident with amnesia or a head injury, none of the stuff you see in movies and read in books. There was no family history of mental illness, and he didn't take drugs. No blackouts from alcohol, no multiple personality scares. No, he was perfectly normal, Johann was, and he was scared to death.

The Yukon knew the way to Rady's. Johann, upon arrival, remembered none of the drive. But he did remember studying the rearview mirror block after block while holding his breath and praying the men in suits hadn't pulled their black car in behind him and followed. It turned out they hadn't.

He parked in the employees' lot and tried to act like everything was okay and it was just another day at work as he sauntered inside. He badged the first level of security, the bag checkers, and then went on down the hall to the locked door and entered the passcode. The door buzzed with a sharp eruption, and Johann passed inside and onto the ward.

Johann found Gerry inside his office, making toast in the Toast-R-Oven his wife had given him at Christmas. It was a half-joking gift, but the other half, the serious half, was for Gerry's low blood sugar. He snacked all day. Before it was ready for eating, his toast would be layered with cheese to deliver some high protein into his system. All part of the deal, Gerry said. "Hypoglycemics like me gotta eat," he proudly told Johann as he entered to find him taking his first bite out of a toast and cheese. "Did you mail my package?"

"I did." Johann shot a look back into the hallway. "Has anyone come around looking for me?"

Gerry was a long, thin man who dressed in jeans and turtlenecks every day. He was bearded and wore frameless eyeglasses beneath a close-cropped head of black hair. He shook his head at the question. "No one came looking for you. Did you shoot someone at the P.O.?"

"Funny man. No, nothing like that. At least I don't think so."

"Ha ha. Your life is pretty sheltered, dear Johann. Had you shot a member of our community, you would've noticed." He was joking with him, of course.

On the personal side, Johann lived to play lead guitar in

a band, loved beach volleyball, and was dating a gal named Sally who dealt Blackjack at the Namatukee Casino. Sally was a fun-lover who never missed Johann's closing performance with his band at the casino on Friday and Saturday nights. She was reliable, always in the front row, dancing by herself and stomping in the pit while Johann lit up the air with his Steve Vai and Joe Satriani licks. He was all of that and more, according to Sally and according to his growing fanbase. But now he was wanted by the FBI and, he realized with a shudder, running from the law.

"Gerry, can I ask you something?"

Gerry smacked his lips. "Ask away. As long as it isn't to ask when you're getting out of here to go home. That's the one I hear the most and hate the most."

"Actually, it is about getting out of here."

"Oh, Lord."

"No, getting out of here without getting arrested. I saw my picture on a wanted poster at the post office."

"That's preposterous. Get your vision checked. Next case."

"Seriously, it was me. Down to the little mole beside my mouth. I'm not fooling around here, Gerry. I'm scared to death."

Gerry had been lounging in his chair behind his desk, but now sat up and wheeled the chair forward. "No, I can see you're not kidding. Let's see. Why don't we check my computer and see what we can find out? You got time right now?"

"I do. Where else am I going to go?"

After a few clicks, Gerry said, "Here we go. Let's start with the FBI home page."

Johann watched while the browser loaded the page. When it appeared, all the faces were identical to what

Johann had seen at the post office. And there he was—Johann. There was no doubt.

Gerry's face went pale. He shuddered. "It says you work in mental health in Los Angeles. But we're in San Diego. What the hell? Do you have a second job, fellow?"

"No, I don't. When would I? We're doing tens and twelves every shift right here."

"It says you were born in Amsterdam, moved to the US when you were five, private school in La Jolla, and then University of Wisconsin in Madison where you received a BSN. How we doing so far?"

"Perfect. They know everything about me. What am I wanted for?"

"You're been charged with participation in the bombing in Mexico where eighty-two people were killed, eleven of them FBI agents."

"Holy shit! I was there with my dad, but I didn't do anything! My dad died there!"

"This can't really be happening," said the psychiatrist. He was remaining somewhat calm, Johann saw. Probably his training at keeping cool in the face of threats. "I-I—I'm just not following. Tell you what, Johann. Why don't we call security and get ourselves calmed down here? You're about to explode, and I'm frightened. I need this sorted by smarter people than the two of us."

"You're calling security on me? I haven't done anything, Gerry!"

He sat forward in his chair and ran his palm over his cropped hairline. "We can't make decisions without more clarity here. I'm dialing now. You can stay and walk through this with me, or you can leave the premises, Johann. I'll give you a ten-minute head start, though I don't know why I should. I guess so you won't tarry and hurt anyone. I'm not sure what I'm thinking. I'm losing it here. Protocol, doctor, think! I have to call security. Your head start begins right—now!"

Johann didn't hesitate. He leaped from his chair and ran outside the office into the hallway, heading directly for the exit at the far end of the hall. There was no procedure for exiting the ward other than logging out, so he burst through the exit and ran for the hospital elevators. He was on the second floor; the elevator was on the seventh and stalled. He ran for the stairs and headed down as fast as his feet could move.

Outside he flew, his ears on the alert for the wail of sirens. Nothing heard, he ran for his own car parked in the second row in the hospital employees' parking lot. His smart key was sensed by the small BMW, and the doors unlocked. He dropped into the driver's seat and screeched out of the parking spot and headed for the exit. His ID card raised the security arm, and then Johann squealed the old BMW up a row and then left onto the freeway frontage road.

vinci-books.com/postoffice

About the Author

For thirty years John defended criminal clients across the United States. He defended cases ranging from shoplifting to First Degree Murder to RICO to Tax Evasion, and has gone to jury trial on hundreds. His first book, *The Defendants*, was published in January, 2014. John is presently at work on his 31st thriller.

Reception to John's books have been phenomenal; more than 4,000,000 have been downloaded in 6 years! Every one of them are Amazon best-sellers. He is an Amazon All-Star every month and is a *U.S.A Today* bestseller.

John Ellsworth lives in the Arizona region with three dogs that ignore him but worship his wife, and bark day and night until another home must be abandoned in yet another move.